BOOKS BY TAMMARA WEBBER

CONTOURS OF THE HEART® series:

Easy

Breakable

BETWEEN THE LINES series:

Between the Lines

Where You Are

Good For You

Here Without You

here without you

(between the lines #4)

tammara webber

Cover design by Sarah Hansen at Okay Creations

Cover image used under license from Shutterstock.com
Copyright © Dubova, 2012

Interior design elements used under license from Shutterstock.com
Copyright © Aleks Melnik, 2012

ISBN: 978-0-9856618-4-7

To Charles

who was the dad he didn't have to be

Chapter 1

REID

My girlfriend hasn't told her parents about me.

It's been a week, but we're still a secret—hanging out but never going out, just like we did last fall. Despite my appreciation of how she's willing to spend that time, I don't want to be confined to my house with Dori. She's like a new toy that I can't show off—which was a dick thing to slip and say, but she just rolled her eyes at me for it.

As it is, John is the only friend I have who knows about my new relationship status, although my costar on my last film—Chelsea Radin—smirked perceptively whenever she saw us together during the last few cast volunteer days at the Habitat house. I'm guessing she knows. Especially after she caught us emerging from an alcove on the side of the house, Dori's ponytail loose and her face flushed, me wearing a shit-eating grin.

John and I are hanging courtside when he decides to bring up my clandestine affair, because his concern for timing is identical to his regard for tact—nonexistent.

"So when are you revealing this so-called relationship to the world already?"

The level of noise in Staples Center keeps our exchange confidential, but that doesn't mean I want to discuss Dori in the middle of eighteen thousand people—never mind several hundred cameras broadcasting the game to millions more. Plus, he pronounces relationship in a tone most people reserve for STD. When I shoot him a look, he blinks innocently. I suspect this guise worked on his father for years before he figured out that John really was a next-generation version of himself.

"What? Reid Alexander has a girlfriend." His voice dips at this last word—not like he's obeying my gag order—more like this fact is too appalling to divulge at full volume.

I stare at the three-point shot, lined up and missed. We both curse.

"It's Perez-worthy news, bro! What's with the containment?"

If John is waiting for my answer, he can fucking keep waiting.

Kobe gets penalized for traveling—which never happens—and I slump back in my seat, crossing my arms tightly over my chest. "Shit." That expletive defines my current feelings for the Lakers and Dori, both of whom I love, both of whom are pissing me off.

Elbowing me, John smirks. "C'mon, man, you know I'm the soul of discretion." Oddly enough, that's true. When I don't spill immediately, he starts guessing. "So it's over? Is that it? Dude, I said it wouldn't la—"

"She hasn't told her parents yet."

From the corner of my eye, I watch him frown in confusion and peer at me like I've just spoken in a foreign language and he's waiting for the translation.

Staring at the game, I add, "I feel like I'm stuck in a fucking Nick-at-Night sitcom."

John arches a brow. "Wait. You're serious. That's the reason? Because she hasn't told her parents? I could line up a hundred girls who'd be jacked as hell to go out with you—once. You've made this girl your girlfriend, and she's not telling everyone she knows?"

I shrug, but it stings when he puts it like that. Like I said—tact is not John's thing.

He shakes his head. "Never thought I'd see the day some girl got Reid Alexander pussy-whipped—Ow! Dude!" Glaring, he rubs his arm where I punched him. "What is it about this girl that makes you so fucking violent?"

I laugh, because now we're on the screen over center court. Time to appear as if we're screwing around rather than beginning a private brawl that would unseat the Lakers and the Jazz as tonight's primary entertainment. "Camera."

At that word, John switches gears and plays along with the horseplay ruse, shoving me back.

"That was your last warning, man." My on-camera smile doesn't conceal the sharp threat in my voice. "Don't talk about her like that." He's lucky I gave him a deep bicep bruise instead of rearranging his face.

"I was talking about you," he growls in return, his fake smile mirroring mine.

Brooke

"Ms. Cameron? Bethany Shank here. I've located him."

I shouldn't have answered her call in the middle of a pedicure, but when I saw her name pop up on the screen, my curiosity was overpowering. No way that was going to voicemail. When I hired a private investigator, I expected her to find my kid. I mean duh—of course I expected her to find him. Even so, this news floors the hell out of me. My heart is thrashing like I'm mainlining espresso.

"That was fast."

The woman currently patting my feet dry is pretending she isn't listening to my side of this conversation, and I wonder if she can hear the thundering slam of my heart.

"Yes, well, I told you it would go quickly once you gave me the go-ahead to conduct the search."

"So what's next?" I've found him. Despite my superficial confidence, my hands start to tremble. I wish I was at home, alone, so I could lie down or pace in circles—anything but sit here with my foot on some stranger's knee, shaking like my mother's inbred Pekinese, which pees if someone sneezes.

"There's a lot of sensitive information here. Too much to relay over the phone. Would you prefer to come by the office tomorrow, or would you prefer that I come to you?"

Okay, he's *four*. How much information can there be? *He finally stopped wetting the bed. Throws an occasional shit-fit tantrum. Learned how to write his name in preschool. Has a normal life.* That last bit is all I care about: I just want to hear that he has a normal life, so I can go back to mine in peace.

Part of me feels like a hundred kinds of idiot for doing this at all. Except that for months now, I've had a recurring nightmare about the baby I'd refused to see or hold before my attorney and the social worker transferred him to the adoptive parents. In the dream, I'm holding him and he's staring up at me. And then he bursts into tears, crying like his heart is breaking, and I wake up buried in a landslide of guilt.

There's no reason for me to feel guilty—*no reason*. Why the hell am I dreaming of him crying? And why do I wake up with tears on my face?

I just want closure, finally. Closure, and maybe a photo.

"I assume he's fine. Right?"

If she provides that one syllable of reassurance, I can stop here. If he's *fine*, I don't need details. A photo is probably a bad idea, even. I don't really want to know if he looks more like me or Reid.

"It would be best for us to meet in person. I'll just transfer you to my admin to set up an appointment." Bethany Shank is all detached and impersonal—typical for her. But her clipped demeanor is more grating—and alarming—than usual. There's a small thread of something unsaid, and I can't help but tug at it.

"Is something wrong?"

There's an unexpected pause in place of the quick denial I expected, and suddenly I need privacy. Like *now*. I direct a scowl toward the pedicurist's head—because how goddamned long does it take to dry a *foot* for chrissake?

Glancing up as though she feels my eyes bore into her, she blanches.

I slide my fingers over the phone. "Could you give me a moment? *Thanks*."

Once she shuffles away, I ask Bethany Shank to repeat herself.

"I'd advise an office meeting for this exchange, Ms. Cameron." Her keyboard clicks in the background. "I believe I have an open spot tomorrow afternoon at three."

I don't like this at all. She's not answering my question, which means there *is* something wrong. Now my brain is off on a new loop: *mental disability... terminal illness... dead?*

"No. Today. And come to my apartment."

My PI sighs into the phone as though I give a shit that I've just disturbed her Very Important Schedule. I wait, silent, until she concedes defeat. "I won't be free until seven this evening—"

"Seven's fine. I'll see you then."

She's mid-sigh when I click off. If I wasn't in the middle of a Beverly Hills spa with the nosiest pedicurist on the planet, I'd have forced her to tell me what the hell she found out right *now* instead of having to wait three hours.

"Ready for the oil massage?" The pedicurist returns, a little cowed.

"Sure. But I changed my mind about the French tips. French tips are for summer. It's almost February. I want red. *Blood* red."

She nods. "Yes, of course, Ms. Cameron."

Chapter 2

REID

"Stay." I roll Dori beneath me and pin one wrist above her head, kissing her deeply so she can't tell me no right away—though I know she will. Which makes how ticked off I feel when she does that exact thing a bit unreasonable.

"Reid," she groans into my mouth, "you know I can't stay."

I stare into her very dark eyes, the frustration leaping into my throat, ready to do battle. "You're not a child, Dori. You're almost nineteen. So yes, you *can*."

I release her wrist and she raises her hand to my face, pushes her fingers into my hair, curls them against my scalp.

"I'll tell them. *I will*. Don't you trust me?"

Of course then my temper goes and fucks everything up.

"No, actually. I don't. Because you're leaving for Berkeley *next week*. And because the last time I trusted you about your parents and *us*, you bailed on me."

Her hand falls away and the faintest crease appears between her brows. "This isn't like last time."

I roll off her and onto my back, because I want to believe her, but right there in the back of my mind—and none too far back, either—is the fact that I recently spent one of the most miserable months of my life thinking I'd never see her again. I'm not willing to accept that again.

"Right," I say.

And yeah, it does occur to me that being an asshat isn't the best way to get what I want with her. Realistically, nothing with Dori fits the mold of what usually works for me with the rest of the world—one of the things I love about her—but I can't think logically when I'm this pissed off.

She slides from the bed and straightens her clothes, which are gratifyingly askew from our interrupted make-out session. Damn my temper to hell, too, because she would stay at least another half hour, which I'm blowing by acting like a clingy *chick*. That thought sparks another round of useless anger. I can't seem to make it stop.

"It's late. I'm going to go," she says then, standing next to the bed while I stare at the ceiling.

My new more-perceptive alter ego is pleading with me to just let it go already, but the arrogant prick inside is sulking. *I'm* not wrong. *She* is. She knows it, too—that's why she sounds like she's crying when she turns and leaves.

Ah, fuck.

Ten minutes later, I'm calmer and admitting to myself that I'm a self-absorbed dumbass. I call her but she doesn't pick up, and I hang up when the call goes to voicemail. Fantasizing about confronting her parents and getting this all out in the open—just getting in my car and following her home—I can't help but chuckle. The way she drives, I'd beat her there, even with her ten-minute head start.

After grabbing a snack from the kitchen, I screw around on the Internet, effectively wasting at least forty-five minutes, and then try her again. Voicemail number two. *Click.* I answer an email from George and check out my fan page, where John appears to be correct about the amount of girls who'd chop off a limb to go out with me even once. But none of them *know me.* I'm just a pretty face, a hot body, a fantasy stand-in, and though I appreciate their support, such as it is, I couldn't care less about the shallow praise.

Listening to Dori's cheerful, musical voice tell me to leave a message for the third time, I hang my head and wait for the beep, one hand gripping the phone and the other gripping the back of my neck as if I could shake some sense into myself.

"Dori, I'm sorry. I told you we'd go at your pace, and I broke that promise. Just… I trust you more than I've ever trusted anyone. Maybe that's not saying much—or enough—but I do."

My jaw clenches. What I mean by trust and what she means by it are two different things. We're quite a pair, trying to find the middle ground between our temperaments, our beliefs, our lives. While she tries to repair her broken faith in *everything*, I'm stumbling over learning to trust at all.

"Don't give up on me." I press *end* and lie back in the middle of my bed, wishing I could just learn to shut the fuck up when I'm that pissed off.

Barely resisting the urge to pitch the phone across the room, I focus and count silently. My therapist (another novelty) is adamant about using the focus-and-count thing to uncoil my temper instead of acting on impulse. He insists it's a habit that requires persistence. It works sporadically, at best—especially when I forget to use it. Like when Dori was lying next to me *minutes ago*. Dammit.

When the phone rings, relief floods through me. "Hey."

"I have some news. Are you alone?"

It takes me a second to catch up. Familiar voice, *not* Dori. "Brooke?"

She sighs heavily. "Don't you *ever* look to see who's calling before answering? Are you alone or not?"

I close my eyes and restart the mute therapeutic counting. *So not working.*

"I'm alone." Teeth clamped, I wait for her to say whatever she's going to say. I'm not in the mood for Brooke Cameron. A reserve of composure is essential to my ability to tolerate her, and at the moment I'm all tapped out.

"My PI found him."

Him?

Oh, shit. The kid.

"That was fast."

"Yeah. We need to talk. Can you come over?"

Brooke has always put the *high* in high maintenance. I swallow a retort—my theory on the real reason phones were invented—namely, the avoidance of in-person meetings with people we don't want to see. Ten to one Alexander Graham Bell had a problematic ex or an overbearing mother-in-law.

"When?"

"Now?"

I glance at my watch. "Brooke, I'm tired." *More importantly, I'm hoping Dori will call me back any minute.* "Can't you just tell me whatever it is over the phone?" I'm not used to us speaking amicably—or as amicably as Brooke and I are capable of. That's bizarre in itself.

"Well, shit, Reid. Never mind, then." I hear the drawl creeping into her words and know that despite efforts to avoid setting her off, I have anyway.

"Don't be that way."

"What the hell does that mean?" She huffs out a breath. "This is important and you're blowing me off. I should have expected as much. Are you really alone or just saying you are?"

I shove a hand through my hair and close my eyes. There's not enough focus-and-count in the world to deal with Brooke Cameron. "Why would I lie about that?"

"Why won't you answer the question?"

"Because I already *did* answer it, goddammit."

When she doesn't snap back right away, I get my first clue that something has her pretty freaked out.

"Fine. Here it is." Her voice sounds off—now that she's speaking more quietly, I realize she's been crying. What the hell? Is there something in the air today? "He's in foster care."

"What?" I sit up, the gears in my brain catching and stalling.

"Apparently, the people I chose to give him to transformed into shit-for-brains tweaker meth-addict losers and CPS removed him."

"*What?*"

"Quit saying that! Don't you have anything else to say?"

"Well *no*, actually. Give me a minute, Jesus, I mean—CPS? As in child whatever—the people who take kids away from parents when they're being *abused?*"

I imagine the exaggerated eye-roll I thankfully can't see.

"Yes, Reid. That's what I mean."

My life flashes before my eyes—what's left of it. Because it hits me right then that I've not told Dori about this yet. Not *any* of it. There hasn't been an appropriate time in the past week to bring up the fact that Brooke and I had a son four and a half years ago. A son I'd denied was mine to Brooke's face and in my own head until a few weeks ago. A son she gave up for adoption right after she had him.

With what happened to Dori in high school, this wasn't a piece of my past I could disclose offhandedly, and I've never been the king of insightful situation management. Not to mention the fact that I've never told a living soul about this. Not John, not my parents, *no one.*

"God-fucking-dammit."

"Yeah," Brooke says. She has no idea.

Into the silence of our mutual shock, my phone beeps, and this time, I check the display. Dori is calling me back. "Look, I have to go. I'll call you tomorrow."

"Fine." Brooke hangs up, and I flash over, shelving our conversation for later.

"Dori, I'm sorry—"

"I'm telling them tomorrow, first thing. Please try to understand—this is difficult for them, especially after Deb's accident. It's not about you, really. They don't know you. They're only afraid I'll be hurt, and that's all this response is based on." She blurts her words like a practiced speech, defensive and placating. "They may want to talk to you."

Parents who want to talk to me. Huh. And I'm not only considering it, I'm determined to do it. This is the stuff of alternate universes.

"I'm not going to hurt you, Dori," I say, meaning it. "And I shouldn't have pushed you to tell them," I add, half-meaning it.

"Yes, you should have. I haven't kept my promise to you, either. I told you I would never be ashamed of you—and I'm not, Reid—but this must have seemed that way to you. I'm sorry."

I hadn't realized until the moment she verbalizes it that this was *exactly* how it felt to me. She can hurt me in places I didn't know I was vulnerable, soothe aches I didn't know existed. How does she manage this sort of empathy?

"I wish you were here right now," I say, unable to concentrate on anything but the need to pull her under me and shut the entire world out.

"I was just there, you know," she retorts.

Smartass. God, I want her.

"Yeah, I know. Jesus, I'm a fu—uh, idiot."

Her hoarse little laugh at my interrupted curse yanks at my heart.

"What if I sneak over to your house and climb into your

bedroom window?"

Laughing again, she says, "You can't sneak anywhere in that car—certainly not in my neighborhood. And there's no tree or trellis for you to climb to my second story window."

I chuckle softly. "But you're thinking about it, aren't you?"

Her exhalation sounds like a smile. "Yeah."

"Want me to tell you what I'd do, if your dad had been more obliging and installed a trellis or planted a tree just under your window?"

"Maybe," she says softly, and I imagine her sucking that fat lower lip into her mouth.

"Maybe?"

"Okay. Yes. Tell me."

This is the thing about her—this, right here. She doesn't play coy. That's why the thought of her pushing me away is unacceptable. It wouldn't be a play for attention like it always was with Brooke. Goodbye is *goodbye* to Dori, and I won't let that happen.

"Close your eyes and imagine those perfectly situated branches, right outside your window."

"Um, okay."

I lie back, relaxing, breathing in the subtle trace of her still on my pillows. "You'll leave your window open—the one the fish are swimming toward. It'll be late, and try as you might, you can't stay awake waiting for me. I'll slip quietly across the room in the dark, following bars of moonlight to your bed." I entertain the thought of her, curled up under the covers, and my fingers twist a knot into the unmade bedding beneath me. "What do you wear to sleep?"

"Just a T-shirt," she whispers.

Air hisses through my teeth and I take a slow breath while my body riots. For the first time in my life, I'm hoping the new will wear off soon—just a bit, at least—because whenever I think of touching her and how she responds when I do, I can't think of anything else.

"I'll pull my shirt off before peeling back your covers. Run my fingertips over you, carefully. Wake you so, so, slowly." Every nerve in my body is wide awake. "What will you do then?"

Her voice is so quiet that I strain to hear her. "Reach for you. Take your hand and pull you into my bed."

The hot-factor of this conversation just vaulted up several notches. "Ah, I like the sound of that. But I'm still wearing my jeans, and you're wearing that shirt." I wonder if she's brave enough yet to continue this sort of game, though six months ago I would have had to be high to think she'd *ever* do this. Or that I'd end up wanting a committed relationship with her.

After last weekend, all bets are off on what either of us is capable of.

"Are you—are you wearing the ones with the button-fly?" Breathy and soft, her words are like a caress.

"If that's what you want, then yes."

"Then, um, I'll unbutton your jeans..." Her voice husky and sweet, she hesitates, and I picture the blush spreading across her face.

"You'll shove them down with your foot, grazing my leg as you go," I say, helping her out, "while my hands are sliding under that T-shirt."

"Oh?" She sounds almost breathless, and I'm *completely* turned on.

"Your M.A.D.D. T-shirt," I qualify, pausing when she laughs. "It's a little threadbare, you know. I'll stroke your breasts with my fingertips... and then lean down and taste you right through that thin red knit."

"Ah..." she breathes.

"One hand will drift down, over your ribcage, across your hip, nothing between us... what then?"

Damn if she's not panting. So am I.

"Are you... are you wearing boxers, or briefs?"

I smile. "In the interest of fairness, let's say *no*."

"Oh, fudge."

I repress a laugh.

"Um, what about...?"

I chuckle softly. "Dori, Dori—so responsible, even in the middle of our little fantasy. I'll bring a whole strip of them. You're *protected*. Now what?"

"Reid. I want you." Her voice is pure frustration, and I love it.

My groan echoes her longing. "Baby, let me give your gifted little fingers a few suggestions to follow while I tell you the many, many ways I want *you*."

Brooke

Despite the fact that Reid had nothing useful to say, it helps to have someone to talk to about this. About *him*. Who better than his sperm donor?

I may have to stop referring to Reid like that, assuming he means to be a part of this, which isn't a given. I can't imagine him stepping up and admitting to anyone that he's the father of this kid. Not really.

Earlier tonight, I learned my son's name. *River*. Identical to the up-and-coming young actor who powerballed his way to a flatline on the sidewalk outside an LA club. A promising life cut short—by drugs, no less. Fabulous.

Bethany Shank brought an eight-by-ten print of the photo I'd been longing to get my hands on, rather than sending me a jpeg. I fully believe she just wanted to witness my reaction. That flagrant intrusion wasn't a point in her favor with me. When she slid the photo across the glass tabletop in my kitchen, I stared, but couldn't touch it. My first thought was *No. This can't be him.* Hours later, that kneejerk reaction hasn't changed, even though I know it's wrong.

Staring at his likeness again now, alone, I don't have to worry about my visible reaction. I can study every detail of him.

He squats just inside a cyclone fence marred by patchy streaks of rust. There's a stick in his hand, held like a tool, not a weapon—used, I think, to dig or draw in the dirt. In the background there are a couple of other children, a few pieces of ancient playground equipment, and a mousy middle-aged woman talking on a cell phone.

Compared to my stepbrother, who's a few months older, this child looks slight. Undersized. His clothes are mismatched and his face is dirty, as are his small hands. His hair is shorn so close to his scalp that I can barely make out the color—though given his DNA, it must be blond. Light brows endorse that guesstimate. His nearly-bare head makes him look even more vulnerable than his size.

When I was young, I hid behind my hair. Tilting my chin

forward, I watched the world slide by between the pale strands, pretending indifference to the resentful body language of my increasingly miserable parents and their halfheartedly cryptic conversations, so easily decoded. I anticipated their end before they saw it, and made plans to go with my father when they finally split.

But I was missing a few crucial pieces of the puzzle, and stupidly, so was my mother. Neither of us predicted that other woman—the soon-to-be third wife. The son she would give my father, beginning his third tiny empire, negating the second. Negating *me*.

Now, from the static image in my hand, River stares straight into my eyes as though he knows a high-powered zoom lens is trained on him. As though he knows I am on the other side of it. His eyes aren't the ice blue I share with my father. They're Reid's deep blue. Dark, like the sky at dusk in that split second after the sun disappears for the day. His mouth, too, is Reid's. His button nose is mine.

What an unfair trick God decided to play on me. This dirty, scrawny, ill-clothed child is mine, and the vision I've carried of the life I gave him—when I've thought of him at all—was a lie. I thought he'd be cared for. Wanted. Loved.

Sitting across from Bethany Shank four hours ago, I refused to cry no matter how my eyes stung. "I want to see him." I heard the words I said aloud, followed by her intake of breath. She was no more shocked at me than I was at myself.

"Well, let's not make emotional dec—"

"I. Want. To. See. Him," I said, my subzero gaze freezing her in place. "Find out what we need to do to make that happen."

She cleared her throat and smiled blandly. "Arranging meetings is not a function of my investigative services, Ms. Cameron."

A good decade older than me, Ms. Shank is yet another woman who wrongly imagined me to be a vaporous young Hollywood plaything. I tend to allow the world to think I'm spoiled and gullible. Not only is it mildly amusing most of the time, it makes for satisfying expressions of shock on the opposite side of the table during contract negotiations. Behind closed conference room doors, I am my father's daughter. My agent and manager know this. A handful of studio execs know this, too.

I cocked an eyebrow. "I suggest you make it part of your services, Ms. Shank."

She drew herself up in the chair, her mouth falling open slightly.

Leaning forward, I fixed her with a concentrated stare. "You're an investigator. I'm asking you to investigate. Are you concerned about further compensation? Do you require an advance of some sort? I was assured you were the best in the business. I would hate to have to report otherwise to potential clientele."

Her face took on the mottled appearance of someone newly disabused of unjustified superiority. Ten minutes later, she left my apartment after assuring me that she would be in touch tomorrow with more information.

Once she took off, I fell onto the sofa and dredged up memories I'd never intended to exhume.

I went to live with my stepmother in Texas for the six months it took to get from the blue stick to the birth. My parents were irate and disbelieving when I refused to get an abortion, as though I was staging a rebellion for the sake of extra attention.

"What do you *want*, Brooke?" My mother threw her shoes across the room—yet I was the one being accused of throwing tantrums. "Whatever you're trying to prove, it'll backfire. This will ruin your life. *Ruin it.*" A beat of silence followed, the dots connected with little effort.

I didn't say *Like I ruined yours?* Too easy. I'd long since learned not to offer up my vulnerabilities like a senseless sacrifice.

"I don't want to *keep* it," I sneered. "I'm not *stupid.*"

Her eyes narrowed. She was as proficient at reading the antipathy threaded through our words as I was. "Where are you planning to live as a single, pregnant teenager? Because you're not living here in my house."

She'd intended to deliver a jarring dose of reality, and I felt it, along with the sting of threatened consequences. I was more scared than I let on, but that was nothing new.

Lifting my chin, I said, "I'm staying with Kathryn."

I hadn't talked to Kathryn yet, hadn't thought my mother

would go this far.

Nothing drained the color from my mother's face faster than a reminder of my relationship with my stepmother, the woman my father ditched when my mother got herself pregnant with me. She'd begged him to leave his wife and two daughters, and he had.

He fulfilled his visitation duties to Kelley and Kylie—but elsewhere. His other daughters never came to our house, so my father's previous family skated on my peripheral awareness for the first few years of my life, not quite real. I was too young to comprehend that my mother was a home-wrecking twat until kindergarten.

Kelley, then eleven or twelve, won a statewide writing award, and Kathryn insisted that her father—my father—attend the ceremony to show how proud he was of her. My parents fought bitterly over this atypical plea from his ex. Moving room to room, my mother proclaimed her rights as his current wife while his guilt—heavy and sticky as only overdue remorse can be—compelled him to dismiss her demands.

In the end, all three of us attended a program that had nothing to do with my mother or me. Mom took me to her salon that morning and we had our hair and nails done, as though we were attending a gala event. At the mall, she chose coordinating outfits for the two of us, giggling into the dressing room mirror that we'd look like sisters instead of mother and daughter.

My father and his ex-wife sat next to each other, more congenial than my parents were with each other. We sat in a tense row, a phony testament to post-divorce cooperation: me, Mom, Dad, Kathryn, and Kylie, who leaned up to give me dirty looks until her mother leaned down and said something that made her face go scarlet.

The final straw, I think, was my father's exuberance when Kelley's name was called and she crossed the stage. Sticking his fingers in the sides of his mouth, he whistled as he did on the soccer field when I hijacked the ball from an opponent or kicked a goal. I hadn't known he could feel that way about anyone but me.

"*Kenneth*," Mom hissed, yanking his arm down.

They began to argue, first in softly spit words and heated scowls, and then louder until my father gripped her by the elbow and steered her into the aisle and out of the auditorium. Kylie's wide eyes told me that she wasn't used to witnessing the sorts of outbursts that were commonplace to me. Kathryn worried her lip, glancing back toward the exit three times as the program came to a close and my parents had not returned.

Kelley appeared at the end of the row with a wooden plaque in her hands, her name and accomplishment carved into the brass plate affixed to the front. "Look, Mama, they spelled my name right! Where's Daddy? Can we get milkshakes now?"

Kathryn glanced at me, the two empty seats between us, and the aisle where neither of my parents was visible. "I'm not sure where your father is, but we can't leave Brooke here alone."

Kelley and Kylie stared at me and I stared back. Their clear blue eyes were the same color as mine. The same as my father's eyes. *Our* father's eyes. For the first time, I realized I had sisters. Kylie glared, out of her mother's sight.

I had sisters, and they hated me.

"Let's just bring her!" Kelley said, shrugging.

Thus began my odd relationship with my father's former family.

Eleven years later, it was Kathryn I begged for help. It was Kathryn who took me in, hired an attorney to oversee the adoption, and helped me leaf through scrapbooks made by prospective adoptive parents—all white teeth, spotless homes and financial portfolios, and promises of a future full of love for some lucky infant.

I chose wrong, didn't I? I couldn't have chosen more wrong.

Refusing to read up on post-pregnancy, I didn't know what to expect after he was born. Kathryn tried to warn me about the possible physical and psychological side effects, but I ignored her warnings, insisting that my personal trainer and I would deal with the physical issues, and as for the so-called mental distress—I wouldn't miss a baby I didn't want, because that would be crazy.

After I signed the forms the next day, my attorney and the social worker left with the baby. I lay in the birth center bed, my hands kneading my sore, once-flat stomach like bread dough, feigning indifference to what that new emptiness signified. I hadn't wanted to see or hold him, but I'd grown accustomed to him moving around inside me. Only a week before, I'd seen the shape of a foot pressing out just under my ribcage, plain as day.

Fascinated and horrified, I'd poked at it with my finger and it had pressed back.

Tears stung my eyes and tracked down my face, and I gave myself that one time to cry over the loss of a child who would be better off without me, along with the coldhearted boy I was better off without. Staring at the unused rocking chair in the corner of the homey little room, I swore I would leave that place and put it all behind me. I would go live my life and establish my brilliant career. I would forget all of it, starting the moment I stepped out of the hospital.

Two days later, my breasts were swollen and leaking. The doctor had mentioned this probability, but I didn't count on the reality of it. My stupid body assumed it had a baby to feed. Or a dozen babies, from the looks of things.

"What the hell?" I wailed to Kathryn. "What the hell is this?" I felt like someone had shoved soccer balls beneath the too-stretched skin of my once-perfect breasts.

"Honey, your body doesn't know you don't have him."

I sputtered with indignation. "This is disgusting! Make it stop!" My nipples dripped painfully, soaking my T-shirt, and I sat on the floor and cried, all previous strength vanishing under hormonal shifts I couldn't bring under control. My body was betraying me.

Kathryn called the doctor, who refused to prescribe anything but painkillers, which I refused to take. For three weeks, we bound my comic-book giant boobs, and Kathryn gave me packages of frozen veggies to hold against them while I watched television and read scripts.

Observing this, Kylie, home for the weekend, suggested I think of it as a bizarre sports injury. "Basically, your tits are on injured reserve," she said, and we laughed hysterically as Kathryn just shook her head at us and brought me two new bags of frozen peas.

"I will never be able to look at peas the same way," she observed, pressing the cold bags to my chest and carrying the thawed, squishy bags to the trash.

Kathryn. She's who I need now. Without another thought, I grab my phone.

"Brooke, how are you, honey?" Just those words from her and I'm bawling. *Dammit.* "I'm here," she says, waiting while I give up the search for a box of tissues and use a decorative hand towel to soak up the spontaneous tears and stop up my runny nose. Good thing I wasn't planning on going out tonight.

"I found him, Kathryn. I found him, and I think maybe... he needs me."

"Slow down, Brooke. You found who?"

I sniffle into the phone, unprepared to speak just yet.

"Oh. *Oh.*"

This is why I called my stepmother. She's so perceptive, and always so attuned to me. I hadn't even told her I was searching for River, but I tell her *I found him*, and she knows.

Chapter 3

river

I am small. I am quiet. I wish I was invisible.

In my old house, I hid when people came. One time, I was asleep on the couch next to Mama when her friend Harry came over. Harry is mean and loud, and I hate him the most. I pulled my blankie over my head. I held my breath and didn't move.

But he pulled the blankie away. "This worthless critter's still here?"

When he grabbed my arm, I shook my head until he was blurry. *I'm not a critter. I'm not.*

He laughed, and his mouth smelled like the trash under the sink. "Critters like this are even scrawnier when you skin 'em." His hand was like a claw, and I couldn't make him let go even though I tugged hard as I could.

"Harry, let him be." Mama's eyes were squinty, but her lips weren't pressed together, like when she was about to yell or hit. She never hit me very hard, but I didn't like her to be mad. Sometimes she hugged me after and said she was sorry.

Harry squeezed my arm harder, like he wanted to snap it into two pieces. I wondered what sound it would make if he did.

His fingers looked like bones from a skeleton.

I found bones in the yard one time, under some old boards. They were a bird shape, but flat. I was real careful when I dug it loose and took it to show Mama, but her mouth made a flat line and she squinted and yelled to get that dirty dead thing out of her kitchen. I dug a hole in the dirt and put the bones in and covered it, because you're supposed to bury dead things in the ground.

Skeletons are a lot of bones that make up a whole thing. I saw a person skeleton once, at Halloween. It was sitting in a chair, like it was waiting for somebody. There were big holes with no eyes, but it looked like it was smiling. No guts or brains or heart, either. It was empty.

Harry was like a skeleton wearing a skin T-shirt stretched over his whole body. Mama told him all the time he didn't have a heart. When he wasn't around, she told me he didn't have a brain. I don't know if he had guts.

"Don't he ever talk?" Harry stared at me like I was a bug. Like he was thinking about squashing me.

"Not really." Mama sighed, because I made her sad.

"A boy his size that won't talk? So he's a *retard*? You should give him to me for a week or so. I'd learn him to talk."

I stared at Mama, telling her *no* with my eyes. My eyes promised her that I would be good every day. I would do everything she said.

"This little shit don't even look like you. You sure he's yours?" When he laughed again, I tried not to breathe in the stink.

"He's adopted."

"You *adopted* him? Why the fuck would you wanna do that?"

Mama looked at me and shrugged her shoulders. "I wanted a baby, I guess. A family."

"Shit, woman—you better not start whining about your old man again, because I will up and leave right now—"

Mama's eyes got wide. "I won't. I wasn't." Her voice was shaky.

"Uh-huh."

Harry's fingers let me loose a little bit and I yanked my arm away and ran to the stairs. My heart was bouncing inside me like it wanted out. It swished so loud in my ears that I couldn't hear my footsteps or his. I got to Mama's room and her closet door was open. I slipped into the dark and pulled the door shut behind me. I fell down on my hands and knees and crawled through the shoes and clothes and trash on the floor.

I found my spot in the corner and pulled my knees up to my chin. I wanted my blankie, and my stomach growled that it was hungry, but I wasn't going back downstairs. Not until Harry was gone. Not until Mama came to find me.

Wendy never forgets to make dinner. I eat until my tummy's full, but I hide food in my napkin and take it to the room that I share with Jerry and Sean. Sometimes I look in the kitchen trash can and find food in there, too. I hide it all in my room. In a box under my bed, or in my closet inside my shoes.

Wendy breathes out a big breath when she finds it. She almost always finds it, but sometimes not for a few days. "Phew, what a horrible smell! Good Lord almighty. River, you don't need to hide food anymore. You get three squares a day here. Don'tcha know that?" She pinches her nose and throws the chicken sandwich into a trash bag. I had to tear it into three pieces to hide it in my shoes.

I nod and stare at the floor.

Wendy doesn't squint, and she never hits me, but she looks sad when she finds the food. When I have bad dreams, she shakes me a little to wake me up. She always says, "You're safe here." I don't say anything back. I don't say anything ever. She's sad about that, too.

But I still hide food, and cry at night, and miss Mama, even if I feel bad for making Wendy sad. Just like I made Mama sad.

Dori

I just told my parents what Reid did for Deb last fall. They're shocked, and grateful, but it hasn't changed their opinion of him where I'm concerned.

"He's using his money to buy you." Mom shakes her head, aghast. "He has an endless supply of financial resources—as impossible as it would have been for us to pay for that private room, how is it a sacrifice for him? He's not stepping out onto any limbs for you."

I peer at her. "What do you expect him to do to prove himself to you?"

Her arms crossed over her chest like a shield, she slumps back into her chair and scowls at the tabletop. "I don't know if it's possible, to be honest. We're always going to be worried that you'll end up hurt."

"Mom, horrible things happen, and we can't prevent them. There isn't some grand destiny controlling it all—"

"Oh, Dori." Dad has tears in his eyes. "Have you lost your faith? Have you really?"

I stare at my hands, because I can't look at him and answer truthfully. "Maybe what I have faith in right now is the fact that Reid loves me, and that I love him. And maybe someday that, too, will no longer be true. But we all had faith that Deb would become a doctor. We had faith that Bradford and she would get married, and they would be happy together. She had faith in those things, too. I always thought that someday, when I lose you and Mom, I would have Deb to lean on. We'd share each other's grief. And now, I'll go through that alone. Or maybe tomorrow someone will run a stoplight and you'll lose me, too—"

"Dori!" Mom gasps, and I glance up and see the shock on her face. "*Don't say that*. Please don't say that."

"But it's true, isn't it? Deb just slipped and fell, and now her life is basically over." At the agony painted on their mirrored faces, I amend, "She's not who she was, and I can't pretend she is. Nothing is certain. Nothing is preordained." Dad closes his eyes, and I hate knowing I'm causing him pain. But I have to make them understand how I feel, so they can learn to accept who I am. "All I know is this—I'm loved by my parents, and my dog." I lay a hand on Esther's wizened head and she nuzzles into my hand. "And I'm loved by Reid. I don't want to think about ten years from now, or two years, or next week."

They exchange a glance, and I know they've already discussed their united reaction should they fail to talk me out of him. Their Parental Plan B.

"Okay, Dori. Okay," Dad says. "What do you—what do you expect us to do?"

I know that any compromise reached will be strained, but I'll take it.

"I want you to give him a chance. You wouldn't object if everything else in this relationship was identical, but it was with Nick instead of Reid."

"*Nick* doesn't have a worldwide reputation for womanizing!" Mom says, her blurted words finding a too-easy target.

My answer is subdued, because of course it hurts to think of all of the girls he's been with, and all he has access to. "Reid didn't love those girls. He loves me."

"You're darn right he didn't love them. Or respect them." My father shades pink, but doesn't stop there. "How do you know what lies he may have told them to get them into bed?"

"I only know what he's told me."

"Exactly," he huffs.

"He wouldn't have to lie, or say an untrue thing, to get girls into his bed."

Mom eyes me. "And that doesn't worry you just as much? If not more?"

Esther's muzzle sits lightly on my thigh, her eyes staring up at me, anxious. I reassure my dog with careful strokes, but I can't convince my parents that their fears are misguided. The atmosphere is unbearably tense, and their protectiveness—a shield behind which I've always moved freely—has become a thick bridle. Even as I try to relax within it, I'm pulling against the restraint.

"I believe what he's told me. I believe what he says he feels. And when it comes down to it, what he says he does or feels is mine to believe or not. No one else's." My voice strengthens with these declarations, and I see that this is how rebellions of all kinds gain strength—inside the avowals.

My mother narrows her eyes, and I know her question before she articulates it fully. "Dori. Are you and he—"

"*Mom.* Please don't ask questions you don't want answers to, because I won't lie to you. Not anymore."

Her face is a picture of defeat, individual features downturned in surrender. "So you expect us to sit by while you begin a sordid relationship with a... a celebrity." Her voice cracks, but wobbles on. "A young man who'll use you and cast you aside when he tires of you—"

"If that's what you want to believe. If that's what you think I'm capable of."

"I don't know what you're capable of any more, Dori," she snaps.

I sigh. "I see that. But maybe you never did."

Those are perhaps the truest words any of us have just spoken. When I open the door, he pulls off his sunglasses and steps inside, as beautiful as always. He's toned-down—as regular-boy as possible, for him: beneath his favorite Lakers cap, brim pulled low, wisps of blond hair fall across his forehead and curl around his ears and temples. He's wearing his button-fly jeans. His navy T-shirt isn't too closely fitted, but even still, it can't hide the solid curve of his wide shoulders and sculpted torso.

I press my face to his chest. Pulling me close, he wraps his arms around me and takes a deep, easy breath as I curl into him. I know that nothing is static. Nothing remains the same forever, no matter how much I wish it would. But in this moment, I love this boy, and I know he loves me, and I don't care if at some point that will no longer be true.

But my parents? I recall the words we exchanged and all the ones we held back, and I can't picture them ever coming around to accepting him—accepting *us*.

"Hey." He turns the brim of the cap backward and tips my chin to examine my eyes. "What's this?"

I duck my worried face back to his chest, muffling my words. "I can't believe I thought this would work."

He cups my shoulders in his palms, angling me away from his chest and peering into my eyes. "So little confidence in my charm, Dori? I won *you* over, didn't I? Although I suppose we'd fare better if we don't reveal a few of my more appealing attributes to your parents. Your obsession with my button-fly jeans, for example, might lose something in translation."

I choke an incredulous laugh. *This is never going to work.* Without loosening my grip on him, I chew my lip and he quirks an eyebrow, waiting.

"Can we just run away from home?"

His mouth breaks into a grin, eyes flashing mischief. "Sure. Where to? Paris? Madrid? It's summer in Melbourne, you know."

I'm so not used to these surreal sorts of conversations. I know he's playing along with my apprehension, giving me an out he knows I won't take, but if my request was serious, none of these are impossible destinations. A couple of days ago, he asked me about my birthday, which is a month away. In a humorous attempt at subtlety, he brought up cars a half hour later, quizzing me about transmission types and favorite colors.

Not quite believing he was seriously considering such an

outrageous gift, I mentioned that I won't need a car at Cal. "Hmm, yeah," he said, preoccupied with a video game. I thought that was the end of it until later, sitting at his kitchen table, he asked me how I intended to get around in Berkeley without a car.

"Awesome public transportation. And I'm taking my bike."

He paused, a forkful of pasta halfway between his plate and his mouth. "A bike, as in a bicycle?"

I laughed. "No—the other kind of bike. I'm actually a closet Hell's Angel. Wanna go for a spin on my Harley?"

I squeaked when he pulled me from my chair onto his lap.

Hands gripping my waist, he bowed his mouth to my ear and breathed, "Yes. Yes, I do."

And then his father strode into the kitchen, announcing his presence by clattering dishes onto the butcher-block island while feigning ignorance of our PDA-laden presence at the table.

Now, I tap a finger against my chin and pretend to consider running away from home to *Melbourne*. If only. "I guess I should pack my swimsuit."

"Mmm. Better and better. Do you own a bikini?"

"Well, no."

That single dimple appears at the edge of his lopsided smile. "Then I guess we have some shopping to do first." He lowers his mouth to mine just as my dad—who refuses to pretend he doesn't see us—emerges from the hallway to his study and clears his throat.

"Well, *that* went well." Sarcasm is a favorite line of defense for Reid.

I knew Mom and Dad might be inflexible. I couldn't very well expect them to feign delight when they're so opposed to the notion of Reid and me together, but I never thought they'd be openly prejudicial. My altruistic parents urged their daughters to reject racism, bigotry and intolerance, and our entire lives, Deb and I learned by following their examples. Now I'm facing the fact that their broad-mindedness only exists so long as the individuals aren't famous and affluent.

I'm afraid to look up at him—to see how he's dealing with the short, denigrating interview my parents just put him through. He seems remarkably unperturbed by what they said and how they said it—more so than I am. I'm livid and embarrassed.

"I'm sorry. I didn't know it would be that unpleasant."

He chuckles. "Unpleasant, huh?"

"Understatement?"

"A bit, yeah."

My parents have gone to their room, leaving the brightly lit living room to us. The soft mumble of their voices signals their open door at the top of the staircase—an unspoken edict that Reid is not to set foot on the stairs, let alone into my bedroom.

They weren't this watchful four years ago, when I was dating Colin, who pretended to be trustworthy and decent, not that I blame them for failing to see through his façade. I just wish they could understand that one of the things I respect about Reid is— oddly enough—the fact that he's honest about who he is and what he wants, no matter what it is. I guess that's why I believe him when he says he wants me. When he says he loves me.

"Hey." He bumps my knee with his, and then turns to draw my legs over his and pull me closer. "You okay?"

"Are you?"

He half-smiles. "C'mon now. You don't think I'd let a little parental reproach stand in my way, do you? You know me better than that. I *live* for disapproval. It's expected of me. My fans would think I was dying or something if parents started randomly approving of me."

Chapter 4

Brooke

Travel is nothing unusual for me. Though getting from one place to another via various airports is tedious as all get-out, it's just something to endure. It's not panic-inducing, for chrissake. Even so, my flight leaves in three hours, and every time I think about landing in Austin, I feel like I'm going to puke.

One wheeled Louis Vuitton bag waits by the front door, and in ten minutes the other will join it, ready for the car service to transport me to LAX. I've put off calling Reid back, still unused to voluntarily sharing information with him. Doing so borders on trust—something altogether unnatural in conjunction with Reid Alexander. But I said I'd keep him posted, so I dial his number, fully expecting to go to voicemail.

Instead, he answers, annoyingly cheerful. "Hey, I was just about to call you."

Balancing the phone between my shoulder and ear, I sweep a load of cosmetics from the vanity counter into a travel bag and zip it shut. "You know this is *Brooke*, right?"

"I looked this time. Aren't you proud?"

What right does he have to be so fucking happy? Oh, yeah. Because he's Reid Alexander, who checks out of any sense of responsibility over anything ever. "Glancing at your screen before answering your phone is a debatable source of pride, Reid, though I guess you have to take it where you find it."

He ignores the barb. "So what did you find out?"

Am I actually talking to *Reid*, or has some alien taken over his body? He's too happy to be ill. Though I sure as hell know crazy

29

people can be irrationally happy. "Uh, well, Bethany brought a photo of him—"

"Really? Wow."

"—and like I told you, he's in foster care. Long-term foster care."

"What do you mean—'long-term'?"

"The parental rights of his adoptive mother were officially terminated months ago. Her husband died a couple years ago—Bethany's checking on how, not that it matters. It looks like she started using meth after that and didn't care who she took down with her. She's been through court-ordered treatment twice and blew it both times, so she's never getting him back." I think about a two-year-old River, left with no father and a drug-zombie of a mother—and I stuff two pairs of jeans into my case with more force than necessary. "I don't know where she is now—jail, crack house, on the streets hooking for daily hits—and I don't care."

"Jesus. Wow."

I roll my eyes at his second *wow*. I'm so not in the mood for his incredulity. Not when I'm damned sure he's going to drop this cold as soon as he knows what I'm about to do.

"I'm going to Austin."

If question marks were audible, I'd have just heard one from his end.

"That's where he is—just south of Austin."

"So you're going to go to Austin to—what?" Suspicion laces his tone, not so glib now, like he's finally getting it.

I told Kathryn and Bethany Shank that this trip was part responsibility, part curiosity, but that was stretching the truth. This child I've never seen or held exerts a deep, gravitational sort of draw. Against all odds, I feel a bond between us that has for four years surfaced on his birthday only. It isn't mere curiosity pulling me to Texas and I know it.

"I'm going to check on his situation. I'm going to find out if I can get him back."

Silence. Dead silence. I wish I could reclaim the words and leave them unsaid. It figures that Reid would be the one I blurt the whole truth to.

"Brooke, the kid's not a pair of Lanvin slingbacks. You can't just put in an order at Barney's and pick him up later. You gave up your rights to him. He can be adopted by someone else now, right? You gave him away—"

"I know that, Reid. Don't you think I fucking know that?"

I hate that he put it that way—*gave him away*. As if I sacrificed nothing to do it and traipsed off scot-free, like he did.

"Yeah, okay, okay—but no one's going to let you disrupt his life now just to—"

"Disrupt his life? He's in foster care. And I'm his *mother*."

More silence, and I think I'm as stunned as he is by my declaration. It's clear that he doesn't feel the same obligation I feel, but this has never been his burden. It has only ever been mine. His twelve-step apology, no matter what it stems from, doesn't extend that far.

"Look, I don't expect you to be involved or anything, okay? I didn't claim that you were his father four and a half years ago, and I won't now—not that there might not be some media speculation—"

"*Brooke*. You can't seriously mean to go to Austin and bring him back to LA? What about your career? Or the fact that you're twenty? And single?"

I should have known he wouldn't understand.

"What, like there's no such thing as a single mother? Besides which, I can't think that far ahead right now. All I know is he needs me and I'm going and I don't give a shit who thinks what about it, including *you*. Just deny you're his father, if it comes to that. I'm sure Graham and Emma won't tell, and they're the only ones who know. I have to go now. Later, Reid."

I press *end* and toss the phone onto the bed.

I still hate saying Graham's name. Or thinking about him. I press my fingers to my sternum, hard, because it hurts. It always hurts when I think about him.

The weather in Austin is close to that of Los Angeles this time of year, though it's a bit more volatile. I roll up a jacket and cram it alongside the jeans. And then I stop dead, thinking about River. He'll need clothes. And toys. And soap. And whatever else kids his age need. Special food? A nanny? I have no idea. *I have no idea*. The enormity of this decision swirls around me and fills the room, insinuating that I can't possibly do this.

I'm going to fail. One way or another, I'm going to fail.

I've heard these same sorts of prophecies inside my own head my entire life, and I learned long ago to ignore them. At fifteen, I decided to become a movie star, and now I am. I run my career and my personal life as I see fit, and no one—*no one*—tells me what to do. I screw up occasionally—like I did with Graham. That failure cost me my best friend, and I'll never come to terms with it. "Dammit," I mutter, yanking the second case from the bed and shoving Graham Douglas from my mind. Again.

If I get to Austin and believe there's a viable alternative to me taking my son back, I'll consider it. Otherwise, I'm just going to have to figure this single parent shit out.

REID

Shit. Shit, shit, shit.

Tonight, Dori and I have our first public date. We have literally days until she leaves for Berkeley, which is an ass-numbingly boring five-hour drive from LA. The last thing I want to do is drop *Oh by the way—I'm a father, sort of* on her right before she goes.

The longer I don't tell her, the worse it becomes that I haven't.

Unless she never finds out.

The probability of Brooke actually bringing the kid home with her like he's a puppy from the pound is doubtful. Aside from the legal implications of her having relinquished her rights to him, there's the simple fact that Brooke Cameron doesn't voluntarily interact with children. Even Graham's kid seemed like no more than a means to an end to her—an inconvenience she knew she'd have to tolerate to be with him. She's got a younger half-brother, I think, born after we split, but I've never seen a single photo of her with him. Although that could have as much to do with avoidance of her father, whom she loathes.

Would Dori do that for me? Though I don't plan to claim paternity publicly, no matter what I plead guilty to privately.

Christ, I can't even go there right now. Dori was abandoned by that guy in high school, and on the surface, what happened between Brooke and me looks no different. Except that Brooke told me she was pregnant, and *then* I abandoned her.

Fuck. If I were religious, I would cross myself.

Life was so much easier before I had a conscience.

Brooke has complete control over what happens now, and I'm never fond of that scenario. She's volatile and impulsive—not a safe combination, though she said she wouldn't tell. Graham and Emma aren't going to out me, either, though I can just imagine their united disapproval, if I happen to run into them.

Once I find out what Brooke plans to do, I'll tell Dori.

Or not.

Good plan.

Dori:	What are we doing? A hint, please? Or just tell me? I don't know what to wear.
Me:	A casual dinner, then a party at my friend John's place.
Dori:	A party??
Me:	It's not a big deal. If you don't want to go, we don't have to.
Dori:	No. If this is how you want to do it, then let's do it. What should I wear?
Me:	Whatever you want.
Dori:	You always say that!
Me:	And I always mean it.

Chapter 5

Dori

There's been no change in my sister in the five months since her accident, and according to her prognosis, none is expected. Locked in a persistent vegetative state, she continues to exist, but nothing more.

My parents finally stopped asking God for a miracle with every dinner table prayer, so I no longer have to bite back words that keep my stomach twisted into knots. Now, they simply request God's care of her—a prayer that still swells from the last traces of faith in my heart, even as I deem it incompatible with the fact that she's in this condition at all.

I'm spending time with Deb this afternoon, killing time before meeting Kayla and Aimee for another of their Cinderella transformations. While trimming the stems of the tulips I picked up on the way over, I relay the latest developments in my life. I'm getting better, but these one-sided conversations still feel contrived. When Mom, Dad or Nick comes with me, I'm silent except for replies to something they say. I'll stroke Deb's arm, help feed her, sing her favorite songs, brush her hair—but I only speak to her when we're alone, like we are now.

"I'm going out to dinner with Reid tonight," I tell her, followed by the clip-clip of my scissors pruning an inch from each stem.

The day after Reid's return to my life just days ago, I'd confided the truth of our newfound relationship into Deb's silent room. I felt like such a coward—confessing secrets to my mute, unresponsive sister and no one else. Now, my parents are aware of it, but their biased judgment of Reid means my sharing stops there. Deb, once again, is my confidante.

What I would give for her fair-minded advice instead of this silence. I don't know what she'd think of Reid, or our relationship, but she would tell me straight up, without any candy-coating. And in the end, she'd support whatever decision I made. Instead, I hear only the views of distraught parents and celebrity-awed friends. Neither feels credible.

"We're also going to a *party*. Crazy, right? Me, at a Hollywood party. His friend John isn't a celebrity, but he sounds like sort of a social climber." A sobering thought hits me then, as if Deb had stated it. "I guess I shouldn't judge, though—most people are going to think the same of me. Or worse." *Gold digger*.

I straighten the soft blanket on Deb's bed and perch next to her. "I have no idea what to wear tonight, so I invited Kayla and Aimee to come over and do their worst." Laughing softly, I recall my friends' doubly silent response when I phoned to tell them about Reid and our impending debut. I don't think I've ever known either of them to be stunned into silence—certainly not both of them at the same time. Five seconds later, they erupted into a breakneck dialogue about designers, color palettes, shoe trends and hairstyles, and all the reasons I'd been reluctant to tell them came rushing back.

The last time I'd allowed them free rein with my clothes and makeup, I'd woken up in Reid's bed with the worst hangover imaginable.

There were worse alternatives than that, though—one of which almost happened. I almost left a nightclub with a possibly psychotic stranger due to my alcohol-compromised state. Instead, I woke up to the beginnings of a fairytale love. One I still can't quite believe is real.

After arguing with each other for ten minutes as though I'm not standing there, Aimee and Kayla settle for a turquoise silk top with beading around the hem and neckline (Kayla's), a pair of dark, pressed jeans in an unfamiliar brand (Aimee's), and fuzzy chocolate boots (also Aimee's, and flat-heeled, thank the Lord). Naturally, they refuse to consider any of *my* clothing for more than half a second.

"No," Aimee says. "*Noooooo*. You should never wear your clothes when you go out with him. I'm not kidding. *Never*."

I decide to panic about that later. Right now, I don't have time.

Trying to talk Kayla out of using her mammoth case of cosmetics on me is futile, but we compromise with a semi-natural look when I remind her that Reid has only ever seen me with next-to-no makeup. "Except for the hangover night," I add, and they both avert their eyes, each reproached for letting me out of her sight at that club.

"You guys, stop with the guilty faces!" They peer back at me, sheepish, and I shake my head, insisting, "I made my own foolish decisions that night. I got luckier than I deserved when Reid spotted me. I don't blame you and I never did. I'm just not used to a lot of makeup, and I want to feel comfortable tonight."

Did I just say comfortable? What a totally unrealistic request.

"Did you notice how she just went, 'Reid,' like you'd say, 'Clark' or 'Josh'?" Aimee asks Kayla, who nods. They both sigh, and I struggle to resist an eye roll.

From the moment Aimee and Kayla arrived and even when Reid arrives to pick me up, Mom is conspicuously absent. She vanished behind my parents' closed bedroom door before I came home from Deb's and hasn't come out. Dad does his fatherly duty, opening the door and uttering his unfailingly polite, if clipped, "Good evening, Reid."

I hear Reid's response as I reach the top of the stairs, Kayla and Aimee at my heels. "Good evening, Mr. Cantrell."

"*Reverend* Cantrell," my father corrects, not meanly, but not in the playful manner in which he'd have spoken to Nick—whom he directed, *Call me Doug*.

"*Reverend* Cantrell," Reid parrots, unfazed, releasing my father's hand as I come into view. I soak in the sight of him, despite having seen him yesterday. His blue button-down and jeans seem understated, but I'd bet twenty dollars he knows exactly what wearing that particular shade of blue does to his eyes.

I'll be lucky if Kayla doesn't press so close to my back that I end up in a heap at the bottom of the staircase.

"Aimee," she squeaks. "That's. Really. *Him*."

Reid's eyes sweep over me from head to toe and back,

unhurriedly, with no care of his rapt audience—my father or either of my star-struck friends. "Beautiful," he says, taking my hand, and I'm immediately thankful for my friends and their fairy godmother skills.

REID

"Ready?" I ask her, and it won't be the last time tonight I do so. We're in a short line of cars waiting for the valet.

Unhooking her seat belt, she takes a deep breath and squares her shoulders, as if she's preparing for a challenging Olympic performance instead of a night out. Her huge brown eyes turn to me as she nods. "Ready."

I suppress a laugh and lean to kiss her temple. "This will all be over soon, and we'll be old news. I promise." These words have a fifty-fifty chance of becoming truth. Same chance of turning out to be entirely false, but I prefer to be optimistic about my promises.

"Okay," she says, so very serious. And trusting. Which is why tonight, I chose one of the places celebrities go when we want to feel a bit like ordinary people—ordinary, wealthy people who don't have to endure being photographed everywhere they go: Chateau Marmont.

Paparazzi aren't allowed into the long bricked drive, let alone up the steps or inside. Cameras are completely prohibited in the restaurant, in fact—and unlike some Hollywood spots, that decree is strictly enforced. Not that obsessive fans don't ever break the rules and get away with it—but dinner on the patio is a dark, candlelit affair. Good luck getting off a perfect shot with a cell phone and no flash.

The valet exchanges keys and a ticket with the driver in front of us and I slide my fingers down Dori's arm, taking her hand. "Have you been here before?"

She laughs as though that's the most ridiculous question ever posed. "Uh, no. I've heard about it, though. Does that count?"

"Hmm. I'll allow half a point for knowledge of it. Sounds like we might need to schedule a weekend in the penthouse, though. Or maybe you'd prefer one of the cottages."

She smiles up at me. "A cottage?" Of course she'd be more intrigued by a creaky, cloistered 1930s bungalow than a sumptuous, high-ceilinged suite with patio views of Sunset Boulevard and the West Hollywood hillside. "That sounds like a storybook suggestion. Should I bring my red hoodie and a picnic basket?"

"Only if you're going to say, *Oh, Reid, what a big*—"

"Stop!" she laughs, pressing her hand to my mouth. "Don't you dare finish that thought!"

I run a finger over the curve of her ear, knowing it would be bright pink if I could discern the color in the dim confines of the car. "I'm afraid it's too late for that."

Adorably prim, she purses her lips and changes the subject. "Staying at a hotel in the city where you live seems like an impractical thing to do, though I guess that's normal for celebrities."

"You've never done that?" My last in-LA hotel stay was at Brooke's insistence, when her whole convoluted plan to lure Graham away from Emma blew up in her face.

Dori shrugs lightly, glancing forward as I pull up to the valet stand and remember that her high school jerk of a boyfriend took her to a motel when she turned fifteen, and then dumped her a month later—when he turned eighteen and she became jailbait.

I'd like to beat the shit out of that guy, even if it has been nearly four years.

"Looks like I have a new goal: *Teach Dori to be impractical.*"

She shakes her head, bemused. "I don't know, Reid—that sounds like an unattainable goal." The valet opens her door and she starts before taking another deep breath and accepting his hand. She's a bundle of nerves. I doubt she's going to relax all evening, and God knows I probably won't be able to talk her into loosening up the Reid Alexander way—with a shot of something old and expensive.

"Challenge accepted, Dorcas Cantrell," I murmur, jumping out of my side of the car and coming around to encircle her shoulders and lead her inside. *Challenge accepted.*

I order the chilled crab and avocado for an appetizer, and a bottle of torrontés. Dori asks for a glass of water. At my nod, the waiter fetches a trendy bottled water, decanting and pouring it into her glass while maintaining a perfectly blank expression. Dori arches a brow and mouths *impractical* at me with a smirk. I smirk back. She has no idea what impractical things I can come up with where she's concerned.

By the end of the meal, she's more relaxed. Despite the crush of people, the lush vegetation and flickering candles render the patio cozy and intimate instead of congested. There've been no camera flashes, of course, and no one's paid us any particular attention, other than the wait staff—all of them serving us with the same pleasant but impassive expressions.

It won't be this way in other LA haunts. At some point soon, Dori will be fully initiated into the public scrutiny that comes with being or dating a celebrity. She had a minor taste of it last summer, after the patio incident—but that was nothing.

Not that I'm telling her that.

John's high-rise apartment is bursting at the seams by the time we arrive, which wasn't exactly what we agreed on when he begged me to let him host Dori's coming out party. (Another thing I'm not telling her—that John and I devised the party specifically to introduce her to our crowd in a less public venue.)

"Wow," Dori murmurs, leaning close. "Your friend has lots of friends."

John doesn't have friends as much as he has a network of useful acquaintances, and those acquaintances are all not-so-slyly eyeballing us the moment we hand our jackets to the girl at the door and begin to make our way through the crowd. I follow the sound of John's laughter over the music, feeling Dori's hand clamped to mine like our palms are permanently bonded.

"Reid—hey, dude. Where's—? Oh, there she is," he smiles, spotting her behind me. "Even smaller than I remembered."

Dori has only the vaguest of memories of John, since their only meeting occurred during the most inebriated night of her life—if not the *only* inebriated night of her life. She smiles back at him, but her grip on my hand doesn't loosen. I bend that arm behind her back so I can pull her closer. She may be curvy and strong, but John's right, she feels small tucked to my side.

"Hey, John. Lots of people here," I say pointedly. We'd agreed on twenty or so, and there are easily two or three times that many wandering around his place and spilling onto the balcony.

He shrugs and grins. "What can I say? I'm a popular guy." Snatching two champagne flutes from the bar's countertop, he hands them to us. "Welcome, Dori. I hear you've made an honest man of my bro, here."

I take one glass while Dori shakes her head infinitesimally. "Oh—I don't—"

Deftly separating her from me, John smiles and leans close, pressing the glass into her hand. "Just hold it. You can sip it. Or not." His hand at her lower back, he says over his shoulder, "I'll return her in a bit, dude. Maybe." His brows waggle and I glare at him.

"*John.*" My voice has an edge, but he's set on ignoring me, damn him.

Stopping at the first huddle of people, he asks, "Claude and Nichole—have you met Reid's girlfriend? This is Dori. LA native, Cal undergrad, way too smart for him. I'm just waiting for her to wise up so I can swoop in."

Eyebrows rise, eyes widen, and a couple of mouths fall open. I hear my name whispered, along with the repetition of the word *girlfriend* and speculations of *Who is she?* John is strategically blocking Dori's view of a couple of girls whose eyes run over her, one whispering to the other, their joint scorn palpable. I'm pretty sure I've slept with at least one of them. Shit.

The couple he addressed, though, smile and recover quickly. They're both semi-working actors, each patiently awaiting a turn in the spotlight, and it's standard John to keep his eye on up-and-comers like that. Just as he did with me.

"Oh! Dori? So nice to meet you," Nichole says.

"Thank you." Dori smiles, holding that glass of champagne like an ornamental shield. John's still got her opposite arm tucked into the crook of his elbow.

"I didn't know Reid had a girlfriend," Claude says, addressing her with curiosity. "This is recent?"

"Not only recent, but virtually unprecedented," John answers, proud to be the one to divulge this newsflash. As he escorts her to the next group, she throws an amused glance over her shoulder, and I'm convinced she can handle just about anything.

Chapter 6

Brooke

Kathryn offered to drive in and pick me up, but the flight is due to land close to midnight, and I have a downtown appointment at 9 a.m. There's no reason to trek out to the sticks just to turn around in a few hours and come right back, in rush hour traffic, no less. I set up car service and a hotel with an open-ended checkout instead—something my agent or manager would normally do, but I'm not even telling either of them I'm leaving LA, let alone the reason why. They'd freak out and blow up my phone with all the reasons I shouldn't go.

What's that thing they say about apologizing later instead of asking permission now? That could be the official Brooke Cameron motto.

My favorite part of flying first class is that I'm first on and first off—which means little to no interaction with my fellow passengers. That's a luxury I'm happy to pay for. Tonight, my row mate is some musician's kid. I vaguely recognize him, but can't recall which legendary lead-man-whore fathered him. He ogles me with interest, but I'm not sure if he recognizes me. I check him out while he's engrossed in an argument with the flight attendant over whether or not he can be served alcohol ("But this is *first class!*" he whines, as if she isn't aware of that), and my short perusal leads to the conclusion that he can't be a day over sixteen.

I slip my ear buds in, stare out the window, and ignore him. Soon he's playing an all-boobs-and-blood video game on his laptop, confirming his probable age.

By the time we land, all the airport shops are closed and the linked seating outside every gate is empty, the wide expanse of polished floor reflecting the methodical dots of yellow lighting in the main concourse. A large metal sign under a colorful collection of guitar art declares my hometown the "Music Capital of the World."

Pieces of this collection stand watch over empty baggage carousels, all but one of them motionless—probably my flight. I didn't check a bag, so I don't have to stop. I'm creeped out in such a huge, nearly unpopulated place, and my absurd imagination—courtesy two hours' worth of gory video game imagery—suggests a zombie apocalypse.

I hightail it through the nearly deserted airport to the appointed exit, where a car waits at the curb to transport me into the city I used to know so well.

I've only been back three times in the past six years—the first to give birth to River, the second to film *School Pride*, and the third to do a photo shoot promoting the film. Austin and I have grown and changed since I lived here, whether we welcomed those transformations or not.

I might be able to retrace my steps, but I can't go back and choose an alternate path. Far too late for that.

I was fifteen when I went on location without parental supervision for the first time. Reid, a year younger, was the only cast member near my age. As minor characters, we had few scenes and were too often left to our own devices. We quickly formed an alliance against being bored out of our minds.

One afternoon during the first week, I sat on my trailer steps and watched as he attempted to perform a routine trick on the longboard he'd brought along. Over and over, he glided across the concrete, hooking the edge of the board and jumping simultaneously, but never quite landing it.

He was so pretty. So cocky. So determined. So doing it *wrong*.

The fifth time he screwed up, he fell on his ass and I chuckled. Scowling, he swiped blood from his elbow and dared, "Why don't *you* try it, if you think it looks so easy?"

I didn't tell him that my stepsister, Kylie, was a skilled skateboarder, and I'd known how to pop-shove it like a pro since I was ten. Pretending ignorance, I listened as he explained the how-to. When I got a running start before jumping onto the board and pumping it even faster, he looked startled. With a practiced flick of my foot, I flipped the board, landed it smoothly and glided by him wearing a cocky grin of my own.

As he walked up, I stepped off the board and popped it up and into my hand to give it back. Placing his hand atop mine instead of taking the board, he pushed right into my personal space, eyes bright. "That was *awesome*," he said. "And *so* freakin' hot. It makes me want to, like, kiss you or something."

"Okay," I said, heart pounding from the physical exertion, the anticipation of my first kiss, or both.

If he was surprised by my instant acquiescence, he didn't show it. Instead, he stepped closer, bracketed my waist with his hands, and leaned to give me a kiss that was more like several small kisses in a row, each one better than the last.

I didn't know then that he was experiencing his first kiss, too. And his second. And his third.

Dori

The farther I get from Reid, the more anxious I am. I don't know any of these people, and I don't know this roguish boy guiding me through the crowd with his hand at my lower back, either. I know he's Reid's best friend, but any time Reid tries to describe their relationship, he ends up shaking his head and shrugging. "You'll see when you meet him. He's just *John*."

So far, I've concluded that John is a habitual flirt and a shameless celebrity suck-up, and his language is as atrocious as Reid's was—or more likely as atrocious as Reid's *is*—I have no delusions that I've changed him, only that he attempts to abide by my limits when he's around me. Judging by tonight's spate of accolades concerning my education and social service record, John is also determined to get on my good side. Or elevate me to sainthood by the end of the night.

I clear my throat to correct the erroneous statement he's just made to a couple of girls lounging on his sofa—girls who are now appraising me curiously, as if I have extra limbs or a blue skin tone.

"I'm not actually a missionary."

He frowns. "But Reid said you went to Puerto Rico or Brazil to hand out shoes or bibles or something."

"Uh, I went to Ecuador to work as a volunteer music teacher at a mission school—"

"Mission school. Right. So you're like, a missionary."

Oh my *word*. I take a breath. "Well, no—missionaries usually accept long term or even lifelong assignments; they're dedicated to doing evangelical work as well as practical objectives like establishing schools or hospitals—"

"But you just said you were helping run a school in Panama."

I sigh, recalling Ana Diaz, my program director in Quito who fights a daily, year-round battle against poverty, crime, and uneducated parents who can't imagine anything better for their children—who send them out to shine shoes or pickpocket or anything that might put food on the family's table that night.

"She said Ecuador," one of the girls says, scrutinizing my face. Like all the other girls here, she's dressed casually, but something about the way the fabrics drape over her says *money*. Her eyes are dark and alert. I'm certain she can tell that I'm completely out of my element.

John shrugs. "Po-tae-to, po-tah-to."

She rolls her eyes and mutters, "Idiot." John feigns an insulted gasp, voicing his unconcern over her opinion wordlessly. Ignoring him, she asks, "So, you're Reid's girlfriend?"

My heart flips over at the word and I nod, absorbing the disbelief in her crooked brow and swiftly repeated head-to-toe inspection.

"I'm sorry, it's just—you seem really… not his type."

I flush and John turns me, saying, "No need to be a bitch, Jo—"

"No." She leans forward. "I mean, she's totally unlike his *last* girlfriend."

John stops, turning back to her. "I *know* you don't know Emma Pierce."

"Not her." Her lip angles in a sneer of disgust. "Brooke Cameron."

My mouth falls open. Brooke Cameron—the beautiful star of *Life's a Beach* with whom Kayla and Aimee have a love-and-hate-from-afar relationship. The girl who played Caroline in Reid's last movie. *She* was once his girlfriend?

"Jesus, that flaming disaster was like a hundred years ago. And you remember it?" John laughs. "Obsessed much?"

"Fuck you, John," Jo says, surging up, eyes flashing, drink sloshing onto her hand. "I'm not the one content to be his man-whore sidekick. No offense," she tosses at me.

"Uh..." I glance over my shoulder, looking for Reid and fighting claustrophobia.

"God, okay you two—that's enough." The other girl pipes up, her voice as tiny as she is. She stands, hands on hips, glowering up at John. "I thought you were going to be nice."

He pulls her in close with his opposite arm. "Maybe you should keep your roommate on a leash, Bianca. Or muzzled."

"John!" She shoves him in the chest halfheartedly, the attraction between them obvious.

"C'mon, Bianca." Jo stomps toward the bar setup in the corner.

Bianca heaves a groan, shakes her head and follows her friend.

Watching them go, lips flattened, John mumbles, "Well, that was nasty."

"Is Bianca your—?" I stop, unsure how to classify her.

He takes the fluted glass from my hand, quaffs half the bubbly contents—champagne, I assume—and hands it back. "We're on-again, off-again. Can't stand her charming roommate, though, in case you didn't catch that."

"Hmm. I hadn't noticed."

He smiles wolfishly at my sarcastic tone, and I begin to see the place where he and Reid connect. "I like you, Dori."

"Hey." Reid's eyes are dark, one brow quirked as he draws me from John's side. "Hands off, man. I don't want to maim you at your own party." His threat is all for show, as is John's theatrical palms-up. Reid's voice goes softer and he angles his head in the direction taken by the girls. "And, uh, what was *that* about? Why is Jo even here?"

"Bro, seriously—be realistic," John scoffs. "I can't just invite a bunch of *guys*."

The implication is unmistakable: there's no avoiding some things, like the ghosts of Reid's sexual past. There are too many girls in his social circle, in this city, in this *country*, for us to avoid them all. His Hollywood Lothario reputation precedes him. My friends and even my parents are all too familiar with it. I've made it clear that I don't want or need to hear the grisly details, and I think he was grateful he didn't have to confess them.

I expect the general public to wonder what in the world he's doing with me—I got a taste of that when I tripped and fell on top of him at the Habitat project last summer, sending the tabloids into merciless speculation. I expect to run into starlets and fans who want him, who've *been with* him, even, who might hate me on sight.

Pretty sure Jo is one of those.

But finding out that he was involved with Brooke Cameron for long enough that it was a known relationship? *He may have loved her.* That unforeseen possibility wells up, a reflux of the only fear I've refused to face. Despite the rumors that he's bedded half of young Hollywood—and the fact that he's never refuted those allegations, I hoped his heart was mine alone.

I want to reject the jealousy and insecurity that begins to boil in the pit of my stomach. I need the truth, whatever it is, but I can't ask him. Because deep inside, I don't want to know.

Chapter 7

Brooke

Norman Rogers, Kathryn's attorney—more of a family friend at this point since he's been her attorney since her divorce from my dad—sputters, incredulous, when I tell him I want River.

"But. Are you sure?" he asks, as if I would set up this appointment and travel from Los Angeles to Texas on a whim.

I grind my teeth. I survived the shocked reactions of Reid, my private investigator and my stepmother. What's one more? "Yes. I want my son back." On second thought, I should probably get used to this response. Maybe I should call Angelina and ask her how she fielded these sorts of skeptical reactions.

Eyeing me over his glasses, Norman says, "Alrighty, then." Tapping his gold-plated pen on the pad, he gets down to business. "The first thing we need to do is get in front of a judge and get a home study ordered. I assume you plan to move him to California? If so, we'll need to get an ICPC to coordinate the case between Los Angeles County and the State of Texas." He scrawls his lawyer chicken-scratch across a legal pad, plotting our plan of attack, I assume. "It'll be up to the judge whether the adoption takes place here in a Texas or is transferred to a California court."

"Adoption?" I throw some incredulity of my own at him. "But I'm his mother. Can't I just have him back?"

Norman stares down at the pad and underlines a couple of things, rubbing one thick finger back and forth on his forehead as if he's trying to buff away the premature creases this conversation will leave there. The silence stretches until at last, he clears his throat. "Brooke, River is in foster care. The State of Texas holds guardianship over him. There are specific procedures in place to make sure what's done now is in the best interest of the child."

"But I'm his mother," I whisper, repeating myself, the guilt swallowing me up like quicksand. I can barely breathe.

"Technically, Brooke, you aren't."

This statement slaps me in the face, stealing the remainder of my breath. I feel my mouth fall open and watch Norman's brows draw together in contrition, his lips tightening. He's given me the blunt truth, and as much as I appreciate him doing so, I didn't anticipate this answer.

"How long? How long until I can have him?" A tremor runs through my entire body, starting at my neck and shooting painfully to the tips of my fingers and toes. "Or are you telling me I can't—I can't get him back?"

Norman's rueful expression blurs while the rest of the room swims. "Brooke, you gave him up when he was born because you believed that to be in his best interest."

I seal my shuddering lips together. I gave him up because I didn't want him. I didn't even want to hold him before I gave him away. My relinquishment was no selfless act on my part—I just wanted my life back.

"The court will take that into consideration," he continues. Overriding my buzzing thoughts, his voice is tinny, as though his words echo through a can. "Best-case scenario, we're looking at four or five months—"

"Four or five *months?*" My words resound and twang and I don't care who hears or how I sound. "I can't leave him in that dirty, flea-infested place for *months!* I can't just go back home and leave him here like I did last time!"

Like explosives detonating a dam, something cracks inside my chest and to my utter horror, I'm bawling.

Norman stands and sits, twice, finally seizing a box of tissues from his tidy credenza and thrusting it at me as Kathryn bursts into the room, dropping into the chair next to me and pulling me to her shoulder. "Honey, you aren't abandoning him. We're starting a process here. Look—we want them to be meticulous. We want them to be careful. We don't know if there are grandparents who want him, or aunts or uncles who've already started this process. Maybe he's weeks or days away from a new home."

She knew. That's why she insisted on coming along today, and why she installed herself in a chair right outside the office door. That's why she was so restrained this morning on the drive from the hotel, venturing no opinions about what Norman might say. She already knew, or at least suspected.

"You want what's best for him, right?" she asks.

I nod and bury my face against her like I had as a child. How many times had I come to her when my own parents failed me? She'd kept me sane when no one else cared what I thought, felt or wanted. But if River has grandparents or aunts or uncles, where the hell were those people when he was suffering?

And where was I? Partying, or shooting another insipid *Life's a Beach* episode? A second wave of sobs washes over me, but I steel myself against it, like a sharp high face of rock against the tide.

What's best for my son is me.

As if I'd said these words aloud, Kathryn says, "Even if what's best for him might not be coming home with you right now? Even if what's best for him isn't you?" Kathryn's words light the landscape of my memory. Graham. The loss of his friendship and that sharp, buried pain in the center of my chest. I thought I was what was best for him, but really, I hadn't cared what was best for him.

I'd wanted Graham because Graham would have been best for *me*. I still believe that, though I see now—more clearly than ever—that I was not best for him. I wasn't what he wanted.

I want to be what's best for River. But what if I'm not?

I pull myself together. Breathe. Sit up straight. Press the tissue tight under each eye. Clear my throat.

"Yes."

REID

No paparazzi shots emerge, but one shadowy fan-submitted cell-phone image pops up on one of my fan sites, and within the hour, it's on all of them, as is speculation about Dori. John texts me the link.

John:	Word is out on your soooper-secret GF.
Me:	Is it ok to murder some of these people? What makes them think their stupid opinions about who I date matters to me?
John:	Come on dude. You've seen this a million times before. Literally.
Me:	I know. I just feel more protective of her.
John:	AWARE.
Me:	Yeah yeah. I'd say I'm sorry, but I'm not.
John:	Are you getting her a bodyguard?
Me:	I hadn't thought of that. God, she would freak. Can I do that without her knowing?
John:	Probably. But then she can't tell him who's safe. He might beat up some poor fucker who's just talking to her.
Me:	And that would be bad, right?
John:	Sounds like a question for Lawyer Dad.

When I show up for our second public date, I'm greeted by the sight of the media camped out along Dori's street. Not many—but enough to rattle Dori and her parents. A rental van sits in the driveway, backed up to the garage and probably already loaded. Her parents are driving her upstate to Berkeley tomorrow, and I'm not invited.

"They've always assumed they'd take me to college, move me into my dorm, meet my roommate, suffer through the tearful goodbyes—all that stuff—just the three of us," she told me.

I don't expect to be part of every segment of her life, but I feel like I'm in a tug-of-war with them. Consenting to assume second place is not in my nature, and chucking her parents' wishes out the window isn't in Dori's. The current stalemate is a fucked-up sort of compromise, but at this point—whatever works, works.

"How much do you trust me?" I ask just before we head out her front door.

She looks up at me—a little less made up than she was last time we went out. Her friends aren't here tonight. Her outfit—pale pink button-down shirt, gray cords, and generic loafers in a nondescript color—is less hip, a more girl-next-door than her previous (no doubt borrowed) ensemble. As happened with her collection of extra-large, philanthropically mindful T-shirts, though, it turns me on knowing that I'm the guy who knows what's underneath her plain veneer.

"Do you need to ask?" she says.

"I'm still getting used to it."

"I trust you, Reid."

Subduing a brief surge of guilt over the rather significant thing I'm still withholding, I tell her, "I'm going to hold your hand on the way to the car, which will be interpreted—correctly—as deliberate confirmation of our relationship. Try to erase that apprehensive little frown. Have you ever been on stage? School play, class skit, anything?"

She nods, the crease between her brows more pronounced and her lower lip drawn fully into her mouth—firm evidence of her anxiety. "I've done my share of class skits. Why?"

"Don't panic—I'm not giving you any lines. You just need to try to look *happy*."

The frown deepens. "I *am* happy."

I can't help but laugh. "Very convincing, Miss Cantrell." I trace the little furrow with my index finger, continuing down her nose and gently pinching her chin between my fingertips.

She takes a slow breath, closes her eyes, and relaxes her face into my hand.

Rewarding her with a deep kiss, my thumb strokes her cheek. "Perfect. Now hold that satisfied expression, and later this evening, I'll make good on the promise behind that kiss."

Before she can lose her nerve, I take her hand and we emerge into the first real shit-storm of paparazzi she's been subjected to. They call our names and a barrage of questions. "Reid—are you and Ms. Cantrell in a relationship now?" and, "How long have you two been together?" while cameras whirr and flashes erupt into the violet twilight. She's never squeezed my hand so tightly.

Making certain she's safely locked in before circling the back of my car to the driver's door, I open the door and flash the photogs a smile—a show of gratitude that they left us enough room to maneuver from the front door to the car.

"What about Emma Pierce?" a voice calls. "Does this mean you're over her? Moving on?"

I shake my head and chuckle. Man, they just do *not* give up.

It's been eight months since I delivered Emma right into

Graham Douglas's arms. When I met up with the two of them in Vancouver last fall, they were revoltingly happy—but seeing them together then only made me think of Dori, the infuriating Habitat girl I didn't think I'd ever see again.

Brooke: Call me. I have news.
Me: On a date. Will call tomorrow.
Brooke: A "date"? Is that what you're calling them now?
Me: Off limits topic.
Brooke: Fine. TTYT.

Chapter 8

Dori

Reid is trying to talk me into sleeping over as I slide my feet into my faux leather Payless loafers and he pulls on a paint-splattered Ralph Lauren hoodie.

"Did you wear that to the Habitat project last week?"

Glancing down, he shrugs. "Nah. It came like this."

"Huh," I say. "So it looks like that on purpose? I guess a good portion of my wardrobe is more hip than I thought." Silly me, wearing the less-shabby stuff.

I'm glad to be leaving town today for at least one reason—the fact that Kayla and Aimee will *kill* me when they see photos of what I wore last night. They've both admitted to stalking Reid online now, though I suspect they were following gossip about him long before he ever wrecked his car and stumbled into my humble social circle. They'll be appalled once they get an eyeful of my drab Fashion Don't, days after their warnings that I should never wear my own clothes out with Reid.

They never told me what, exactly, I'm supposed to wear in place of what I own.

He pulls me up from his bed and slides his arms around me. "I don't want to hand you over yet."

Trailing one finger down the jagged, over-sized metallic teeth of his hoodie zipper, I say, "We've already—*you know*. Twice." His arms tighten in response and he nuzzles my face with a low *hmm*. Forget what people say about makeup sex—I've decided going-away sex doesn't get nearly as much credit as it deserves. "If I stay, we'd probably just sleep anyway."

"And that would be bad because?"

I press my face to his chest and breathe him in. There's nothing I'd like better than to kick off my shoes and climb back into his bed. "It's my last night at home, at least for a while. Plus, Dad promised to make my favorite breakfast—banana walnut waffles—in the morning."

His fingers encircle my wrist and he pushes the cuff of my shirt back to kiss the pulse thrumming there. "I can get you home in time for breakfast," he whispers.

Eyes downcast, I can't swallow the lump in my throat. "I'll miss you."

"No you won't," he says. My eyes flash up and give my misery away, and he sighs. "God, Dori. You won't miss me because I'm going to see you as often as I can get there or fly you here. In fact, the premiere for *Mercy Killing* is right before Valentine's Day. I want you to come with me."

I almost forgot about the romantic action flick he'll be promoting with Chelsea Radin over the next month. Thank goodness I met and liked Chelsea and her husband, Chad, last week. Some of the steamy film stills of her with Reid are unbearable to look at. I don't know if I'll be able to take the live-action scenes. I'd love to ask Chad how he copes with his wife doing scenes like that without wanting to pulverize her male costars.

"During the week? I'd have to skip at least a day of classes, Reid—I don't think that's a good idea, so early in the semester."

He groans. "How did I know you would be that academically conscientious type of student? Bet you got straight A's in high school, too."

"No, I didn't." When he crooks an eyebrow, I admit, "I have to study incessantly to do well. Learning new things doesn't come easy for me like it does for some people, and cramming doesn't work, either. I did earn mostly A's, but I got several B's and two C's."

"Oh, no!" he mocks. "*Two?* We might have to break up. In what subjects did you make these abysmal grades?"

"Pre-AP geometry and biology. Freshman year."

After Colin dumped me and I had an abortion. When I could hardly stomach going to school and seeing him every day. When I

sank into a depression so deep that only Deb was able to reach me.
His expression darkens. "Freshman year—spring semester."
I nod, and he pulls me tighter.

It's pre-dawn dark when Dad comes into my room bearing coffee. "Wake up, sleepyhead," he says, setting a mug on my night table and gently jostling my shoulder.

I grumble incoherently, having only had four hours of sleep after Reid dropped me off. He wanted to walk me to the door, but I asked him not to because it too closely recalled our final farewell—or so we thought—before my volunteer mission to Ecuador. Before Deb's accident. Before I lost myself, dragged under by the implicit loss of my sister and my faith. I didn't even begin to resurface until Reid found me.

We kissed goodbye in his car for half an hour before I could make myself go inside. I waved once before slipping inside the darkened house, and as soon as I shut the door, silent tears began skating down my face. Treading carefully up the staircase—the last thing I needed was for Mom to get a look at my dejected expression—I chided myself for being ridiculous. I would see him again in a week or two. Three at most.

Dad settles on the edge of my bed now and sips his coffee while I sit up and reach for mine.

"Ready for a long, boring day on the road, followed by a million trips from a pint-sized rental truck to your new dorm room?"

"Ugh. Dad, sometimes your propensity to tell the absolute truth is less welcome than other times."

He chuckles. "You'll find out soon enough, once we get on the 5. Hours and hours of the opposite of a scenic thoroughfare. Although you're in luck—you'll be treated to my witty company the whole way! If you're truly fortunate, I'll bounce my Sunday sermon ideas off you. I'm dithering between either the trials of Job or Hannah's unceasing plea to God for a son."

I crack an eye open. "Gosh, Dad. Gloomy much?"

He shrugs and says, "They both came to good in the end."

"Sure, after lifetimes of suffering and praying for favors that were unobtainable without a miracle." Without waiting for his response, I shift the subject to the one we're avoiding. "So Mom is driving the car, and I'm riding in the truck with you? She's still that angry at me about Reid?"

He stares into his mug. "She's not angry, Dori. She's concerned."

"When I'm concerned about someone, I don't stop talking to them," I counter.

He nods without replying, and I see that he agrees with me in this, at least. Giving up on me, even if he believes I'm making rotten choices, isn't an option. I won't push him further, though, because my parents seldom disagree, and I don't want to be the cause of an argument between them. I just want to live my own life. Mom will either change her mind or she won't. If anyone can change it, it's my father.

REID

Me:	Call me when you're ready to tell me your news. Headed to an appointment with George.
Brooke:	Give me 10 minutes.

Brooke wastes no time on pleasantries when I answer—not that we've actually been pleasant with each other even once in the past five years. "I saw the attorney yesterday."

Ridiculously, I thought I'd braced myself well enough for this conversation. *Wrong.*

"You've retained an *attorney* already? Jesus, Brooke, what are you doing?"

"I'm applying to adopt him."

I nearly rear-end the tiny classic convertible in front of me, the Ferrari's brakes squealing and catching at the last possible second and whipping me forward in my seat. The driver turns and shoots me the finger. I grip the wheel with both hands to keep from shooting it back.

Whatever cracked idea I expected Brooke to disclose this morning, whatever I imagined her finding in Austin, whatever absurd course of action I dreaded she might try to take—this is miles beyond it.

"Oh, my God, Brooke—*why*? You can't be a mother to this kid—"

"Why the hell not?" she retorts. "I'm financially sound. I can provide whatever he needs. And by the way I *am* his mother."

She's lost her mind, though implying that probably won't do any good.

Logic? Worth a shot. "Kids need more than a biological connection and money—they need attention. Two parents, preferably. A family. They need someone to be there full time."

"Oh please—attention? A family—like you or I got? I have more *parents* than I can shake a stick at, and most of them *sucked*. And your parents were so clueless they let you nearly kill yourself on multiple occasions."

She has good points, dammit, though I prefer throwing my dad under the bus to blaming Mom. She's been quietly disappearing nearly every afternoon for about an hour and a half, and I haven't seen her drink a drop in almost two months. I suspect she's attending the AA meetings Dori suggested, but I haven't asked and don't plan to.

"You're right—they pretty much across-the-board sucked ass as parents. And yet you think you'll do a better job than any of them? At your age? By yourself? And with your proclivity for partying and screwing around?"

"God-fucking-dammit, Reid—you have *no* right to preach at me about screwing around—"

"Not to mention your language—and before you try to turn that around, remember that *I'm* not saying I want to raise a kid. And I don't give a shit who you sleep with, otherwise—"

"I party to keep from being bored—or haven't you ever done that?" She knows damned well I've done exactly that. "We're single, young celebrities. Partying is expected. It's practically an unspoken part of my PR strategy. I've never given an actual shit about doing it—I'm more than happy to ditch it. My public relations machine will just have to switch gears. And by the way— my sex life, not that it's any of your business, is heavily fabricated. I'm more particular than the media portrays me to be."

She's making too much sense, and she's thought this all the

way out—which is even more alarming. "Okay, fine, whatever—but you have to admit that having a kid to raise will interfere with your *socializing*, whatever form it takes, not to mention your filming schedule."

"Will it? How? Newsflash—lots of actors have children."

"Not when they're *twenty* and *alone*."

She's silent for two beats, and I think that maybe she'll be reasonable. But no.

"I'll be twenty-one in three months, and I'm not without resources and support. But more importantly, you're missing the point of this call. I'm not trying to convince you of the rightness of my actions or my suitability as a parent. I'm *informing* you, not asking your permission. If you'd rather I didn't keep you informed, I won't. It's that simple."

Shit. "No—I want to know. I mean, he's… he's mine, right? *Jesus*." My heart rate has doubled during this conversation. "Brooke, I haven't told anyone about him."

"No kidding."

"I mean *no one*. My parents don't know. George doesn't know. John doesn't know. God… My girlfriend doesn't know."

If I wasn't maneuvering through snarled LA traffic, I would take a five second timeout and beat my fucking head on the steering wheel. While counting.

"I saw that online this morning—so it's true? *You* have a girlfriend. An actual non-celeb, *pastor's daughter* girlfriend. Who you met during court-ordered community service? I was sure the whole thing was all some sort of clever public relations scam to help you dodge your recent weed-smoking, DUI-allegations image."

"No scam. It's real."

"Jesus. I don't even—I'm speechless. You've actually managed to shock me."

"Well, *ditto*. This insane conversation is jam-packed with shocking. You want to be someone's *mother*, and I want to be someone's *boyfriend*." I can't help but laugh, and she joins in, and soon we're both laughing so hard we can't stop. "We've come a long way, Brooke."

"Yeah," she says, softly. "We have."

"So what now?"

She takes a deep breath before answering. "I meant what I said before—I mean to claim River as mine, but I don't intend to reveal his paternity. So if you want to keep it to yourself, you can."

"River? That's his name? Did you name him—you know, before—"

"No. The people who adopted him named him. I don't know why they chose it. Maybe they knew my name and they thought *River* was a play on it. Maybe they named him after someone. Maybe they named him for the color of his eyes."

"He has blue eyes? I guess that's not surprising in a kid we'd make." I still can't wrap my head around this fact.

"They aren't just blue, Reid—they're *your eyes*. He looks like the photos of you that your mom kept in the family room, the ones on top of that baby grand no one ever played."

My curiosity overrides any sense I've got, and I want to know what he looks like.

Brooke, reading my mind, says, "Bethany only gave me one photo of him, but I'll scan it and send it to you, if you want."

"Brooke—are you sure about this? What you're doing? It sounds like he's had a tough time. You might mean well, but—"

"I'm sure. I'll send the photo in a few minutes. I'll get Kathryn to scan it."

"So how long will it be until you have him?"

"The attorney said four to six months until I can even lay hands on him."

"*What?*"

"I know, right? *Finally*—someone who gets my reaction. I about shit a brick."

This still feels completely unreal. "How will that work? You have to come back to LA to film the show, right?"

"I don't know. I think I'm going to have the home study done here, which means I need to establish residence here. I have to talk to Kathryn and Glenn. I'll have to travel back and forth until it's final, but I can't just *leave* him here. I can't just go back to my life, knowing he's here without me."

"But if you can't see him, what's the point of staying there?"

She sighs. "I'm praying for a miracle."

The thought of Brooke praying for anything is inconsistent with anything I've ever known about her.

Fifteen minutes later, she sends the photo to my phone. I've just arrived at George's office when I pull it up and nearly walk into the glass door.

"Watch out, dude!" a FedEx guy yells, waking me from my stupor in time to swerve.

Inside, I stop and stand motionless in the center of the glass and chrome atrium of my manager's building. As I stare at the photo on my display, I realize one thing. This wasn't real. He wasn't real. None of it was real—not until this moment.

Chapter 9

Brooke

I've been acting for six years and recognizable since the first season of *Life's a Beach* hit the small screen. So I've had rude questions hollered at me by gossip reporters as I try to get from my car to my front door. Probing entertainment columnists have interviewed me in conjunction with costars from films and cast mates from the show.

In other words, I'm accustomed to people asking seriously violence-inciting shit. But their most invasive inquiries don't hold a candle to the eighteen-page interrogation I just got from my case-worker.

Reading over my shoulder, Kathryn sighs. "Norman said they would ask intrusive questions, but *gracious*."

The topic of the current inquiry is my sexual history—first time, how many partners since, type of sex, frequency, protection, birth control, sexually transmitted diseases… and everything I feel, think or believe about any of those things.

"How many partners? Are they *serious?* Do I make an educated guess? Round up? Round down?"

"Brooke," Kathryn begins, "you don't have to do—"

"*I'm doing it.*" Head in my hands, I want to scream. Or break down and cry. Every self-destructive decision I've ever made—and plenty that only look bad because I'm female—rears up and hisses in my ear that I'm going to look as unfit as that meth-addled idiot who had the chance to be his mother and blew it. That no sane person would ever give me a child to raise, even if he is *mine*.

"I'm doing it," I repeat, less abrasively.

Squeezing my shoulder, Kathryn moves away from the kitchen table and leaves me to it, offering to make a fresh pot of coffee. I nod, pressing the heels of my hands to my eyes so tightly that no light sneaks in.

This house has been a refuge for me for so long. Half an hour west of Austin, it's surrounded by acres of scrubby hill-country; the homes here are large, set a distance apart from each other, and constructed from native stone and wood. They don't tower above the native landscape so much as merge perfectly with it, as though they simply grew here along with the sage and desert willow.

Even with my eyes shut, I envision Kathryn's familiar movements from the sounds she makes: scooping coffee from the copper-lidded canister, filling the reservoir, pushing the start button. She pulls mugs from one of the glass-door cabinets and sets them on the artsy concrete countertop decorated with inset bits of china and bottle glass. Along with the coffee, she'll bring me a homemade oatmeal or macadamia nut cookie, which I'll work off with a walk to the thin creek that serves as a winding border on one side of their property.

Kathryn and Glenn have agreed to let me claim their house as a secondary residence, so part of the home study will be conducted here. That means they'll have to submit to the same sort of scrutiny I'm undergoing: drug testing, criminal background checks, character references. Their home will be inspected top to bottom for safety concerns. Their pet immunizations and behavioral histories will be checked. And possibly their sex lives, allergies and what type of toilet paper they prefer will be investigated.

My agent calls when I'm taking the cookie-blasting stroll to the creek, and I almost hit *ignore*. I'm so not ready to talk to her about what I'm doing, but I suppose that isn't the only thing I'll have to do this week that I might not be ready to do.

"Brooke! Are you sitting? I hope you're sitting but not driving. You aren't driving, are you? Be honest."

Ever since one of her clients wrecked his Jeep when she called to tell him about a big audition—fracturing a kneecap and busting his forehead wide open—she's been reluctant to pass on any news to a client who's behind the wheel.

"Not driving, Janelle. What's up?"

"Okay, cool. First, I got a call from Stan this morning."

Stan is the executive producer of *Life's a Beach*. He's been perfectly professional in public, but he was less than enthused when I left the show to pursue a film career, and he seemed to take it personally—something he hadn't done when my costar, Xavier, quit for the same purpose.

Unlike my film, *School Pride*, Xavier's first film—a drama of all things—flopped like a trout in the final stages of death. My ex costar is pretty and beefy—with absolutely zilch going on upstairs. Perfect to star as a guy who runs a beachfront bar. Not so perfect to portray a character who has *thoughts*. Rumor has it he's begging for a chance to get his old role back.

"Oh, yeah?"

"This is totally hush-hush, of course," she adds and I *mmmph* in agreement. "He broached the unsurprising notion of bringing you back for the season finale. I gave him a half-hearted response because *hello*—my girl's got one successful film out and another one releasing next month, right? So then he said—again, totally hush-hush-off-the-record-don't-spread-it—that they're planning to bring Xavier back to the show in the same episode, and the angle would be something to do with the two of you in a way that wasn't kosher before now."

She's referring to the fact that when I left the show, my character was underage, and Xavier's character owned a bar. Every scene we filmed together sizzled with sexual chemistry, but they couldn't expand on it for fear of losing their family-friendly endorsements. Now, my character would be eighteen—legally able to bang the twenty-something stud.

Tastefully, of course.

"But I'm so not done! Are you sitting?"

"Uh, no." I whack long strands of dry grass out of my way with the stick I picked up a few dozen feet back, which makes me think of River, digging in the dirt in that photo. "But I'm good. Please, go on."

The creek gurgles just ahead, where the edge of the property slopes. If it were summer, I'd be kicking my flip-flops off. Instead, I'm hunching into my hooded sweater.

"So *then* I got a call from Hillary." Hillary was Janelle's college roommate, and is now a PA for some studio exec—and Janelle's number one source of studio gossip. "We're going to get a call in the next day or so. You're back up for the role of Monica."

I stop dead at the crest of the incline to the creek, unable to reply. I wanted that role *so badly* last fall when I auditioned. I got two callbacks, but ultimately lost it to my top rival, who'd been born with two golden tickets in her bratty little hands —a movie star mom and a rock star dad.

At the time, three months ago, I told myself it was just one film, and there would be others, but that call from Janelle felt like a slamming door. Or punishment from a higher power for one of many transgressions.

The slow-moving water below is far too frigid for wading, but temperatures in central Texas are seldom cold enough to freeze even the edges of moving water. Soon, it will be warm enough to stake out a corner of the large, flat rock that juts into the creek. I spent most of my fourteenth summer with both feet dangling from that rock, skimming the cool, shallow water with my toes while I read or daydreamed, lying back and staring straight up into a big azure sky dissected by branches from the live oaks growing along the banks.

And then Mom remarried and relocated the two of us to Los Angeles.

"Brooke? Are you there? You'd better not be driving—"

And here's my agent, offering me the role I've been preparing for, pining for, ever since I first set my mind on film stardom.

"Not driving. Just confused—I thought I lost that role when it went to Caren—"

"Yeah, well, maybe Caren shouldn't have decided to go drinking and skiing. She broke both legs and her pelvis!" Janelle is comically gleeful at this announcement; my competition isn't her client, after all. "She'll be in a half-body cast until at least summer, and then *weeks* of physical therapy!"

The thought of Caren in a body cast is so sad. Not. "Wow, so I'm definitely in?"

"According to Hillary, Caren just barely edged you out in the first place. *You're in.* I have to wait until we get the call, of course, and do my own little 'acting job'—pretending to be all shocked and surprised—but they'll want to set up a few meetings before filming, which is going to start in Australia."

"*Australia?*" I can't believe I forgot this factor. But then, I thought I was out of the running.

"That's not a problem, right? It's not like you're tied down to LA—or even the US."

Well, *damn*.

Dori

After a week of orientations, meet-and-greets and becoming adjusted to sharing a room, I'm ready for classes to begin. Entering campus mid-year has made the process more low-key, I think. I've been waiting for someone to identify me from the few public photos and grill me about my connection with Reid—but so far, nothing. The first time he shows up on campus and is recognized, my mundane status will be over. But until then, I'm finally here, at Cal. And for the first time in a long time, I'm contemplating my future.

My roommate, Shayma, is quiet. Whether she's listening to music, studying, or watching clips or videos on her computer, she wears donut-sized, sound-cancelling earphones. I learned the level of sound-proofing the hard way, yesterday afternoon.

After an informal walking tour of Telegraph Avenue, I came back to the room and found her staring at her laptop, headphones in place. I gathered my things to take a shower in the bathroom we share with four other girls, and came back a few minutes later, settling on my narrow bed to read over my course syllabi for the hundredth time.

In an attempt not to exclude her, I asked if she'd like to come out for pizza later with some other people I'd met. When she didn't reply, I realized she couldn't hear me. So I got up and tapped her shoulder—and she screamed like I was looming over her with a butcher knife and murderous intentions.

"*Barnacles!*" I stumbled back, eyes wide, as she yanked the already-askew headset from her head.

"OHMYGOD," she gasped, hand to chest. "I didn't know you were here."

We both jumped again when someone thumped a fist against the door four times in quick succession. "Everything okay in there?" a male voice called.

Red-faced, I opened the door to find two of our suitemates and two boys from the room next door, one of whom was holding a baseball bat. "Yeah. We're fine," I said, my heart still racing.

All four of them looked unconvinced, bat boy cocking an eyebrow and leaning forward to glance into the room. Shayma, giant earpads nesting under her jaw on either side, nodded. "I, uh, just had the volume up too high when I started a video."

"You're wearing headphones," he said.

She scowled. "They weren't plugged in."

"Good thing, or you wouldn't have working *eardrums* anymore." He tapped the bat against his palm, his body flooded with unnecessary adrenaline, no doubt. "Okay, well. Keep it down in here. Unless we're invited." He winked at us before I shut the door.

"I'm so sorry," I said. "I thought you'd seen me come and go from the shower—"

She shook her head. "Didn't see you. You're sure nothing like my last roommate. She was like a whole herd of elephants every time she came into the room. I've never been around a person who made so much *noise*." Gesturing to the headphones, she added, "That's why I got these. Otherwise, I couldn't hear a damned thing when she was around. Not even my own thoughts."

I laughed. "Well, you shouldn't have that problem with me. I'm pretty unobtrusive."

Smiling, she shook her head. "No shit. Me, too. I think we're gonna get along just fine." She narrowed her eyes, still smiling, which made her face look slightly squashed, like a Muppet. "Um. Did you just say *barnacles?*"

Reid:	Last chance to come to my premiere. I'm not going to beg.
Me:	:(

Reid:	Okay fine I'm begging. John thinks he's second in line, and it would be so wrong to make that true.
Me:	What about your mom?
Reid:	Hmm. I don't know that she'd want to go.
Me:	I would if I were her!
Reid:	Then why don't you want to go if you were you?
Me:	I told you, I would love to go, but I don't want to miss class. Stop being a bad influence.
Reid:	NEVER.
Me:	*sigh*
Reid:	I'll think about asking her. Calling you later. Be there.
Me:	Don't tell me what to do, Mr. Alexander.
Reid:	Cut, cut, cut! You're supposed to say "make me!"
Me:	I forgot my lines. Sorry.
Reid:	You're forgiven. Vixen.
Me:	Hahaha – no! You are so sexist.
Reid:	That sounds naughty when you say it.
Me:	You're impossible.
Reid:	Oh trust me. I'm SO possible. Please consent to answer my telephone call later this evening and I shall show you, Miss Cantrell.
Me:	That's better.

"So where are you tonight?" I keep my voice low, despite the fact that Shayma's got her headphones in place and wouldn't hear a word I say, even if I was conducting this call in song.

"New York. We have *Good Morning America* tomorrow."

I glance at the time, which is approaching 10 p.m. "Isn't it getting late there?"

"Yeah, I'm three hours ahead of you right now."

"What time is your interview?"

"Not sure what time they'll do the interview—but we head for the studio in about four hours."

"Four hours—don't you need your beauty sleep?"

"Do I? Hold on—I've got another call—" There's a pause while he checks the display. "Never mind. That can go to voicemail."

"It's not your mom, is it?"

"No," he laughs. "Looking out for my mom now, Dori? God, you're cute. It's just Brooke." He clears his throat. "No big deal. I can talk to her tomorrow—or whenever."

"Brooke *Cameron*? Why is she calling you? Wait. Scratch that. It sounds like something a jealous girlfriend would say."

"Jealous? *Rawr*. I like the sound of that," he encourages, and I wish he wouldn't. "So, classes begin tomorrow? What's up first?"

Outwardly, I launch into a loose explanation of my schedule: intro courses in statistics, psychology, sociology, and cultural anthropology. I tested out of a number of required prereqs. AP English took care of reading and comprehension, and my four years of Spanish—in addition to the fact that I used it nearly daily during community service projects—dispatched my foreign language requirement. I'm not as behind as I feared I would be, starting a semester late.

Internally, I'm wondering why Reid is getting late-night calls from Brooke Cameron, who is exactly the sort of girl I'd have imagined him with months ago, when he showed up—condescending, obnoxious, and oh-so beautiful—on my Habitat project. The fact that they used to date, and I dare not even think about what else, just makes it more difficult to ignore the fear.

What competition would you be, if a girl like that decides she wants him?

"I miss you," he says then, and I mash my insecurity into a corner.

"I miss you, too."

Chapter 10

river

I don't remember Mama's face. I remember parts of it, but not all of it together. Sometimes I dream about her and I know I can see her in the dream, but when I wake up I can't remember. Even if I squeeze my eyes closed really tight and try.

I don't remember Daddy at all.

Harry told me I didn't even have a daddy and that I am a bastard. He told me that a lot of times. I don't know what bastard means, but I know it's bad because Wendy's eyes got big when Sean grabbed my shirt and called me that.

Now he has to do a time-out.

I feel bad because I took Sean's Fruit Roll-Up and hid it in my pajama drawer. I don't know how he knows I took it, but he does. He tells Wendy, "But he *stole* my cherry Roll-Up!"

She shakes her head. "Then you come talk to me. You know that word is on the Never List, and furthermore you can't go all vigilante justice in this house."

"Huh?" he says.

She shakes her head again and sighs like she's tired, and then she takes his arm and puts him on a kitchen chair. She sets the timer for six minutes because Sean is six so that's how many time-out minutes he gets. His face is as red as that cherry Roll-Up and his eyes are angry and looking at me.

"River. Come with me," Wendy says, and I follow her to the bedroom. When we get there, she stands in the middle of the floor and opens her hand. I go to the drawer and get Sean's Roll-Up and give it to her. It still has the wrapper on. I'm glad I didn't eat it.

She slips the Roll-Up into her shirt pocket and takes my hand. We sit on my bed.

Her mouth makes a straight line, like she's holding her words in. You don't have to press your lips together to hold words in, though. I opened my mouth wide one time to see if the words I was thinking would fall out, but they wouldn't. If words don't want to come out, they don't. I don't understand when people say things and then they say, *I didn't mean to say that*. Words don't just fall out. You have to push them out. And sometimes, you can't push them out, even if you want to.

I count to nine in my head before Wendy says, "River, you can't take other people's things. It's bad enough when you hide your own food, but you can't take other people's food and hide it, too. Do you understand?"

My eyes get full of tears and I nod once and look down at my lap, which makes them run down my face. I wipe them on my T-shirt sleeve and chew my bottom lip. It tastes like the tears now. Like salt.

"Alrighty then." She pats my knee and looks at her watch. "You sit right there 'til you hear Sean's timer ding. Time out. Four minutes."

I want to ask her what a bastard is. Maybe a bastard is somebody who steals other people's food. Or just somebody you hate.

I hate Harry, and I would like to call him a word from the Never List. I remember his face, and I wish I didn't. I remember his face, and I can't remember Mama's. Harry is a bastard, I think. I wish I could forget him.

REID

On the elevator up to my manager's office, I was at war with myself. Should I tell him about Brooke, the kid, the adoption, or not? I knew from the start that if there was any possibility of my alleged paternity going public, George would have to know to have any shot at doing career damage control.

I've never worried that what I tell him will leave his office—it's like a confessional, without the claustrophobic booth or the Hail Marys. Even so, uncomfortable revelations made to George—or my parents—have always been on a need-to-know basis. There's a shitload that none of them know, but the fact that I have a four-year-old son dwarfs everything else to hell.

Undecided one way or the other, I found my manager in a rare, unfocused frame of mind. He didn't inspect me for indications of suppression, though I knew it was rolling off me like overzealously-applied body spray. If he was paying attention, he'd be able to tell, every time. Sitting back, he'd just eye me patiently and wait for me to come clean.

I realized uneasily that he was starting to trust me.

All I could think was *Damn, what crap timing for that.*

George detailed the bitch of a promotion schedule for *Mercy Killing* (killer promo is a good thing, because if no one wants to talk to you, your movie is dead in the water), while inside the front pocket of my jeans, my hand gripped my phone like it was either a grenade or a gold bar. Damn if Brooke wasn't the queen of mind-blowing text photos. As my manager droned, I struggled to concentrate on the three weeks of heavy promotion Chelsea Radin and I were about to do and prayed that something would stop Brooke from her insane resolution.

George and I spoke about Dori, of course—he'd seen the gossip sites, and I told him that yes, we were dating, and yes, it was serious. After a moment spent eyeing me like he was waiting for the punch line to an unfunny joke, his mouth quirked. "Huh."

I told him I was inviting her to the premiere, but called five minutes ago to let him know I'm taking my mother instead, at Dori's suggestion.

After a moment of silence, he scoffed, "Who is this, and what have you done with Reid Alexander?"

"Haha," I said.

Standing in the hotel bathroom post-shower, I wrap a towel around my waist. My razor is charged and ready to give me the perfect shaved-yesterday trim. While I wait for the steam to subside, I shift between watching myself gradually emerge in the steamed-up mirror, like a suspended, developing image in a darkroom, and staring, again, at the photo Brooke texted.

Some children don't resemble their fathers. I look almost nothing like Mark Alexander, for example. But this child, next to me, would be like seeing John next to his Dark Lord CFO father—too much resemblance to be anything but related.

Zooming in on the kid's face, I compare his features to mine. Similar face shape. Same eye color. Same mouth—full, almost feminine. I got into my fair share of fights as a boy over my *girly* lips. Until I got to be around eleven and it became clear that girls weren't bothered by that fullness. Quite the opposite, in fact.

I wonder if anyone will tell him that.

River's mouth isn't smiling, and I wonder if he ever laughs. The straight, pale lines of his eyebrows are barely there at all, and their shape, too, matches mine. But where my straight brows express confidence, and when necessary, conceit, he just looks solemn.

As though summoned, a new text appears from Brooke. I never called her back after I ignored her interruption during Dori's call. She called again this morning—also ignored. She didn't leave a message either time.

> Brooke: I need to talk. I can't talk to anyone else about this. Please.

Reluctantly, I dial her back, imagining some sort of ill-omened soundtrack in the background, intensifying with each ring like a swelling threat of doom.

"Thanks for calling," she answers. "I'm not—not asking for your opinion or your advice. I just need to talk, and I need you to listen."

Seriously? Just listen and keep my opinions to myself. When has that *ever* applied to me?

"Brooke, you can't just unload on me and expect me to *not* tell you what I think."

She's quiet for a moment, and I think maybe she's about to deliver a terse *Never mind* and dead air. Or *Fuck you* and dead air. Or just dead air.

"Okay. But that doesn't mean I'm going to follow—or even

consider—what you have to say."

"Then why tell me? Why not tell Kathryn, or—"

"Because it's a career thing. And usually, I would call..."

Graham. Damn that fucker. I get it, and we're even cautious friends, now—but damn.

"Okay, okay. Fine." I run a hand through my hair. The fact that she just wants to discuss a career crisis is sort of a relief, though I have to wonder what she'd have to say to me that she wouldn't much rather talk over with her agent or manager. "Spill."

She breathes a sigh and tells me how last fall, she nearly landed the lead in *Paper Oceans*—an upcoming film that has Hollywood buzzing, even pre-production. Impressed, I have no problem commiserating at the loss, especially since it went to Caren Castleberry, one of the industry's most talentless, well-connected twits.

"That sucks. Don't they know they need someone who can express multiple emotions for that role? She's basically got one expression." I switch on the razor and start a quick once-over.

"I know, right? If they did a graphic representation of her accessible emotions, they could use the same fucking photo for all of them. The most accurate one would be labeled *stoned*."

"Speaking of—didn't she just break her pelvis or something, drunk skiing?"

"Yeah. She totally did. Pelvis and both legs, according to my agent."

"Ouch. That'll put her out of commission for a few weeks for *many* things."

"*Gross*, Reid. Jesus."

"I'm just sympathizing!"

She huffs a breath. "*Anyway*—and this is totally classified because it's not on paper yet—I got the role."

"*Wow*. That's awesome." I recall her *I don't want your opinion* speech, and I'm guessing this isn't the dilemma she felt compelled to share. "So what's the problem?"

"Filming starts in Australia. This summer."

Ah. Talk about suckass timing. "Brooke, you might not get another shot at a film like this—a role like this. If this is the career direction you want, you don't have a choice."

"See, that's the thing. I do have a choice. And I think I have to turn it down."

My mouth hangs open for a moment and the razor buzzes in my hand. "You're going to turn it down? Because of—what you're doing in Austin? Isn't there some way around flat-out turning it down?"

"I don't see a way. I have to be here. In the US. I can go back and forth between Austin and LA, as often as needed, but I can't adopt a child and then disappear to the land down under for a month or however long—if the court would even allow me to do that, which it *won't*."

"What do you expect me to—"

"I told you I don't expect even an opinion from you, and I was serious. I just need to talk this out. *Fuck.* I mean—God, I'm going to have to stop saying that—Stan also wants me back for the season finale of *Life's a Beach*. I think I can work that into an offer for next season."

"Speaker." I set the phone on the counter and start shrugging into my interview outfit. "Let me get this straight, Brooke—you're going to throw away a major role in a possibly Oscar-worthy film to be on a teenage cable version of *Baywatch?* Have you completely lost it?"

"If this opportunity hadn't come back around—"

"If the opportunity hadn't come back around, your agent would still be looking for film roles, right? *Hearts Over Manhattan* is coming out in three weeks—I've seen clips, by the way, and it's going to kill at the box office. You'll get auditions for more rom-coms from that alone. But I can't believe we're even talking about *that* because you can't be serious that you want to turn down this role."

"It's not always about what I want. At least, not any more. If I mean to be his mother, then he has to start coming first."

"That doesn't mean throwing away your career."

"I don't consider this to be throwing my career away—"

"Okay, crippling it, then. This whole thing could hit a brick wall, where either you or the court says it's a no-go. What then? What if you turn this role down for *nothing?*"

She's silent, and I don't know if I've landed a point or pissed her off.

"This is why I didn't want your opinion."

Guess the answer is *pissed her off.*

"What, so you wouldn't have to hear the truth?"

"No, so I wouldn't have to hear how people talk themselves out of being the parents they should be. The excuses. The selfishness. Don't you think I want to play Monica?"

"*Yes*, I think you want it—that's exactly why I'm arguing—"

"Reid. *He needs me.*" She chokes up. "He needs me, and I'm not going to fuck this up—dammit, I mean *screw* this up—not this time. I've never done anything in my whole life that wasn't selfish—"

"Brooke," I sigh, lacing my black Prada boots. "Five years ago, you were a pregnant teenager. You moved to Texas. You had him without your parents' support, without *my* support. I don't know why you made that inadvisable choice, but you did. That wasn't selfish."

"You're wrong. It wasn't some moral judgment or an unselfish choice—I just knew that when we made him, I loved you, and I couldn't… there was no other choice for me. That decision was about *me*, and I can't pretend otherwise."

Weeks ago, when she told me that he was unequivocally mine and I finally believed her, I was dumbfounded. But this kicks the breath out of me. *When we made him, I loved you.*

"There's no choice for me this time, either. Thanks for listening, Reid. I know what I have to do, but I'm not going to tell Janelle right away. She hasn't even gotten the *Paper Oceans* offer yet. I think I can get through the premiere of *Hearts Over Manhattan* first. God, she's going to go off like a roman candle."

A slight drawl—it was never thick—threads through her words, almost imperceptibly. Must be a by-product of her being back in Texas, living with her stepmother.

For a moment, I drift in the memory of it.

And then my phone beeps. It's Dori.

tammara webber

Chapter 11

Dori

"I was in class when you texted—I just got out and thought I'd call instead of text since I'm wearing mittens. So you're going to come up this weekend? Are you sure you have time?" After an hour in an overly warm classroom, I exit Barrows and immediately begin shivering in a gust of north wind.

"I can escape from the promo tour overnight Saturday, but I'll have to fly," he says. "I don't have time to drive it. I can't leave LA until after 7 p.m., and I have to be back by noon."

We'll barely have twelve hours inside those parameters.

Like the swipe of a hand across a fogged windowpane, I see clearly, abruptly, that this is how it will be between us. Berkeley is where I'll be for the next four years, and when I try to imagine him, or us, after that, I can't. I visualize myself, applying to earn my master's in social work. Possibly leaving California to do it. Alone.

My teeth chatter—from cold or fear or both—and I struggle to dispel the ache from my voice. "What do you want to do while you're here?"

His low chuckle initiates warmth in the pit of my belly that spreads like a slow blaze. "Do you need to ask? It feels like months since I've gotten my hands on you."

Entering the library, my voice drops to a whisper. "It's been ten days, I think."

"*Months*," he insists. "And did you say you were wearing *mittens*? Photo. *Now*."

I shake my head and laugh soundlessly. "You'll just have to

wait and see them in person."

"Is there a matching hat? And scarf? Hmm, I like the thought of a scarf. Scarves are so handy for draping or blindfolding or trussing—"

"*Stop that,*" I hiss softly. "It's abnormal to blush like this in the library, you know. Maybe you should bring your own scarf and I'll use it on *you.*" When he doesn't reply, I say, "Reid?"

"Sorry. I'm *way* too turned on for a proper comeback."

I was certain my research on social interaction in groups and organizations would be more productive if I spent my time in the library around other equally studious undergrads. Instead, the hum of low voices and rustling movements of books and papers keeps lulling me into thoughts about the social interaction of two people, connected. Thoughts about the nature of love.

People in a group attempt to fit together like puzzle pieces to make a uniform whole. A recognizable representation of the efforts and goals of the organization itself.

I used to think of two people in love like that. Like puzzle pieces, fitting together. But it's not like that at all. Love pulls a part of you out, and it pulls a part of him—like taffy, stretching but not separating. The tendrils of each one wrap around the other, until they meld together. One, but not quite. Separate, but not quite. Like my parents.

And then there are those like Colin and me. He never shared a shred of himself, but I didn't know it. I'd imbedded myself into him because he wanted me to, and thought he did the same. But when he broke free, he ripped a part of me away. He retreated, unaltered, and I came apart, fractured and incomplete.

What Reid and I have, right now, is enough. I love him, and he loves me in a way Colin never did, but that's no guarantee of forever. I don't know when it will end, only that it will, and I want to protect us both. I can't let myself become a part of him, and I can't let him become part of me. So I won't whisper the words to him, even if they're true.

Shayma is tossing a change of clothes and her toiletries into her backpack. She's spending the night with a friend, and leaving the room to me—and my boyfriend.

"Are you sure it's okay? You're sure you don't mind? We can go to a hotel—"

She shakes her head and laughs. "Will you stop? If I say I'm good—I'm good. Hotels are expensive."

"Uh…"

"One tiny stipulation, though."

"Yeah?" I say, distractedly glancing around the room. I can't imagine Reid here. Our low-cost dorm room, the size of his closet, looks like a set of a movie in which he stars as an average, albeit very beautiful college guy—not somewhere he'd deign to spend the night.

"I need to meet him. *Wait*. Two stipulations. Second stipulation: not on my bed, *mmkay*?"

My face goes sunburn-hot and my mouth falls open. "I—I would never—"

"Wow." Her brows shoot up. "I don't think I've ever seen somebody blush that hard. You're like *maroon*."

I hide my blazing face behind my hands, mortified.

"So he's driving from LA? Flying?" She plops onto her bed, four feet across from me.

"Flying."

"And you don't need help picking him up, since you don't have a car?"

"No. I'm meeting him at the Starbucks. He's going to get a car from the airport."

Her head angles. "Get a car. Like a rental? Like a taxi?"

I shrug. Shayma is one of the most low-key girls I've ever met. This level of curiosity from her is as weird as if the stuffed Cal-cap-wearing Golden Bear Deb bought for me two years ago—now sitting on my overcrowded desk shelf—suddenly struck up a conversation. I take a deep breath. If Shayma is going to meet Reid tonight, she might as well know it ahead of time.

"Not exactly. More like the kind of car driven by a chauffeur."

One eyebrow quirks up and her chin shrinks back. "A who? A what? Girl, you've got a man with *money*? No wonder you can afford to be a social welfare major."

Shayma is studying international business, and plans to head for London or Hong Kong for graduate school.

I frown.

"So he's what—trust-funded? Or old? Oh shit—he's from LA—is he Hollywood?"

My eyes widen. "Are you psychic, Shayma?"

She rolls her eyes. "You know I don't believe in that crap. The only things that don't lie in this world are numbers. My mawmaw thinks she's a seer. Daddy says she's always claimed to have second sight, but ever since I was a little child—when she predicted Kelly Clarkson winning the first *American Idol*—she's sworn she's a bona fide clairvoyant."

We laugh, and then I take a deep breath. "So. My boyfriend. He's..." another breath, "Reid Alexander."

She stares, blinks once, and shakes her head a little, like she's trying to clear water from her ears. "Did you just say *Reid Alexander*?"

I nod.

"Well. Forget what I said about 'not on my bed.'"

Brooke

Rowena: You in Austin?
Me: Visiting family. I'll be back in LA for promos soon. Will text with details.

Shit. Even for an industrious and thriving—thanks to me—paparazza, Rowena is scary-connected. I don't like when she knows things I'm not ready for her to know, and this is too close. I don't want the media getting wind of River—not yet. She knows better than to cross me, but it may be time for us to have a *come-to-Jesus talk*—a favorite phrase of my mother's, which is odd considering her lack of a personal moral compass. I think even Jesus would pick up his skirts and run the opposite direction if he saw my mother coming.

My stomach drops when I think about this news coming to

light, and how it will be portrayed. Of course I knew there'd be no escaping public conjecture about River, but I haven't considered the best way for it to go public in the first place.

I've always believed that my sex life and sexual history is no one's business, but that freaking questionnaire stripped away that delusion. The media will be just as interested. More so. To them, everything is possible news fodder and nothing is sacred. The number one thing they'll want to know: *Who's the daddy?*

Five years ago, I scrawled *unknown* on the form. I didn't care how it looked to leave that line blank on his birth certificate. For myself, I still don't care. But for River—how will that affect him?

I'll have to control it, and the best way to do that is Rowena.

Everything has been turned in to the court—questionnaires, criminal background checks, and drug tests (thank God it's been months since I smoked a joint and years since I tried anything stupider). Norman urged out-and-out candor about everything—the shoplifting to spite Mom at fourteen, the random recreational drug use, the abundant underage drinking, my sex life—the real one and the publicized one.

Lord knows there's probably detailed evidence of every one of my sins somewhere. If I lie, something is sure to come back and bite me in the ass.

Now, according to Norman, we wait. Before we leave his office, he asks us to give him character references—three related, three non-related. Kylie and Kelley are going on my "related" list, and grudgingly, I decide my father would be better than my mother, given a choice between them—and Kathryn agrees.

Daddy. *There's* a fun phone call for later. I doubt he'll be pleased, but Kelley is pregnant, so it's not like impending grandfatherhood could induce heart failure. I have no idea if he and wife Number Four plan to propagate, but with three ex-wives and five children, one would think he'd feel kind of been-there, done-that by now.

On the other hand, whenever he wants an empty nest, all he has to do is *leave*.

I nearly draw a blank on the three non-related sources, because the first person to come to mind is Graham. But of course, we're not speaking. I stare at the form in my lap, swallowing the hot mix of guilt and grief. I print *MiShaun Grant* and copy her contact information from my phone. She's the only actress in my age range for whom I have both respect and a working phone number. I add Dana Scatio—the director of *Hearts Over Manhattan*. She loves me, and (bonus) was my most recent boss, of sorts.

"What about Janelle, my agent?" I ask. Note to self: *I need to inform Janelle about River.*

Norman frowns. "She's an option, if you can't think of anyone else." His expression says *That can't possibly be true, can it?* "Technically, she works for you and has a vested interest in getting you what you want, so she's deemed a less reliably candid source. The caseworker will likely contact her when they do the sweep through everyone with whom you've had substantial interaction. These six are merely the ones you deem most likely to give a favorable, yet realistic depiction of you."

I'm gripping the pen in my hand so hard that the metal clip bites into my palm, and my world goes a bit fuzzy at the edges. "Sorry—did you just say they're going to speak with *everyone*?"

In what's left of my peripheral vision, Kathryn's head pops up. Her gaze swings between Norman and me, and both she and Glenn have stopped writing. I'm sure they're both having a tough time narrowing *down* to six people who will speak favorably of them.

"Family, work relationships, close friends, ex-boyfriends—I'm afraid so." Norman regards me kindly from behind his folder-buried desk. "Not to worry—they don't expect you to be perfect or universally loved."

Universally loved? Can there be anything in the history of catchphrases that applies to me *less*? *Oh, God.*

"They conduct these interviews to evaluate whether (a) you're truthful and (b) you've got no detrimental personality disorders—anything that might prevent you from being a dependable parent to the child. It's all about his best interest, as I've said. I know you're tired of me repeating that phrase over and over, but it's what matters to the court. Best get accustomed to it early on."

Oh. My. God.

They're going to call both of my parents. My ex-stepmothers and ex-stepfathers. They're most likely going to call Reid.

And they're definitely going to call Graham.

"Hello?"

Emma's voice is exactly as I expected—clipped. Cold.

"Emma, this is Brooke," I reply needlessly. She obviously recognizes my number.

Silence. Okay.

"I'm calling..." I close my eyes "...to ask a favor."

She sputters a little. "A *favor*? How—what would Graham's mom call it? How *cheeky* of you. But since Cara isn't around, I'll just say how goddamned *presumptuous* of you. What do you want, Brooke?"

What do I want? I want to hang up. Last year, I made a huge miscalculation where Emma was concerned. Where Graham was concerned. I never said anything to either of them afterward, of course. Never tried to account for what I did, or beg forgiveness. I knew I was automatically evicted from his life. I didn't need to hear him say it.

I rarely apologize. It's not that I think I'm never wrong—I just don't care to admit it out loud. The only time I say *I'm sorry* is when there is literally no other way around saying it, or to get out of penalties that are possible to circumvent. Most consequences stick. That's why they're called consequences.

Eight months ago, there was no evading Graham's banishment, and my way around a pointless *I'm sorry* was avoidance, plain and simple.

If I take that approach now, I could lose River. I take a breath and square my shoulders.

"I need to talk to Graham—"

"Of all the—"

"Emma, I'm sorry. I fucked up. I totally fucked up. I wouldn't bother you—either of you—and look, I'm calling *your* phone, not his. I'm asking your permission. I'm begging you for it. Please." My voice splinters at the end of this appeal, the last word sounding more like a sob. Fucking *hell*.

More silence.

"Are you dying or something?" she asks, and I can't tell if she sounds more hopeful or regretful at the prospect.

"Not yet."

"What do you mean *not yet*?"

"I'm not—this isn't about me, as such. Well, it's only about me secondarily. It's about my son."

"Your what?"

"The baby I gave up for adoption. His adoptive father died and his mother turned into a meth addict and now he's in foster care and I'm trying to get him out."

Way to go, Brooke. That wasn't word vomit. That was word projectile vomiting.

"Does Reid know?" She says his name as though they've been in contact, which I suppose is possible. Maybe she was part of his twelve-step apologyfest last month.

"He knows. He's not involved. Which is fine. This is my choice. When I told you about the pregnancy—" I sigh. "I only told you so you'd hate him. But he was just a kid. I was just a kid. I'm not asking him for anything now, but yes, he's aware." Stop talking. "We're even sort of getting along. It's kind of weird, actually." *Stop talking.*

"Huh."

I roll my eyes, remembering how Graham and I had an infuriating conversation once upon a time about Emma and how she said *huh* whenever she couldn't think of anything else to say. He thought it was so adorable, and I wanted to gag him with a knee sock.

"I'll, um, talk to him. No promises. He'll call you if he wants to talk. If he doesn't, he won't call."

I grit my teeth, feeling powerless. "I understand. Thank you."

"Goodbye, Brooke."

After we disconnect, I pull up the photo of River I scanned into my phone and sent to Reid. Every time I look at it, I feel more overwhelmed, more terrified I'm going to fuck this up, and more sure that I can't let that happen. If I have to go around Emma to beg Graham not to ruin this, I'll do it. But I'm patient enough to bide my time and wait, and hope she doesn't hate me as much as I deserve to be hated.

If our positions were reversed, I'd have told her to fuck off and blocked her from Graham's phone.

But Emma is not me. And that's just one more reason why Graham is hers, and not mine.

Chapter 12

REID

I have the driver drop me a block away from the Starbucks on the corner, pulling the beanie over my ears and hunching into my jacket before grabbing my shoulder duffle. It's dark out, so I can't wear my sunglasses, but it's not like anyone expects Reid Alexander to pop up here, either. Even if I'm recognized, most people will merely assume I bear an uncanny resemblance to "that one guy from that movie."

"Nine tomorrow morning?" I say, opening the door, and he nods.

"Yessir."

I didn't realize how much I'd missed the sight of her until I see her. She sent a text fifteen minutes ago to tell me she'd arrived and staked out a chair on the second level. I was supposed to call her when I got there, but I didn't. I wanted this moment. I hoped she'd be caught up in reading, not looking for me. That I could take a few precious seconds to drink her in. That I'd get to witness the exact moment she notices I'm there.

Dori never disappoints.

As though she feels my eyes grazing over her, she glances up and right at me. She snaps the book closed without marking her page and tosses it toward her bag on the floor. Springing from the chair, she's clamping her mouth shut to keep from saying my name and giving my identity away—but her smile is a mile wide. One second later, she's in my arms, on her toes, offering her lips up for a kiss. I'm happy to oblige.

"I wholeheartedly approve of that welcome," I murmur into

her mouth, kissing her once more as she regains her composure and recollects where we are—in public.

Sweeping her hair back on one side, I cradle her head in my hand and smile down at her now-demure expression—pursed lips, faint blush pinkening the curve of that exposed ear. My voice restrained, low, I say, "Let's go be alone, beautiful girl, where I can ravish you without the audience that bothers only you." I feel her pulse speed under my fingertips and tighten my opposite arm around her, pressing her closer. "Or I'd be happy to back you up against a wall, right here, right now, and kiss you breathless. For a start."

"I'll get my bag," she says, her warm breath gushing against my neck.

I nod, and she ducks her chin low and steps away to collect her book and bag from the floor, and her sweater from the chair. Shrugging into it, she leads the way down the narrow staircase, across the expanse of main floor, and out the door. I reflect that this may be the only time in my personal history in which I entered a Starbucks and didn't buy anything.

Outside at the curb, she pulls to a sudden stop. "Oh, did you want something?"

I arch a brow. "Not anything *they* sell. Let's go see this tiny room of yours. And say hello -and-goodbye to your *very* considerate roommate."

Glancing up, she bites her lip and smiles at the same time, pulling me across the street to the campus. Her face is a perfect picture of the inner mischievousness with which I'm oh-so familiar. Avidly familiar.

We don't get far before we're in a thick grove of stories-tall trees, which I make a mental note of for some future encounter. When it's warmer.

The campus is well-lit and well-populated for a Saturday night, which makes me feel easier about her being here. No one pays us any mind. We are two more students crossing the campus grounds, in search of entertainment—or privacy.

As though I'm playing a character, I immerse myself in a storyline where Dori and I have parallel goals, parallel lives. Where we meet for coffee in between classes, commiserate about professors and assignments, take walks and weekend trips and lie out in grassy common areas on sunny days. Where we study between make-out sessions, and make love between study sessions.

"What's the matter?" she asks, and I realize I'm frowning.

I stop, pulling her fully against me and tip her concerned face up to mine. "Absolutely nothing," I say. "I just need to do this before going any further." I lean to kiss her in the semi-darkness. Someone hoots in the distance—at us or at something unrelated—I don't know or care.

I'm always amused by people's reactions when I'm recognized in entirely incongruous, unexpected places for movie star viewing. A state college dorm elevator is, predictably, one of these places. Dori grips my hand when a couple of girls with laundry bags get on. They're whispering while giving me not-so-covert sidelong glances. Wrapping my arms around Dori, I pull her back against my chest and into our own personal space bubble.

When the girls exit one floor up and the doors begin to close, they turn back and stare, bug-eyed. I wink, and Dori catches me doing it.

The doors slide shut, and she smacks my hand where it lays across her abdomen. "You're a bad boy, Reid Alexander."

Chuckling, I whisper into her ear, though we're alone now. "Baby, you just wait until I get you into that room. Unless you don't want to wait."

Breath catching, she shudders against the length of me, from my thighs to where the back of her head rests under my chin. I close my eyes and breathe through my nose, which only intensifies the cake-sweet smell of her invading my senses.

Fucking *hell*. She has no idea how close she is to me slamming that *emergency stop* button and backing her into a corner.

Then again, maybe she has a very clear idea. Her fingertips stroke my hand, feather-light, where she slapped it seconds ago. When we reach her floor, she grabs hold of my hand and makes a sharp right, pulling me into the hallway. We may only have the next twelve hours, but I'm going to make good use of every single one of them.

Dori

Seated at a corner bistro table by the front window of the Starbucks, we wait for the car that will take Reid to the airport. He checks email and messages on his phone, facing away from the other Sunday-morning patrons, while I sip my latte and make note of every visually accessible detail of him. It could be weeks before we see each other again, unless he can slip away from his crazy promotion schedule—something he's promised to try to do.

The late-January sun glints off the waves of his movie star hair, burnished gold with darker natural lowlights. Falling over his forehead, curling over his ears, marginally flattened by the knit cap he wore on the walk from my room, it begs to be touched. His dark lashes, too, are somehow gold-tipped. When those lashes sweep up and his gaze connects with mine, I catch my breath. In the clear morning light, his typically dark blue eyes are vivid enough for me to perceive every individual facet, his irises becoming mosaics of broken sea glass.

Angling his head, he says, "What?"

I shake my head faintly. "When I didn't like you, the fact that you were so hot played against you."

He smirks. "You don't say."

Struggling to find the right words, I lean onto my elbows. "If I was already angry at you for something you said or did, I'd look at you and just get angrier. Because it seemed so unfair to be given a face like that and use it for nothing but egocentric causes. I'm guessing that's not how it normally works for you—or I guess I should say, not normally how it works *against* you."

His mouth pulls up on one side and he shakes his head once. "Uh, no. That's usually not the case."

"People find themselves letting you have your way, because you're so beautiful that they don't want to deny you anything."

"I feel so cheap now."

"You shouldn't. It's not your fault you were born looking the way you look—"

He barks a laugh, hand across his mouth, weirdly self-conscious. "Thanks for the sympathy?"

"What I mean is, how you look just intensifies everything else about you, which didn't work with me, because I was raised to weigh people's actions, to rank them higher than their looks. Superficial people can be swayed by surface beauty alone. It's basic human nature to like pretty things, after all."

"I'm not so sure I'm enjoying the turn of this conversation, to tell you the truth. I feel like I should go rub some dirt on my face, or at least change into polyester plaid."

I shake my head and try again. "When you showed up at Habitat with the cast of *Mercy Killing*, I'd already experienced, firsthand, what it was like to be cared for by you. By the time I left that day, I knew what you'd done for Deb, and the knowledge of that beautiful part of you—the real you, apart from your looks— stunned me. But the combination of the compassion you were capable of and your physical beauty, right in front of me, was so overwhelming."

His mouth drops open just slightly, and his brows draw together just as disconcertedly. "Dori, I'm no angel—"

"I know, and I don't expect you to be. You know I like the, uh…" I feel the blush creeping over my ears, and with my hair in a messy knot at the nape of my neck, I know that tell-tale signal is visible. My voice drops to the lowest possible level. "…the *naughty* side of you, too."

He takes my hand from the table between us and holds it loosely in his, splayed open, tracing loops on my palm with the tip of his thumb. "Is that why I was able to say a few words I'm not allowed to say in the daylight, when I whispered them to you last night?" His voice is low and rough, dragging something deep inside me to the surface. He leans closer. "When I told you what I was going to do to you before I did it? When I told you what to do to me?"

My face floods with heat and memory. I had been beyond shocked to discover that those forbidden words—some of which he's *never* spoken in front of me—made my body go liquid under his as he whispered them in the dark, his voice husky and demanding.

When he sat on the edge of my cramped bed this morning, stretching, his shoulder blades bore the evidence of my enthusiasm. And he seemed to have a bruise or two in curious spots. I was mortified.

"I hurt you," I said miserably, tracing my fingers over the thin lines on his back.

He turned and flattened me against the bed in the space of one blink, his chest pressed to mine, his elbows bearing his weight. "If you *ever* apologize to me for doing," he closed his eyes and then flashed them open, "*anything* you did to me last night, I'll have no choice but to punish you."

"Oh?" I whispered, my imagination running rampant.

He smiled wolfishly. "In the heat of the moment, it appears we forgot to employ that scarf you were promising to produce. The next time you give me a few hours of your time, Dorcas Cantrell, I think we have a few new things to try."

His soft laugh brings me back to the Starbucks. "I always feel like doing a quick fist-pump when I manage to say something that makes you blush well beyond the ears," he says.

"Meanie."

"You know you love it."

"I'm a glutton for punishment, apparently." Another wave of pink descends after I realize I just used the word *punishment*, and he chuckles again.

Tapping a coffee stirrer on the table, he stares at it before sighing. "Dori, what you said about the 'real' me—I'm trying to be a better human being, but I'm still the same guy. People can only change so much."

My heart aches at the truth of those words, and how they apply to the thing I'm dreading most—losing him. But I know he's referring to other, more personally important changes.

"You underestimate yourself, Reid. As always. You have a good heart, and now your eyes are more open to other people, to suffering you can do something about. All you have to do is not close them again. I know, better than anyone, that everything isn't fixable."

Everything isn't fixable, and miracles are only happy twists of fate. Fate can so easily twist in the opposite direction. I face that fact every time my sister looks right through me.

Chapter 13

Brooke

"Brooke, where *are* you? I heard a rumor that you're in *Texas*. Is that *true*?" Janelle's voice is a bit overly-screechy before my second cup of coffee. Truthfully, it's screechy all the time. I love her, but *Christ*, when she's worked up, her voice could pierce steel. I hold the phone a foot away from my ear, only bringing it close to speak.

"Okay, what the hell. Where are these rumors coming from? You're the second person who's asked me that."

"So you aren't in Texas? You and Chandler have multiple promo commitments in the LA area this week, starting tomorrow—"

Glenn shuffles into the kitchen, but stops and turns when he hears the voice blaring from the receiver. When I roll my eyes and mouth *Janelle*, he shakes his head and chuckles.

My stepfather is in the oil business. After decades growing his career in the field, he moved into management a few years ago. He's good at his job because he's firm but easygoing, traits that served him equally well as a stepfather to Kelley and Kylie. All things Hollywood confound and amuse Glenn.

"Yeah, Janelle, I know."

"—so I just need to ascertain that you'll be there," she continues as though I haven't spoken, "unless something needs to be rescheduled?" Her tone says that had better not be the case unless someone is dying. Namely, me.

"No rescheduling necessary, Janelle. I had to run home to deal with some family issues, but I'm coming back to LA later today."

Over the rim of his coffee cup, Glenn's brows rise. I shake my head. I'm not ready to spill everything to my agent just yet. Especially knowing that conversation is going to include me telling her that in all likelihood, I'm going to turn down *Paper Oceans*. She may attempt to have me committed.

"Oh, thank goodness," Janelle says. "I was just telling Amaris…"

My phone beeps and I check the screen easily, since I'm holding it away from my head.

Graham.

My mouth goes dry and I have to remind myself to breathe.

"Janelle," I interrupt. "*Janelle*—I've got another call—I've got to take this. I'll call you when I'm home tonight." I'm already grabbing what's left of my tepid coffee and walking back to my room when I flash over. I try and fail to sound composed instead of freaked out. "Hello?"

"Brooke. Emma said you called." His tone is guarded, noncommittal, but his voice is so very familiar. My eyes fill and I swallow, suddenly at a loss for words.

"Brooke?" he repeats.

"I'm here. I guess I didn't think you'd call. Thank you."

"I just want to know what you want. Don't thank me yet."

"Okay. Okay." I take a deep breath. "A few weeks ago, I hired an investigator to check on the baby I gave up—just to make sure he was okay. I was having nightmares about him. I thought if I could find out he's happy and healthy, the nightmares would stop and I could just go on with my life."

He makes no comment. The old Graham, in our old friendship, would have made an inquiry or offered an observation. But I destroyed that relationship. I killed his trust and his care for me.

I close my bedroom door and sit on my bed. I have to do this for River. What I've lost is not of any consequence.

"He's in foster care. He was removed from his adoptive home by CPS."

Hesitantly, he says, "That's what Emma said. Do you know why?"

I feel a rush of gratitude for his question, and for the first time, I entertain the hope that he'll listen. That maybe, for River's sake, he can stop hating me long enough to not prevent me from getting him.

"I don't know all of it. I know his adoptive father died, but I don't know how. I know his adoptive mother became a meth addict, that she went into court-ordered rehab at least twice, and that she failed both times. I know that no relatives have stepped forward to take him—my PI is working on information about them. He's been in foster care for months." Tears are rolling down my face. "Bethany Shank—my PI—gave me a photo of him."

When my voice breaks, I hear a soft whoosh of breath from Graham and I think, *Please-oh-please don't think I'm faking this.* "He's so small. And he looks so sad. He needs me, Graham. That's why I applied to adopt him—"

"What?" I know that he's frowning now. Combing his dark hair back with one hand. Closing his eyes and shaking his head twice before opening them. "Emma said you told her you were trying to get him out of foster care—but we didn't know what that meant, exactly. Adoption, Brooke? *You?*"

I'm trying so hard not to sound like I'm crying. My fingers press against that characteristic pain in my sternum, but nothing soothes the sharp burn of it, like a newly-lit match, flaring to life just under my skin.

"Yes. I'm all he's got. It has to be me."

He sighs. "It sounds like you mean well, and I can appreciate that you feel responsible for him, believe me. But he needs someone stable, someone devoted to him. He's just a little younger than Cara, right? You have no idea how much energy it requires to look after her, and I have my parents and my sisters. I have Emma."

And you have no one. He doesn't say the words, but they hang there between us, as though he has.

"Emma said you wanted a favor?"

"Yes. His caseworker is going to call you. Maybe his ad litem, too. I don't know what they're going to ask, but please, just… just don't say anything that will make me lose him. Please, Graham."

I count my own heartbeats as they pulse through my ears. *One. Two. Three. Four.*

"You really want this, don't you? My concern is—why? He's a child, Brooke. He can't fill your need for affection. Children are owed love from their guardians—not the other way around."

I would be offended, but in light of our history, and what he knows of me, it's a valid question. "I understand why you'd think that. But if I'm getting anything from this, it's a sense of doing the right thing. I'm scared. I'm terrified thinking about all I don't know, and everything I could screw up. But he needs me. I have to do this."

"What if he has needs you can't fill? What if he's been hurt so badly that you can't help him?"

"Then I'll get him the help he needs. I'll keep trying. I'm goddamned stubborn, Graham. If nothing else, you know that about me."

I envision the wry, reluctant smile on his face. "Yes. I do."

REID

I could say I looked for an opening, sometime in the twelve hours I spent with Dori, to tell her about River.

But that would be a lie. And right now, my only lie is of omission.

I could say that every day that goes by, the guilt is heavier, but that's not exactly true, either. What I feel is fear. Fear that if she finds out—no matter how, from my mouth or someone else's—she won't vacillate. She won't bother with the semantics of *telling* a lie versus *not telling* the truth. She'll see in black and white. She'll ignore the gray.

This is a girl who seems to have lost a lifelong faith in *God*. Discarding her tenuous, newfound faith in me would be nothing next to that.

Besides, there's a chance that Brooke will change her mind—as slim as that chance may be. Or that someone else will step up and take responsibility for him. That this secret will stay in the closet, where secrets belong. And maybe someday, I can tell Dori—when I don't have this feeling that there's a time clock ticking over my shoulder. Or maybe a bomb.

I don't want to lose her. She's more important to me than a boy I've never seen. A child I didn't even think was mine, biologically, until a few weeks ago. I can't be a father—not yet, and maybe never.

Dori said I have a good heart.

And there is where I find the guilt.

By a week prior to the premiere of *Mercy Killing*, I've been asked by multiple interviewers if I'm dating someone—though they hint about it slyly rather than framing the question plainly, to get around the studio's constraint on the subject being broached directly. I give evasive answers and an oblivious smile. Today's interviewer was a little pushier.

What's funny is I don't give a shit what the *studio* wants or doesn't. This is about Dori, and her parents—and not giving them reason to hate me for dragging their daughter into my *debauched world*, as they like to term it. Not that I can argue. I've debauched with dedicated regularity and zeal for years.

I have more sympathy now for Emma's ordeal during the *School Pride* promo tour last spring—not only having to deny the existence of her relationship with Graham, but having to pretend one with *me* at the same time. While I was doing everything in my power to sabotage their relationship.

Christ, I was such an asshole.

George began negotiating the "official" stance on my love life with the studio last week, when I made it clear I had no intention of denying my relationship with Dori once it comes to light. "And it will," I added. "I'm just easing her into the spotlight." *Along with her parents.*

"So you'll agree to wait until after the release to announce the relationship publicly?" he asks now, *again*. George knows me too well.

"Yeah, sure—in theory. But if someone shows me a photo of Dori and says, 'Is this your girlfriend?' I'm *not* saying she isn't." I park in the gated lot of Brooke's exclusive complex and let the engine idle while we wrap up.

"Noted." He clears his throat. "One more thing—I've been contacted by a social worker in *Texas*—and asked to pass along a request for you to return the call. Something to do with a court case? He said it involved confidential information that he couldn't discuss with anyone but you. I don't suppose you want to let your *manager* in on what that's about, if you happen to know?"

The blood in my veins turns to ice, and my hand grips the gearshift as though it will keep me from being sucked out the open window of my car. Brooke said she wouldn't connect me, but clearly, she lied. This is my chance to tell George everything, but I'm immobilized.

"Uh, I don't know—I can give him a call and see what it's about."

His sigh reveals his suspicion that I'm withholding something critical. "I'll email his information. Give me a call back if there's something I need to oversee."

I go from fuming to dumbstruck when Brooke opens her door. Brooke is like my mother in a few ways—one of them being the fact that she always looks as though she could grab a bag and go straight to a club or some posh event without so much as checking the mirror.

My mother wears designer clothes around the house. She always has. Even when she's drunk—when she *was* drunk, I correct myself, because it's been so long since I've seen her that way—she was stylish and well-groomed. A little off, but not by much.

It's not that Brooke looks *off.*

She's Brooke—from five years ago.

Her hair is pulled into a messy ponytail, tendrils escaping around her face. Thin gold hoops dangle from her ears, but she's not wearing makeup. Her eyes are big and blue in her very young face.

When we were going out, she would occasionally dig through my dresser drawers and take a pair of jeans, and I was content to let her. She'd ditch whatever trendy pair she was wearing—shimmying out of them while I watched her, breathless—and pull mine on. They'd hang perfectly on her slim hips, fitting her the same way they fit me when I had a boy's body—the one I outgrew a couple of years ago.

"Ahhh," she'd say, dropping onto my bed. "Much better."

All I could think about was how to get her back out of them.

The worn jeans she's currently wearing could be one of the

three or four pairs she appropriated from me back then, though I'm fairly certain she either shredded them with a giant set of shears or burned them in some sorcerous ritual after we broke up. She's barefoot—her toenails polished blood red—and wearing a plain, fitted white T-shirt.

Silent, she gestures for me to enter, and I follow her through a maze of boxes and into her living room. I don't remember exactly what her place looked like when I was here last, because I've only been here once, and it's been almost a year—but several things appear to be missing. And then there are the boxes.

Frowning curiously, I turn back to her. "Moving?"

She nods. "I'll need two bedrooms. And most of my décor isn't exactly child-friendly."

She says this as though it's normal for such sentences to be said between us. Or for the phrase *child-friendly* to come from her mouth, *ever*.

She perches in a black leather chair and I take its twin—these make up the only furniture in the room, aside from a nearly-empty bookcase.

I begin first, preempting whatever plan she had for the direction of this conversation. "My manager got a call for me from a social worker in Texas. He wouldn't tell George what he wanted, but I'm pretty sure it has to do with you—or, you know, River."

She takes a deep breath, staring at the interlocked hands in her lap, and a distinct feeling of unease creeps over me.

"Yes, that's why I asked you to come over." She sighs, and I think, *Oh, no.* "I had to tell them."

"Excuse me?"

"That you're his birth father."

My jaw drops. "What do you mean you *had* to tell them—"

Her eyes flash up. "I had to fill out an eighteen-page questionnaire, Reid. It asked the most personal questions you could imagine, and Norman, my attorney, warned me to be utterly truthful, or I could risk a denial before we even got started.

"So I told them about my home-wrecking mother, and my cheating father. The fact that I was illegitimate because my father was still technically *married* to Kathryn when I was born. The fact that my mother frequently slapped me across the face when I pissed her off, starting so young that I don't remember the first time she did it. I had to reveal my sexual history and experience—all of it. My relationships with my stepfathers and stepmothers and my experience with children—which is of course zero."

I shake my head. "You keep saying you *had to*, but that's not true, Brooke—no one is forcing you to do this."

She narrows her clear blue eyes and they blaze. "We are *done* discussing the decisions I'm making concerning *my* child, Reid Alexander." Backlit by the wall of windows behind her, pale blonde hair haloing her head, she looks like an angel spoiling for a fight.

"You're making decisions for *me*, Brooke—why can't you see that?"

"I don't have a choice."

"You do—"

"Fine! Then I'm choosing our *son*."

My jaw clenches and I stand, hands fisted at my sides. "You've called me his birth father. Now you're calling him my son—like I have some sort of connection with him. I don't. I didn't think he was mine when you turned up pregnant, and you knew it. We'd been broken up for weeks by then. I never felt anything about him one way or the other, Brooke, and I don't now, and if that makes me a heartless bastard, then so be it—"

"No, Reid—that's you making *him* a bastard."

My hands both go to the back of my neck and I pull my elbows in, biceps shielding my face like blinders. Pacing between the dozens of boxes littering the floor, I count. *One, two, three, four…* I ache to throw something or break something or scream something. *Five, six, seven. Eight, nine, ten.*

I need to leave. But first: "What does the social worker want?"

She blanches like she'd forgotten about that, and then licks her lips. If her head was transparent, I'd see gears working furiously. "A couple of things. They want you to sign a form saying you willingly volunteer to relinquish your parental rights to him. That shouldn't be a problem for you, I gather. It's like clearing a deed to a property, Norman says, so it can transfer easily to a new buyer." She swallows, the muscles in her throat strained. I get the feeling she wants to cry, but isn't allowing herself to do it. So *Brooke* of her. Always calculating something.

"They might also ask you about our relationship. And the

breakup. And the pregnancy. And why I left your name off the birth record. And… they're calling people for character references. For me."

I laugh once, humorlessly, stuffing my hands into my front pockets. "Me? A guy who plea-bargained his way out of a DUI a few months ago as a character reference? I doubt anything I say will hold any weight one way or the other."

She shrugs, her expression earnest. I can't stand to look at her. Not when she looks so much like she did years ago. I conclude that she must have done this on purpose—but how would she know? How would she know that for months after our breakup, I woke up from dreams of her looking *exactly like she does now*?

"Maybe not," she says. "But the worst thing would be if they believe I lied and said he wasn't yours, or didn't tell you about him at all. Will you just back me up on that, and sign the relinquishment papers? Even if you can't say another positive word about me?"

She did tell me she was pregnant, and even if she let me believe he probably wasn't mine, she never told me he wasn't.

"I'll back up your story, because it's true. But relinquishment papers? That's a legal declaration, Brooke." I'm back to pacing. The stacks of boxes narrow the walls, constricting the paths between them, paralleling my emotions perfectly. "*Fuck*. My father will kill me if I sign a legal document without his *expert* guidance." I look back up at her and shake my head slowly. "I'm going to have to tell him. And may God have mercy on my soul."

Chapter 14

Dori

My schedule looks like a sampler platter instead of a meal. Every class I'm taking this semester is preceded by "Introduction to," which theoretically makes sense, considering I'm a freshman, and therefore assumed to be a novice at everything. If I hadn't tested out of reading and comprehension, quantitative reasoning, and four semesters of Spanish, I suppose my schedule and I wouldn't look quite so deficient in experience.

On a bench in upper Sproul, I wait with one member of my Intro to Sociology study group for the other two to arrive. The plan was to stake a spot somewhere outside to study, but that was before the sky became completely overcast and the temperature dropped ten degrees.

Claudia scowls down the plaza, looking for Raul and Afton. "Whose bright idea was it to study outdoors in February? I'm. Effing. Freezing."

I shrug. "I'm sure they'll agree to go inside. And it was nice out yesterday."

"Psshh," she says. "It was tolerable, at best. Have you ever noticed how all campus brochures have pictures of happy, smiling students taken on beautiful, blue-sky days? No matter where the campus is located—Oklahoma, North Dakota, Arizona—whatever. No one is ever huddling into their down-filled North Face jacket, cursing their chapped lips and flyaway hair. No one's ever sloshing across campus in an ugly downpour with no umbrella, a soaked-through backpack, waterlogged shoes and jeans saturated to mid-thigh. No one's got sweat-stained pits and perspiration-covered faces. Oh, no—they're throwing a Frisbee or studying contentedly on a green lawn in perfect temperatures. They're laughing on the way to the food court or chatting on the steps of the library."

I smile. Claudia is one of those people who constantly complains, but she grumbles so humorously that I don't care. She's like a grumpy old lady in an eighteen-year-old body.

A couple of girls suddenly appear in front of us, gazing directly at me, as though I'm about to impart life-saving information. Claudia lifts an eyebrow and looks at me, too.

"Hey," the girl on the left says. "Um, we live in your building? And you were with a guy the other night…"

Uh-oh. I recognize them now—the elevator girls. Darn Reid and his winking.

I attempt to look blankly at them. Reid's told me what his studio wants, but he's also told me that he doesn't care what I say or do—he says that if someone asks me about him, I can say whatever I'd like. But his premiere is tomorrow night, and I don't particularly want to out myself right here, right now, with strangers. Along with Claudia, the world's most acerbic Peace and Conflict Studies major ever.

Girl on the right isn't about to drop this opportunity. "Was he really Reid Alexander?"

Before I can say a word, Claudia hoots a laugh. "Are you guys high right now? Reid Alexander, on campus, and *no one* noticed? Give me a break."

Their faces fall. "Oh."

Then left side girl rallies. "Then that guy—he's goes here? To Cal?"

I shake my head once. "No, he doesn't. He was just visiting."

"Aww," they say in unison, dismayed, and my scowl narrows on them.

"And he's my boyfriend." *Whoa.* Where did *that* tone come from?

Unbothered by any sense of diplomacy, left side girl snorts. "He *is*?"

Her friend tries to save face—by saying the most awkward thing possible. "Well, congratulations—I mean—he looks *just like* Reid Alexander, so obviously he's hot. Aheh."

"Uh. Thanks?"

After they scuttle away, I say, "That was weird."

I feel Claudia's eyes on me. "So you're dating Reid Alexander?"

I look into her dark eyes, and my lips part, but no sound emerges. I can't think of a single thing to say.

"Has anyone ever told you that you *do not* have a poker face?"

Lips twisting, I admit, "Yeah, I may have heard that one a time or two."

She angles her head and smiles. "You're the Habitat girl, aren't you? From last summer."

Oh, yay. I'd escaped two zealous Reid Alexander groupies, only to find out I'm in a study group with the most dangerous of them all. "And you're a Reid Alexander fan?"

"*Hell*, no. My little sisters are. They're *rabid* about him. He seems like a pretentious, untalented asshole to me."

I blink.

"Note I said *seems*. I haven't actually seen any of his films. And he can't be a total lost cause if he's dating you. I think. Unless you care to refute that?"

"Which part?"

She shrugs. "Any of it. I'm open-minded. Sort of."

I laugh softly as our classmates finally walk up, shivering in their jackets.

"Oh. My. Holy. Fucking. Hell," Raul says. "Can we *please* go inside to do this?"

"A man after my own heart," Claudia says, bounding from the bench as though released from a spell and walking resolutely in the direction of the library. "Brr! Dayum. I never thought I'd say this, but I miss San Diego." Turning and pointing a finger, she adds, "You guys did *not* hear me say that."

Afton mimes locking her lips and tossing an invisible key over her shoulder. "We all wanted to get the hell outta somewhere, dude," she says. "But some stuff we take for granted about home just isn't better elsewhere."

Claudia leans closer as we head toward the library. "Psychology majors, *Jesus*. And did she just call me *dude*? That's so not going to endear her to me anytime soon—I don't care how cute her butt is in those jeans. Although she does have a valid point about home and elsewhere. So, About the pretty boy—?"

I smile and meet her eyes. "He's not a lost cause."
She returns my smile. "Good enough for me."

I have Reid's fan sites bookmarked, so I can watch him from a distance, like everyone else has to. My annoyance is increasing, especially when sites claim "proof" that he's hooking up with random starlets or singers he stands next to at some event. Or a commenting fan proclaims her undying love and desire to have his babies. Or someone is trying to figure out who I am and where I'm from and why in the world *Reid Alexander* would even bother with me.

Looking at these pages feels a little stalkerish, too. On the other hand, this is no different than going to friends' Facebook profiles and browsing through photos of them living their lives apart from me. Curiosity is a compelling thing. Where Reid is concerned, I've been curious from the moment he called me a hypocrite for deeming him hopeless, days after we met.

With his mother beside him on the red carpet at his premiere, it's a no-brainer where Reid gets his looks. Their coloring is exactly the same, as well as their features—with exception of the angled jaw bestowed by his father. Lucy Alexander is stunning and elegant, her pride in her son evident in the way she watches him while he signs autographs and leans in to take photos with the beside-themselves fans pressing against the velvet rope.

When I came up with the idea of inviting his mother as his plus-one, I had a good feeling about it. He was unconvinced that she'd want to go, so I told him the only way he'd know was to ask.

"You'd have thought I just handed her an Oscar," he said later, filling me in on their conversation. "First, she gasped and teared up, and I was thinking, *Oh, great, I've upset her*. And then she said, 'Don't you want to take Dori?' So I told her you couldn't get away that night. She stepped forward and hugged me, which she hasn't done in—I don't know—it feels like *years*, and then she said she'd love to go."

"I told you so," I sing-songed, and he laughed.

"You just *live* for the times you're able to say that, don't you?"

"Yeah, and lucky for me—with you, I get to say it a *lot*."

"Haha. Very funny, Miss Cantrell. I'll have to try to hand out those little treats more sparingly. I don't want you to get spoiled."

"Oh, so now you can control the frequency of your wrongness?" I scoffed, trying not to giggle. "How will you do that?"

"Well, I appear to have two choices. I can either be right more often—*stop laughing*—or I can stop saying things that turn out to be wrong. Hmm. This is a tough decision."

REID

Me:	We need to discuss something. In person. Important.
Dad:	I'll be home tonight by 8. Will that work for you?
Me:	Yes. I'll meet you in your study. I leave for the NYC debut tomorrow morning.

Dad is still dressed for work, with the exception of the suit jacket hanging on the peg and padded hanger he had installed for that purpose near the open door. His cuff links are in a small glass bowl he purchased for the express function of holding cufflinks, his red-patterned tie remains knotted, but loose, and his shirtsleeves are rolled to mid-forearm.

I knock my knuckles twice to announce my presence, and his eyes snap up from the paperwork he's scanning.

He pushes it aside and collects a pad and pen. "Reid. Come in." After I take a deep breath and sit, he says, "All right, what's going on?"

Every carefully premeditated introduction to the grenade I'm about to toss into the room has flown out of my brain. Entire perfectly-crafted explanations are just *gone*. I'm thinking in words, like a toddler. Or Tarzan. *Me father. You grandfather. HELP.*

I look him in the eye and he's frowning, waiting for me to state my business. I haven't been scared of my father since I was ten. Intimidated? Yes. Demeaned? Yes. Afraid? No.

Is this what his clients feel like, sitting across the desk from him?

And that's when it hits me. No, this isn't what it feels like to be his client. He doesn't frown at his clients. He may wear a veneer of concern. He may even *be* concerned. But the face I'm seeing—the eyes I'm looking into now—he's alarmed. Apprehensive. Worried.

His clients don't get that puckered-brow expression. My mother does. And I do.

I rub my clammy palms against my jeans. "I have a problem, and I need your advice. Your legal advice."

He takes a breath through his nose and his brow clears, the slightest bit. He's still on alert, but he knows this crisis is in his territory—whatever it is—and I've brought it to him before someone else did. That's possibly unprecedented.

"I'm listening," he says.

I take another deep breath. "You remember Brooke?"

He grimaces. "Brooke Cameron?" I nod, and he answers, "Yes, I remember her."

Grenade time. "After we broke up…" Pull the pin. Toss. "She found out she was pregnant."

I expect him to speak, start sputtering or roaring, something. Eyes drilling into mine, he goes a little pale around the edges, but he holds his fire. He recognizes that there's some reason I've brought this to him, and I haven't voiced it yet. He hasn't scribbled so much as a stroke on that pad.

Swallowing, I continue. "She had the baby, and gave it up for adoption. A few weeks ago, she hired a PI to look for him. She found him—in foster care. And now, she wants to adopt him. She wants me to sign relinquishment papers. I want to make sure I'm not missing something before I do it."

He begins to write on the pad, and I sit, waiting.

Several minutes later, he begins to fire questions at me, one after the other. After each one, there's a prolonged pause as he logs my answer.

"Did she tell you she was pregnant at the time?"

"Yes."

"Did she tell you she was giving the child up for adoption?"

"Yes."

"Did you sign anything—anything at all—taking responsibility for the pregnancy?"

"No."

"No paternity test either, I assume."

"No."

"So you might not be the biological father."

"I'm the father."

"Reid, if there's no proof—"

"I'm the father."

He scratches something onto the pad, and mumbles, "We'll revisit that one later. Do you know if your name is on the birth certificate as the father?"

"No—Brooke says she left it as unknown."

He shakes his head a bit, exasperated. "Then how does she now all of a sudden 'know' it's yours?"

"She always knew. I... I hurt her." He flinches and I throw my hands up. "Not *physically*. Jesus, Dad, don't you know me at all?"

"Sorry," he says, shaking his head. "Hazard of the profession—literal thinking. Carry on."

"We had an argument that turned into a screaming match. I thought she was cheating, and she was so indignant that she let me think it. Instead of talking about it or even arguing more, I just started going out. Publicly. With lots of girls. I didn't call her. She didn't call me—until she found out she was pregnant. God, I don't even know what I said to her—but I made it clear that I didn't care. So she made her own decisions. I had nothing to do with them. I didn't know until a few weeks ago that he was mine."

"A few weeks—Reid, why do you *wait* to tell me things?" He closes his eyes and huffs a breath. "And how do you *know* it was yours? Because she says so?"

"She's not lying—"

His placating lawyer-face sliding into place, he says, "Even if she's not lying, per se, that doesn't mean she's *right*. She may wish it was yours—"

"*He* is mine." I pull out my phone and pull up the photo.

He takes my phone, unaware what I'm showing him. Glancing at the screen, he stops and blinks. Looks at me. And back at the display in his hand.

"His name is River," I say.

"How old is he?" My father's voice catches and he clears his throat.

"Four and a half."

He scribbles on the pad. "We'll have to get a blood test—" He holds up a hand when I start to object. "I'm an attorney, Reid. You're going to have to trust me. No legal entity or governmental agency is going to take the fact that he's the spitting image of you at his age as evidence of paternity—as well they shouldn't."

"So we can't just sign the papers?"

Sitting back, he shakes his head. "Signing relinquishment papers does one thing—it takes away your parental rights to the child. It does *not* remove the state's right to hold you financially responsible and accountable. It's highly unlikely that they'll cross that line, but not unheard of—especially if her bid to adopt fails. Now—where is he? I know people in LA County Family Court, of course."

"He's in Texas. He was born there."

My father does something I've seen him do only once before—during one of Mom's relapses. He puts his face in his hands, and he says, "Oh, God."

Chapter 15

Brooke

Production wants me on hand and looking hot to hype media interest at the Ziegfeld Theatre opening of *Hearts Over Manhattan*, along with my costar, Chandler Beckett. Tonight.

To that end, I'm at LAX before dawn with a front row seat at the gate, facing a boarding agent who's clearly trying to place who I am. If box office predictions are correct, I may be less likely to encounter that expression soon. Critics are calling *Hearts* "a heart-warming little romance"—perfect for Valentine's weekend.

I ignore the boarding agent and hunch over my laptop to keep what I'm doing private from my fellow travelers, who are beginning to fill in behind me. I'm taking required *parenting classes* online. Having worked through seven sections, I've got twenty-three to go. I plan to polish off at least two more on the long flight from Los Angeles to New York. The current unit concerns disciplining your child in public. While reading a section about not employing the use of public shaming for behavior motivation, I reflect that my mother clearly never took a parenting class.

Chandler is bringing his tediously insecure girlfriend, Nan. At the premiere's after-party on Tuesday, I warned him to clip her claws or I was going to point her at the wardrobe girl—whom she has far better reason to hate, according to on-set gossip—which is generally accurate. The guy has ample acting talent, but I should have demanded a bonus for every love scene. He's one of those guys who kisses like he's gasping for breath every second—no concentration, no finesse, no *aim*. How any girl, even Nan, would worry over losing *that* is beyond me. I'd be kicking it to the curb at the first opportunity.

It slipped my mind to line up a plus one for tonight. Janelle said, "Don't you know anyone in New York? You can't just show up at your first opening night in a lead role *alone.*"

First, yeah, I do know someone in New York, but I can't exactly phone him up and ask him to be my escort. Thanks for reminding me. And second—

"Why the hell not? I don't *need* an escort, by the way. I can walk from the car into the theater—and probably even back again!—without being led by the elbow, *thank-you-very-much.*"

"That's not what I—"

"Whatever, Janelle, let's just drop it. I'm going alone, and I'll hit the after-party for a bit, and then I'm coming home tomorrow. And next week, you and I have some things to discuss."

There's an apprehensive pause. "Oh? Like what?"

"*Next week.*"

"*Fine.*" She's not genuinely angry, just exasperated. I've had that effect on her for a while, especially three years ago, when our relationship took a not-so-subtle turn. She woke up to find me in the driver's seat of my career the day I turned eighteen and fired the manager Mom had hired years earlier. The way Janelle accepted instead of power-tripped that day is why she's still my agent.

We hang up, and I concentrate on the multiple-choice questions for the Public Discipline section I've just completed. Question number four: *Your child throws a screaming tantrum because you won't buy him a candy bar at the grocery store. Do you: (a) Explain that a candy bar will ruin his dinner, (b) Plead with him to stop, (c) Swat him on the bottom, (d) Ignore him.*

I guess *Roll my eyes and wonder what the hell I was thinking* would most closely resemble (d). *Click.*

"Whatcha doin'?" a voice says, and I snap the laptop closed, which probably means I'll have to start that section over. I turn and glare—at *Reid*, who's relocated my shoulder bag from the adjacent seat and plopped down next to me.

"What the hell are you doing here?" I whisper much too loudly.

"Looks as though I'm joining you for opening night. Different movies, of course."

"*What?*" I shake my head, cobwebs clearing. "You're going to New York. Today. On *my* flight."

He smirks. "Or—you're going to New York on *my* flight." Pulling his boarding pass from his back pocket, he asks, "So what seat are you? We might as well get this over with."

I know for a fact that Reid prefers the aisle, while I insist on the window. And of course we're both flying first class, alone. I turn my ticket over next to his.

"You've *got* to be kidding me." 3A, 3B.

"What are the chances that I'll make it to New York alive?" Reid has never, ever been a morning person, and yet he is alarmingly wide awake for someone who should be sleeping off a hangover with one or more idiot girls and missing his flight.

If only.

"Better, if you shut up and stay that way," I mumble.

I want to get back to my end-of-section quiz while the material is fresh, but I don't particularly want to do it with him looking over my shoulder. And now the expectation that I can intimidate my row mate into muteness like I always do is shot to hell.

"I don't suppose you can just pretend you don't know me for the next six—" I glance at my phone display "—or oh-my-God *seven* hours?"

He smiles, picking at a fingernail. Without turning to look at me, he asks softly, "Why do you still hate me?"

I falter before hissing, "Like you're all good with *me*?"

Hands moving to grip the seat on either side of him, his shoulders taut and facing straight ahead, he angles his head just enough to look at me. His hair falls forward, hiding his focused expression from everyone but me. "I don't hate you, Brooke."

The gate agent announces the impending boarding process, and Reid breaks our staring standoff, turning to get my bag and his own from the seat next to him. I shove my laptop into the rolling bag, stand and pull the handle as he shoulders his only bag and hands mine over.

"Will our first class passengers please begin boarding at this time," the agent intones robotically, and I march forward to present my boarding pass, Reid right behind me.

When we reach our seats, he automatically takes my bags and

heaves them into the overhead bin, placing his in beside them as I take my seat. As he slides into the seat next to me, each of us pulls a drink menu from the seat pocket, avoiding eye contact with our fellow passengers as they trudge by sluggishly.

It occurs to me that to these strangers, we look, for all intents and purposes, as though we're traveling together.

Half an hour later, we've each downed a coffee, and Reid has requested and eaten a bag of caramel popcorn. The plane taxis down the runway, finally, and judders into the air at a worrisome angle, but we haven't exchanged another word.

An hour later, I clear my throat. "Are you going to sign the paper?" My question is barely audible over the droning of the plane engine.

Leaning closer, but without turning to look at me, he says, "I talked to Dad. We're requesting a confidential paternity test first."

A blaze of resentment rips through me like a flash fire. And then I recall that Reid's father is, of course, an attorney. Like Norman Rogers, he's bound to proceed cautiously—more so in matters pertaining to his son. Proof is a required starting point. And I know better than anyone that the proof will be conclusive.

Checking my resentment, I ask, "How long will it take to get the results?"

"I don't think it will take long. I already did my part of it."

"Oh?"

He shrugs. "It's not that complicated, I guess. Once they have his, it shouldn't be more than a day or two." After another drink service, during which I order a club soda and Reid orders (and is given) a scotch on the rocks, he ventures, "I'm not sure what happens after that. Everything is complicated by the fact that you went to Texas," he lowers his voice to a whisper, "to have him. The relinquishment does no more than take my rights away—"

"You don't have any *rights*—" I hiss.

"Think of the *title* of the form, Brooke. If no rights existed, I wouldn't have anything to relinquish."

Oh, God.

REID

This after-party is the most over-the-top event I've ever attended. The hotel ballroom looks as though someone took a slice of Vancouver's Gastown district and airlifted it to New York. One wall boasts an animated projection of Burrard Inlet, while the remaining three walls are covered in convincing replicas of storefront façades. Bistro tables line the bricked "streets" while globed street lamps cast spheres of light on squares of real grass and walkpaths dotted with light-strung trees. In the center of it all is the Gastown Steam Clock, which—through the magic of CGI—is blown to smithereens in the next-to-final scene of *Mercy Killing*.

I snap a few photos and text them to Dori.

> Me: Isn't this ridonkulous? I wish you were here.
> Dori: I wish I was in LA. Mom just called. Esther isn't doing well.
> Me: She's sick?
> Dori: I don't want to interrupt your night. I'm a mess. Maybe we could just talk tomorrow, please?

"Talk to me." I've found a private niche outside the ballroom. People are milling around in the hallway, and the band from inside the party is audible, but this is as discreet as it will get until I get back to my hotel and in my room.

Dori is crying. No. She's *bawling*. The sound squeezes my heart like someone has reached inside my chest cavity and seized it, and all I know is I would do anything, *anything*, to stop her anguish.

"Reid." Her voice is already hoarse. God knows how long she's been distressed over this while I viewed my stupid film and accepted accolades from the audience and the crowd waiting outside. The sound of her sobs turns me inside out. "I don't... I don't want to ruin your big night. Can we please talk tomorrow?" She's covering the phone so I won't hear the sobs between the sentences. As if I can't feel it anyway when she speaks.

"Baby. Please talk to me. Nothing is more important to me right now. What happened?"

She wrestles with herself to stop crying, her breaths coming in slowing stutters. "I knew this was coming. Esther has lived a long, good life. She's my age. Did you know that? When we adopted her, they knew her birthdate, and it was the same as mine—the same exact day. Dogs don't live this long. I've been so lucky."

I'm about to snap this phone in two, I'm so frustrated that I can't comfort her.

This long-distance thing is complete *ass*.

"She started limping last week, and Dad took her to the vet. She's got—" More sobbing comes from her end, and I turn toward the wall, clenching my jaw. "She's got multiple tumors. All over. The last few days, she's been whimpering when she walks, and she stopped eating yesterday. They're taking her to the vet tomorrow morning." She dissolves again and I curse under my breath.

"It's just—the last time I saw her was the last time I'll ever see her, and I didn't know it. I didn't get to say goodbye. Just like—" More tears.

Just like Deb. Oh, fuck no. No goddamned way.

"Dori. I need to go. I'm going to call you back in like—ten minutes. Maybe fifteen, okay?"

"You don't have to call back. Reid, seriously, thank you for listening—"

"When I call, you answer. Okay? Swear."

She takes a deep breath and squeaks out a heartbreaking, "Okay."

I fight the urge to punch the stone wall in front of me. Breaking my hand will solve nothing.

When she answers, she's more hoarse than before, but not crying.

"Hello."

"Hey, baby. I've got some instructions for you. Do you have a pen?"

She sniffles. "Uh, instructions? What?" There's a paper-shuffling sound. "Okay?"

"Are you in your room?"

"Yeah."

"Okay, good. Write this number down—it's important: 1360. That's your flight number. I want you to start packing. *Now.* A car will be waiting outside the Starbucks to take you to the airport. That flight leaves in just over an hour, and it's the last one of the day."

"What? But you can't—"

"Do not argue with me—you don't have time. Pack a bag. Get to the Starbucks. Get in the car. The driver will drop you at the right gate. Go inside and head right to the first class counter to get your boarding pass. Don't forget to take your license, by the way. I learned the hard way a couple of years ago that they don't let you on the plane without ID. When you land, there will be another car—the driver will have your name on a placard—and he'll take you straight home."

She starts crying again, and I'm afraid she's going to fight me, but thank God, she just rasps, "Thank you."

I bite back the *I love you* on my tongue. I won't ask for the return of those words from her, certainly not as a reward for this, and that's what saying it now would be. She'll say it when she's ready.

"Let me know when you're home. Don't worry about the time here—I won't go to sleep until I know you're there. Call your parents once you're in the car."

"Okay. Thank you, Reid," she says again.

"Go pack. I'll talk to you in a little while. If you have *any* problem, call me. My phone is in my front pocket and set to vibrate the crap out of my leg."

Her gravelly little laugh destroys me. I return the phone to my pocket and take a deep breath. If Dad wasn't sure how serious I was about Dori before, he sure as hell knows now.

Chapter 16

Dori

When I was six, Deb and I lost our last grandparent—my father's opinionated, quick-witted mother, who made the world's best sugar cookies, loved to sing, and fondly recalled her years as a piano teacher. At her funeral, my sister held my hand, and at the end of the day, she put me to bed.

"I love you, baby sister of mine," Deb said, tucking the covers to my chin.

"How much?" I asked, Esther settling in next to me, as she did every night.

Leaning over me, her serious fourteen-year-old eyes shining, Deb whispered, "As many grains of sand as there are on all the beaches in all the world."

"For how long?" I pressed, and she rolled her eyes.

"Forever and forever and forever." When I smiled, she added, "*Duh.*"

We'd repeated this ritual on occasion over the years, though I'd never doubted my sister's love. Hearing her say it was a comfort that I sometimes craved.

I've had to accept that Deb is forever changed. I'll never hear her quirky laugh or her sound advice again. I'll never feel her arms around me. She'll never tell me she will love me forever. She's gone but not gone, and my heart is in limbo, unable to say goodbye.

Because of Reid, I got to say goodbye to Esther. Last night, she slept next to me one last time, nestled against my chest—her intermittent whines, so soft as to be apologetic, breaking my heart.

119

We drove to the vet's office this morning, and I sat in the back seat, stroking her head where it rested on my leg. Telling her in whispers how much I loved her, and what a good friend she'd been. Her big, dark eyes looked up at me, and I knew she was telling me goodbye, too.

On the way home, I held her worn red collar tight in my hands, tears streaming down my face. I read the inscriptions on her tags— her license info, our matching birthdate, her please-return-to number and address, and her name: *Esther Cantrell*.

It may seem odd to think of a dog as having a last name, because they don't need it for school or a job, but it was right. Esther and I shared a surname because she was family, tip to tail.

Kayla:	Dori, have you seen the photos in the link I just sent you? Maybe nothing is going on, but I never liked that Brooke Cameron. She's probably as bitchy and stupid as her life's a beach character.
Me:	I'm sure it's nothing. I'm actually home. We put Esther to sleep this morning. I'm going back to Cal tomorrow.
Kayla:	Oh no! ☹ I loved Esther. I'm so sorry. Can me and Aimee come over to cheer you up?
Me:	I don't think that's possible, but thank you. I'm going to visit Deb tonight. I'll see you guys next time, I promise.
Kayla:	Okay. {{hug}} We'll keep an eye on that Brooke bitch for you.

The link Kayla sent goes to a gossip website. At the top are two photos—clearly cell-phone taken—of Reid. And Brooke Cameron. Together. In one, they're sitting together at the gate, talking and waiting for a flight. In the other, they're sitting together *on* that flight.

I spoke to him earlier today, and he'd not mentioned her. Perhaps he's waiting for me to bring it up. Or hoping I won't. He didn't tell me they were going to New York together, but they clearly did. There are separate photos of each of them there, too— attending the opening nights of their new films last night, both alone. No dates, no plus-ones. The media, of course, speculates wildly over what that means, and the post includes a photo of the two of them from years ago, holding hands, happy. They look the age I was when I fell in love with Colin.

I don't want to ask him about her. This day has drained me emotionally, and I'm incapable of thinking rationally.

There's also my gratitude for the fact that thanks to Reid, I'm at my kitchen table, making a gravestone out of a clay tile and ceramic buttons to place on Esther's spot in the back yard garden. Two hours ago, Dad and I lowered her carefully into the deep hole he'd dug at dawn, before we left. We positioned Esther's body as Mom stood by, holding a rawhide bone and her favorite toy—a squeaky banana—to be buried with her.

Esther loved chasing and roughhousing. She was one of those dogs who discouraged any fragile things placed on low tables for fear of her long, constantly-wagging tail accidentally sweeping them to the ground. But wrapped in a beach towel of mine which she'd absconded with so many times—dragging it to her dog bed like a security blanket—that I finally gave it to her, she'd seemed so small.

"Would you like tea?" Mom asks now, her voice as gruff as mine. Our grief over Esther has revived every anguished memory of Deb's accident. The three of us are wrestling with the tacit loss of my sister all over again, though no one says so.

"Yes, please. Chai?"

Mom nods and moves to the sink with the teakettle. She stares out the back window, gazing at that new mound of earth within the flowerbed, where my identifying tile will go. In a month or so, the dirt will have compressed back into place and the weather will be warmer, and Dad will plant new flowers there.

Deb used to tell me hilarious stories of Esther as a puppy—how she regularly dug up part of Dad's flower garden to bury her treats and toys. She'd then deposit newly uprooted flowers on the back step, like a confession, or a gift—infuriating our usually unflappable father.

"How's Reid?" Mom asks, and her question takes me by surprise.

"He's good, I think. He came up for a visit last week." Keeping my eyes on the tile I'm working on doesn't prevent my ears from growing hot, because I'm hoping she doesn't ask where he stayed the night.

She's quiet for a few minutes, making the tea. When she sets a mug in front of me, she says, "It was a nice thing he did, flying you home last night. Are you planning on seeing him, while you're here?"

I note the slight judgment in her tone and answer defensively. "He's in New York, actually. He won't be home in LA until tomorrow, after I've gone back to Berkeley."

"Oh," she says, considering. She offers nothing more, padding from the room to take Dad his tea. He's in his study, working on tomorrow's sermon. I can't imagine trying to stand up in front of a congregation tomorrow and be encouraging or instructive—but then, Dad had to continue doing his job after Deb's accident. In the face of it, even.

No matter what grief or loss takes place, most of life flows on all around us, as though nothing's changed. At some point in our sorrow, we each make a choice to sink or swim. There's no other alternative.

REID

The paternity test results are in. No surprise—I'm River's father. I anticipated this answer, of course. What I didn't expect was the irrational dread that tore through me, in the seconds before Dad gave me the 99% confirmed answer: I was afraid he was going to say he wasn't mine.

"He's definitely yours." Dad's dismal tone makes it clear that this wasn't the outcome *he* was wishing for. I can't fault him. This can't be how he envisioned becoming a grandfather (assuming he'd *ever* envisioned that), though legally, he's sort of not one. Yet.

I expected this answer to amplify my frustration with the whole thing, foreseen or not. After all, the possibility that I'll have to tell Dori just became a *probability*. Legal concerns—something I thought I'd moved past two months ago when I got my license back—are about to complicate the hell out of my life. And most bizarre of all—I have a sudden, unwelcome sense of obligation toward Brooke.

I should be ticked, but instead, I feel conflicted and *relieved*. What. The. Hell?

So then I think—maybe it's biological. I'm a man, and I've reproduced. Maybe there's a sort of chest-beating satisfaction at the root of this. How fucking lame and archaic—I mean *shit*, seriously? On the heels of that thought is the knowledge that this same kid has turned *Brooke Cameron* into an ardent defender of motherhood—her own, of course—not the institution itself. But still. There must be some primitive impulse to blame.

Six hours later, I'm meeting with Dad to decide what to do next. Dropping into a seat across from him, I wait while he finishes a client email. His home office looks the same as it always has—a near-duplicate of his high-rise headquarters, but I haven't given it a detailed survey in years.

He doesn't meet with clients here, of course, so there's no need for posturing—tasteful artwork, perfectly aligned legal books, smiling family photos. Accordingly, the only artwork hanging on the walls consists of a couple of repulsively gruesome war paintings he inherited from his parents, who died when I was too young to retain a memory of them. The built-ins behind him house a disordered arrangement of California and Federal criminal law volumes, penal codes (the titles of which made me snicker as a ten-year-old), and thick tomes housing Supreme Court precedents.

I thank fate once again for making me an actor, though at times I wonder how far apart my dad's career and my own actually are.

On his credenza is an array of framed photos—all turned to face his desk, as though he glances at them occasionally, or can if he decides to. The largest is my favorite of my parents on their wedding day. Next to it is Mom holding me the day I was born—she, fresh-faced and beautiful, and me, nothing but a cranky face the size of a grapefruit, encased in a tube of blue blankets. Another shows Mom and me on my first day of kindergarten, my backpack more like a giant shell on my back. She smiles down at me, her hand on my head, and I'm all teeth and big blue eyes, laughing straight into the camera.

While Dad taps at the keyboard, I rise and pick up the pewter frame. Looking closer, I mentally compare this photo to the one of River. Only a year older than he is now, I look much bigger. My clothes are new and expensive—a mirror image of what hip adolescents wore at the time, though at five, I couldn't possibly have known or cared. My expression is far from solemn. Even so, I see him in my features. I see him, if he was cared for. And happier.

I didn't want this, any of it, but it's like I'm stuck on a track, and the train is coming, and there's nothing I can do but accept the inevitable and try to mitigate the collateral damages.

"All done," Dad says, and I set the photo back in its place and take a seat in front of his desk, leaning forward, elbows on knees, hands clasped. Mirroring the sensation I got walking between Brooke's box towers a few days ago, the walls are closing in.

"I don't expect you to answer what I'm about to say right away, though we haven't got the time to linger over decisions. You've said that Ms. Cameron intends to adopt the child—"

"River."

"River. Right." His pen scratches across the pad. "Do you know whether she intends to continue to live in LA? Or move back to Texas?"

"She's moving into a two-bedroom condo near the one she's in now. I assume that means she plans to be here most of the time, if not all of the time."

Pursing his lips, he taps his pen, staring at his handwritten notes. "My initial reaction was hope that I could extricate you from this situation, because this isn't something for which you can serve a few weeks of community service or pay a fine, and then it's all over."

He leans up and our eyes lock—his dark, like Dori's, and I wonder how long it's been since he's looked at me so directly. "I'm not going to lecture you about protection—I think you know these things, and you probably knew them then, but not well enough to be consistent. If anyone should be lectured, it's me. Christ, you weren't even fifteen when this happened." He runs a hand through his salt-and-pepper hair, his jaw locked. "The fact remains, you fathered a child, even if you were a child yourself at the time—and instead of living with settled adoptive parents, he's presently in foster care, and it's very likely he'll be living with your unstable ex-girlfriend soon, minutes away."

"What are you saying, Dad?"

"I'm saying that if you relinquish your rights to him now, you may live to regret it."

Okay. This day is full of unanticipated responses. I nod once and stare at my hands as he continues.

"When you were born, I was petrified that I'd be a horrible father. Your grandfather was a hard man, and he taught me nothing of paternal tenderness. I guess in many ways, my fear came true—I made it true. But I never turned my back on you. I don't have to look at you right now and try to explain why I signed away my rights to you. Giving up a baby for adoption is a good thing, almost always, in cases like yours and Brooke's. What's happened to the—to River—is virtually unheard of. It couldn't have been foreseen, and there's little use asking why or how it happened. All that matters is what we choose to do about it now. What *you* choose to do about it now—because I won't make this choice for you. But I'll stand by you, no matter what you decide."

I close my eyes and will the walls to shift farther apart so I can breathe. "Assuming I don't sign the relinquishment, what happens?"

"Three choices. One, you simply refuse to sign it, making the adoption more difficult for Brooke, but likely resulting in an eventual relinquishment by default. Two, join Brooke's bid to adopt and request joint custody. Three, file for full custody. Considering the fact that you were fifteen when he was born, she knew you were the father, and no one saw fit to inform your legal guardians, a case could be made that you never legally relinquished your rights. She signed her rights away, with full parental consent. You signed nothing, and neither did we."

Brooke will be furious no matter which of those I choose. I'm going to drive Dori away as soon as I spill this to her. And I could destroy my mother's fragile sobriety.

"What about Mom? What will this do to her?"

His mouth forms a grim line, and he's silent for a moment. "I've grappled with that all day. I just don't know, Reid. She's been going to meetings every day. She's doing well. Better than I've seen her in a decade. But you and I know that upheavals like this—"

I drop my head in my hands, pulled in a million directions. "I know."

Ever the attorney, he says, "I'll have to consider how to best disclose it to her. That will be mine to handle, however. You have enough on your plate."

Chapter 17

Brooke

My discussion with Janelle goes as predicted—she has a gradually mushrooming shit-fit, insisting that I should have told her about River long before now.

"Why?" I ask, sitting on the tan leather sofa across from her desk. Boasting an impressive view of Hollywood, Janelle's new corner office is located several floors up from her original shoebox-sized cube with its parking lot view.

"So I could be prepared for things like this!" she exclaims.

I roll my eyes. "And how exactly would you have prepared for this? I gave him up for adoption when I was sixteen, and never expected to see him again. If I couldn't have 'prepared' for this, how the hell would *you*?"

"*Fine.*" She spits her go-to I've-had-it-up-to-here word at me. "But I still think you should have told me."

I offer an indolent one-shoulder shrug, which she hates. "Janelle, if you don't know by now that there's a load of crap you don't know about me and never will—then we've got an even bigger problem."

If the pen she's holding was any thinner, she'd be holding two busted pen halves and a face full of ink. Her jaw clenches and she smiles tightly. "Is there anything else you *do* plan to tell me?"

Here we go—the reason for my in-person visit. "Well. Yes."

Her eyes widen. "You look sheepish. I've never seen you look like this. I don't like it. What—" I watch as her quick brain connects the dots and her face pales. "Oh, no. *Paper Oceans*—you're still going to do it, right? Brooke. *Brooke*—I'm too young

127

and healthy to die of a heart attack, even if I want to!"

"I'm sorry, Janelle. I just don't see how I can."

Her blanched face refills with pink from the bottom up, like someone is topping it off. "B-but you said *Get me an audition for something powerful.* You said *Something like Monster, but where I don't have to look ugly like Charlize.* And I did it! I did it, Brooke. You were *so upset* when that Castleberry twit got the role. When she busted her ass—*literally,* hah-hah!—on that slope, it was like a miracle. You don't turn down miracles in this business, Brooke!"

"I can't leave him. I can't leave the process." I hold up a hand to forestall the comment forming on her tongue. "I'm not going to screw this up, Janelle."

Like a boulder tumbling down a hill, nothing stops her. "But screwing up your *career* is no big deal?" Her eyes bug, and I hope she meant what she said about being too healthy to have a heart attack. "Can't we just—we'll get you an au pair! We'll send them with you. Angelina hauls her brood all over the globe!"

Instantly skeptical—sure I'd read something about at-home and filming swap-offs—I ask, "She does?"

"Hell, I don't know—probably. Who cares—because *you* can!"

"Um, no, I can't. I'll have just gotten placement of him. I can't *run off to Australia with him* before the adoption is final."

She's so google-eyed that it makes my eyes water to look at her. "Look. Brooke. We haven't heard from the studio yet. Maybe something in your circumstances will change, and we won't have to turn it down."

"Like—maybe the court will tell me I'd be the most screwed-up mother he could have, and toss me out on my ass?"

"I don't mean *that.*"

I narrow my gaze on her. "Have they called you yet? Because if you do anything even remotely resembling an attempt to keep him from me just so I will do *Paper Oceans,* I will fire you so fast you'll be embers."

She blinks multiple times and then darts her eyes away, tugging at her suit jacket and harrumphing. "I'm supposed to call someone back tomorrow, actually, and of *course* I wouldn't do *that* to you."

Seeing Janelle in person was definitely the right move.

"I know you wouldn't, Janelle," I smile sweetly, my tone conciliatory, with a touch of my native drawl. "I didn't mean to accuse you. I know you would never do anything to hurt me."

The flight to Austin is blissfully uneventful—no broody teenagers or flirtatious businessmen. No Hollywood golden boys I'd like to strangle with my bare hands. When the flight attendant closes the loading door and the seat next to me remains vacant, I mutter, "Oh, thank God," a bit too vehemently, earning me an arched brow from a lady across the aisle. I pretend not to notice. Feeling the effects of the past week in all its stressful glory, I know one more annoyance might result in an air marshal and handcuffs.

Finally free of the breakneck round of promotion for *Hearts*, I'm heading back to Texas to address the final pieces of my application for River's adoption—one of which is my mother, who'll soon be contacted for her opinion on my suitability as an adoptive parent. As if she would have a clue.

Sometime in my pre-adolescence, some jackass came up with the term MILF, and the boys I knew quickly applied it to my mother. Now, Mom's a three-times-divorced cougar, and instead of being mortified at those titles, she wears them like she wore the hayseed beauty queen crowns now stored in a lighted display case—proudly. She refuses to see that her looks are all she's ever had going for her, and now that she's on the verge of losing them, she's become a pathetic stereotype.

Never undertaking any sort of career aside from securing and discarding husbands, she's accepted a multitude of labels over the years, including *trophy wife* and *single mother*. When I was little, she called herself a "stay-at-home-mom" whenever it suited her, though she did little to nothing to earn that designation.

I know how she'll respond to my bid to adopt River. I knew before I came—because out of all the titles she's willingly assumed, I can't imagine *grandma* ever being one of them.

I haven't seen my mother since she showed up in LA last spring, without notice, expecting entrance to the premiere and after-party of *School Pride*—for herself and her latest cougar-bait. I granted them entrance to the film, but pretended I couldn't get her into the party on such short notice. Total bullshit, but there was no way I was dealing with her up close and personal while Reid and I focused on our doomed plan to break up Graham and Emma.

When I arrive at her downtown apartment at our prearranged time—10 a.m., she's fully made up, but still wearing her black dressing gown.

"Hello, Brooke," she smiles tightly. I'm pretty sure she's had work done since I've seen her, because her facial features look a tad *stretched*. Her caramel eyes are the same as always— somehow cold despite their warm color.

Leading me into the familiar living area, she gestures toward the plush sectional and I sit while she grabs her cup of coffee from the kitchen counter and sits without offering me anything. A new yappy dog runs up and barks annoyingly, beginning to nip at my ankles until I lean down and growl—a trick I learned with the last one. Like its predecessor, it runs away bleating.

"I assume there's a reason for your visit beyond terrorizing Tipsy." *Tipsy*?

Where Kathryn's drawl is comforting, my mother's inflections wring my insides like dishrags. I hate the sound of her voice. I hate her calculating eyes. I hate that I came from her, that she tried to make me into her likeness and in many ways succeeded. I hate that I can't escape this connection, no matter what I do.

I fix her with a polished stare of my own. "Yes. I'm here to inform you of a decision I've made that will affect you, though probably not much."

Her mask drops for a moment and curiosity peeks through. "Oh?"

I take a breath through my nose and just blurt it out. "I've applied for custody of my son."

"I'm sorry, what?" Her penciled-on eyebrows would no doubt arch if they could.

"He was taken from his adoptive mother because of extreme neglect, and he's currently a ward of the state. I've applied to adopt him."

I wait while she processes what I've just told her, wondering if I'll have to repeat it with smaller words.

"What the hell are you saying, Brooke? Did CPS come after you to take—?"

"No. This was my choice."

She blinks, her mouth going slack. "You mean to tell me you are—*on purpose*—taking back that brat you gave away five years ago?"

Oh, hell no. I breathe through my nose one more time. "Do not ever call him that again."

"Don't call him a *brat*? People will call him worse. After all, he *is* a bastard—"

The slap shocks us both. I stand, shaking. My hand stings, and the pink print of it is visible on her cheek until she covers it with her palm. Her eyes are radiating indignation, gears spinning behind them, and every defensive instinct I have is on red alert.

"A caseworker is going to call you. Tell them whatever you'd like about me—I'm sure you will anyway. Just make sure whatever you tell them is the truth. If you lie, and I find out about it, I will go straight to a reporter I know at *People*, and she'll happily whip up a sweet little story about my relationship with you that will make Joan Crawford look like Mother Mary." The false threat rolls off my tongue, but I calculate that I can make it true if I have to. "I've turned into the famous little actress daughter you wanted. Now, you can return the favor by staying the hell out of my life. Feel free to claim me in your laughable circle of expendable acquaintances. But fuck with me or my son, and I will make you wish I was never born."

"Oh, don't worry—I'm way ahead of you there." Her snarling face resembles that of her overbred, ankle-snapping dog. "You always were a selfish little bitch."

Her words render me breathless for a moment, and bring back all of those backhanded slaps from my childhood and adolescence. The hair-pulling. The cruel verbal jabs about any imperfection.

"Well. I learned from an expert." I smile, as if nothing she's ever said has affected me, which feels like the biggest lie I've ever told. "Have a nice life, *Sharla*." Marching to the door without a backward glance, I bite my tongue until I taste blood. I will not cry in front of her. That's what therapists are for, goddammit, and I'm getting one as soon as I get back to LA.

I slam her door behind me, and dial my father's number once I get to the pickup truck I borrowed from Glenn. I might as well get all the hell over with in one day.

"Daddy?" I say when he answers. "I have something to tell

you. Do you have a minute?"

REID

In view of what I'm about to tell Dori, and what I'm about to ask of her, I feel like a two-faced asshole when I pick her up the Friday evening before her birthday. All she knows is that I'm taking her across the bay into San Fran for the weekend. I promised her she'd have time to study for a major exam scheduled for Monday—which would be humorous if I wasn't so preoccupied with the coming conversation.

I've decided not to tell her until Sunday. I want to give her the best weekend of her life before I disclose this sort of news. If there was any way around it, I would put it off longer. I hate that I have to tell her at all, ever.

On a bookcase shelf in her library alcove, my mother has a small wood-carved quotation by Robert Frost that says, "The best way out is always through." I've never fully understood that line until now.

The solitary drive on the 5 from LA to Berkeley is even more monotonous than I remember from the road trip John and I took a couple of years ago. I want my own wheels this weekend, though, so we won't have to rely on chauffeured transportation. When I pull onto the side street next to her dorm, almost everyone ogles the car. It's not my yellow Lotus (I think Dori would have appreciated Dad's mocking *douche taxi* title, had she been around at the time), but the feline body shape and headlights and the Ferrari marque are conspicuous, even in a staid gray.

At the corner just ahead, Dori spots me, ducks her chin, and hurries to the passenger side. Her hair is swept into a giant clip at the back of her head, and she's wearing jeans, dark green Chucks and a Cal sweatshirt. She's using her backpack as an overnight bag, which makes me wonder if she has any decent luggage. Something else I need to remedy, soon.

My heart rate jams into high gear as she slips inside and shuts the door.

"Happy birthday," I say, taking her face in my hands and kissing her.

She braces one hand against my chest, twisting it into my shirt and leaning closer as her mouth opens under mine. It's been twenty-six days since I've seen her, and that interval somehow feels like hours one moment and years the next. There's a sense of desperation to this kiss that scares me, because it's not just coming from me.

"Thank you again for last weekend—"

"It was nothing. I wish I could have been with you. I'm so sorry."

Something flares in her eyes, and she lowers them quickly, like a window shade screening whatever she's thinking.

I pull her chin up. "What?"

She shakes her head and tries to smile, but she's no actress. "It's nothing. I'm just sad. I don't want to ruin the weekend you've planned. Let's not talk about it. I'll be okay."

I want to press her to tell me what's going through her mind. I want to tease her about what a horrible liar she is, and how I need to give her lessons, if she means to do it right—but the words stick in my throat. I can't call her on a fib with what I've been hiding from her.

"No problem," I whisper, kissing her again before taking her backpack and placing it in the seat behind her. "I plan to indulge your every desire this weekend, Miss Cantrell."

She's unusually quiet as I maneuver through in-town traffic. Crossing the bay, she stares out her window, silently watching the yachts and fishing boats, her gaze rising to follow the occasional seagull. For the hundredth time, I struggle to find some way out of telling her about River—not *now*, not this weekend—but I may not see her until her spring recess—a month away. Sometime in the next few days, Dad will start the adoption process. After I've told Brooke, of course.

They've accelerated the schedule for my next film, much of which will be shot on set at Universal Studios in LA, with the rest shot in Utah and New York. Filming was supposed to start in April; instead, we're starting next week, with the scenes in Utah up first.

The best way out is always through.

I've made Saturday dinner reservations, so when I suggest that we stay in and order room service tonight, Dori agrees.

"You can even do a little studying," I say, and she crooks an eyebrow at me, dubious. "Maybe like twenty minutes' worth." Pulling up to the valet at the Mandarin, I add, "Once dinner arrives, though, you're mine." Grinning, I grab our bags and hop out.

We're definitely recognized at the front desk—or at least, *I* am. I think the desk clerk is more than a little worried that I'm checking in with an underage girl, given Dori's backpack and makeup-free face—thank God for the Cal-wear she's sporting, which suggests that she's the co-ed she is. Within minutes, we're in the designated elevator, zooming up to the suite.

"Oh my gosh—my stomach," she says, holding onto me and laughing.

"No need for the elevator to waste time when it doesn't plan to stop anywhere along the way. I promise that's the last rushed experience you'll have tonight." I kiss her nose as the doors slide open. "Everything else will be unhurried and deliberate. If you want something faster," I bend to whisper in her ear and she gives a gratifying shiver, "you'll have to say so."

Her lips part when she sees the suite, and she's speechless for several minutes, standing in the doorway and scanning from one side to the other and back. Finally, she leaves the entrance, tentatively, and moves into the room. "This is all ours? This is *one room*?"

I shrug, enjoying her amazement. "It's a suite."

Within minutes, we're enjoying an unobstructed view of a breathtaking sunset over the bay—judging by the fact that she seems to stop breathing, watching it. I couldn't have timed this better if I'd actually scheduled our arrival time to coincide with the sun's measured retreat.

True to my word, I set her up at the desk and let her do her thing while I put our stuff away and order a dinner of champagne, Nasi Goreng and Singapore Noodles—to be delivered in an hour and a half.

"Time's up." I lean over her and nuzzle her cheek. "I've given you a very generous half hour of study time."

She leans her head back on my shoulder and closes her eyes. "I can't study for only half an hour—I'm going to fail!"

I pull her chair away from the desk and kiss her behind the ear, eliciting a soft moan. "If you're a good girl, I'll allow you another half hour tomorrow."

"I'm always a good girl, Reid," she says, and the ear I'm attending to warms under my tongue. "I mean, uh…"

"No explanation needed," I chuckle, kissing down her neck before releasing her hair from the clip and slipping her sweatshirt off. Underneath, she's wearing a white tank with a scooped neckline trimmed in lace—which I can see straight down from my vantage point behind her. A sweatshirt with *this* hidden beneath it?

"Jesus, Dori." My head is swimming with wanting her, and I'm determined to pay her back in kind, and then some. Cupping my hands over her shoulders and sliding forward, my thumbs follow the line of her collarbone while my fingers brush over the curves of her breasts. "You're perfect."

She starts to object and I place two fingers over her mouth, slipping my other hand into the top of her white lace bra. She arches back and gasps, giving me better access to her warm skin, her heart beating against the palm of my hand.

Pulling her up and kicking the chair out of the way, I turn her and am kissing her deeply before she can take a breath. Her tank follows the sweatshirt to the floor. Gripping her hips, I ask, "Shower before, during, or after? Since you're the birthday girl, your wish is my command."

"During?" Her brow creases. "During wha—oh. *Oh.*"

I release her long enough to pull my T-shirt off, and then lift her until she settles her legs around me and hooks her ankles at the base of my spine. Carrying her into the bathroom, I say, "What you're doing right now? *Yes.*" I kiss her. "Exactly this. In about three minutes."

She slides down the length of me when I put her down to switch on the hot water and then turn to remove her jeans. I'm kneeling, tugging her jeans from her feet when she says, "I thought you said something about *unhurried.*" She steps out of them, nibbling her lower lip and standing in front of me in nothing but scraps of white lace.

"So I did," I answer, rising. Unbuttoning my jeans while my eyes skim over her curvy little body, I whisper, "How is it not *my* birthday? Because I'm definitely getting my wish."

Once my jeans are off, I back her to the wall and she squeaks.

"Cold?" I laugh, pulling her away from the chilly marble and kissing her while I unhook her bra and slide her panties over her hips. "It's warmer in the shower. And be prepared to be very, very wrinkly—because if you want slow, by God, you're getting *slow*."

We barely have time to get our robes on before dinner arrives an hour later. Curling up on the sofa with her legs beneath her, Dori pretends to read while the room service attendants set up the table by the window. Her hair is still damp and shoved back behind her pink-tipped ears. I struggle not to laugh at this girl who is the most mind-blowingly responsive lover I've ever had—while also bizarrely *bashful* in the presence of hotel personnel.

While we trade bites of our meals, placing chopsticked morsels into each other's mouths in a way that would be impossible to get her to do out in public, I coax her into sipping a glass of the champagne—just enough to render her languid and periodically giggly after dinner, mostly when I kiss her somewhere ticklish, like the bottom of her foot, or the curve of her waist, or the top of her inner thigh. For the most part, she sighs and smiles impishly, her hands wandering over me, gentle and teasing, until I pin her to the bed, at which point she grips my biceps and makes the most incredibly satisfying sounds I've ever heard her make.

Note to self: stock a case of *Mesnil Sur Oger ASAP*.

Chapter 18

Dori

A month ago, I woke up with Reid in my narrow dorm bed, and it was like a dream—spending an entire night with him next to me. Burrowed under the covers, back pressed to his warm chest, his arms surrounding me—I wanted to stay there forever.

Waking up with him in this suite feels like—what's better than a dream?

A fantasy. That's what.

We left the heavy draperies pulled open last night. Without moving from the bed, I take in the cerulean blue of the bay, blending into the lighter horizon beyond it. Boats cross the water slowly—tiny specs of white or gray from this distance, without form.

The suite is perfectly temperature-controlled, and the pillow-topped bed is huge, so we weren't required to sleep like two spoons in a drawer due to winter chill or lack of space. Still, my ankle is hooked over his. With the arch of my foot, I stroke the soft hairs on top of his foot and he utters a sleepy, "Mmm..." Bare-chested, sheet pushed to his waist, his opposite arm is crooked under his pillow while the arm nearest me is parallel to mine, intersecting at our hands. His hand rests under mine, fingers folded loosely over the back of my hand.

Asleep, he looks so young, which is perhaps odd for me to think, considering the fact that I'm eleven months younger than he is. With his independent demeanor and his successful career, it's difficult to view him as a boy who's a month shy of twenty. Except when he's unguarded, like now.

I slip from the bed to use the bathroom and brush my teeth, and a few minutes later, he pads in, still a bit heavy-eyed, his hair sticking in all directions. He's pulled on the plaid Cal pajama pants I gave him when he visited campus, while I'm wearing his Berkeley tank that completes the set. It falls to my mid-thigh, the arm openings extending almost to my waist.

It's all I can do to concentrate on getting rid of any traces of morning breath instead of turning and twining myself around him like a ribbon. He grabs his toothbrush and the toothpaste, blearily squirting a blob onto the bristles and attacking his teeth. When he begins to brush his tongue, I stare at my toothbrush, running it under the water stream and willing my pulse rate to normalize. My hair looks like chaos incarnate, but thank goodness, it's down and covering my ears, because I can't stop conjuring memories of his tongue. *Sweet baby Jesus.*

Before I can leave the room, he captures my hand and pulls me back, tossing his toothbrush next to mine. "Good morning, baby." Slipping his arms around my waist, his lips meet mine as his hands inch the hem of the tank higher. "Should I call for breakfast now? Or do we want dessert first?"

Scraping my nails lightly over his hard pecs, tracing the sharp definitions and encircling each nipple with an index finger, I watch his eyes darken. "Dessert, please," I say, and he gathers me into his arms, walks to an overstuffed chair in the living area and settles me astride his lap, giving me a floor-to-ceiling view of the bay over his shoulder that I can't quite take advantage of at the moment.

His hands alternately dipping into the sides of the tank or gripping the bare skin of my hips, he makes love to me with slight adjustments of clothing only, pushing his drawstring pants lower on his hips after producing a condom from the pocket.

"That's some confidence, Mr. Alexander," I whisper, closing my eyes as he rains kisses down my throat and pulls the arm slit of the tank to my mid-chest, exposing one breast and making good use of his gifted tongue.

"Um-hmm," he mumbles, completely unrepentant about his smug capacity to dissolve my reticence like a quick, hard summer rain dissolves chalk sketches from sidewalks.

I dig my nails into his shoulders and down his hard, muscled arms, holding him close and almost crying from pleasure. He chuckles, pulling me tighter—his confidence fully justified.

After a late breakfast on the terrace of our suite, wrapped in fluffy robes and soaking up the sun, we dress and head out for a day of attempted incognito shopping. Reid's dark sunglasses, two to three days of facial scruff, and the Cal cap I bought him, along with my standard ordinary-girl appearance, fool the general public just enough for us to remain anonymous, for the most part. We earn a few double-takes—especially from clerks in the shops—but there aren't any mob scenes.

In a boutique shop on Fillmore, he chooses several dresses and tells me to go try them on. "If you hate them all, we'll go somewhere else. But I'm getting you something that will make you feel like royalty when we go out tonight." I start to object, but he hands the hangers to a shop attendant and presses me toward the dressing room. "*No arguments*, because I chose somewhere completely condescending and snooty for dinner, and that's not your fault."

His line of reasoning makes a peculiar sort of sense until I look at the price tags. "*Reid*," I hiss, poking my face out from behind the dressing room curtain. "I can't wear this. It's the price of a *car*." He smirks. "A used car, maybe," I qualify. "But still."

"I bought a car two months ago, and I will personally guarantee that nothing in that dressing room is anywhere near the price of a car. Even if you wanted *all* of them."

"I don't!" I gasp. "But—"

Crossing his arms, he says, "Let's assume that for you, the price of a nice dress is the price of a decent new car, minus a couple of zeros. Yes?" I nod. "That's what this is for me. It's all relative, Dori." He pushes the curtain aside enough to peek inside. "Let me see." Smiling, he asks, "You love it, don't you?"

I chew the inside of my cheek, appraising myself in this dress—a soft, dark royal blue knit cut like it was made exclusively for me. It somehow upgrades every physical attribute I've got—enhancing the good and improving the bad. But I don't want him to buy me something this unreasonable. My life is made up of enough make-believe with him even *in* it.

Stepping into the dressing booth and drawing the curtain closed behind him, he pulls the zipper down at the slowest pace imaginable and catches my gaze in the mirror. His eyes are steely. "I'm purchasing this dress, Miss Cantrell, and you're going to wear it tonight. Understood?"

Caught between wanting to stomp his foot for ordering me around and wanting to throw my arms around him for making me feel like the most desirable girl in California, I simply nod.

"Good girl. As always—like you said." He places a kiss on my nape and leaves the room.

We're driving back to the hotel when my brain clicks everything into place. I turn the music down. "Reid. This car—this car cost that dress, plus a couple of zeros?"

He just smiles out the windshield and I'm glad to be sitting down and strapped in.

Holy cow.

While Reid is showering, Brooke calls him—no last name. She's in his contacts, then, as simply *Brooke*. I assume it's Brooke Cameron, though of course there are other Brookes in the world.

This could be a publicist Brooke. Or an admin Brooke. Or a mechanic Brooke. Frozen in place, I stare at his phone's display while it buzzes. A minute after the buzzing stops, a message alert beeps. She's left him voicemail.

Wandering out minutes later with a bath sheet slung loosely around his hips, rubbing his hair dry with a hand towel, he glances to where I'm carefully removing the price tags from my dress. After detouring to turn me by my robe's belt and steal a slow-building kiss, one hand slipping inside the robe to stroke the bare skin of my hip, he smiles and turns to dig shaving accoutrements from his bag, his phone feet away on the night table.

Trembling from his touch and the words stuck in my throat—*Brooke called you*—I walk into the bathroom.

I pull coils of my hair up with hairpins while Reid shaves, reflecting that he was in the bedroom long enough to listen to the message, but I didn't hear him call her back. He doesn't seem uneasy or concerned. Expression concentrated, he runs the razor over his foam-obscured jaw, pausing to swish the blade beneath a stream of hot water after each swipe.

Maybe it was unimportant. Maybe it was nothing.

"You got a call while you were in the shower," I finally say, watching him.

His brows draw down slightly and his eyes flick to me. "Oh?"

Staring into my own eyes, I lean close to the mirror and run the mascara wand over my lashes. "From Brooke?" I clarify, trying to sound unconcerned. Trying to *be* unconcerned.

He stops cold, staring at me, and I feel as though the air has all just been sucked from the room. "Did you answer it?" he asks, strained.

He must not have looked at his phone, must not have seen the alert. Even before calling her back, he's more on edge than I've seen him since the night he came to speak to my parents. The apprehension is plain on his face—his normally evasive-if-necessary face.

"Of course not, Reid—I wouldn't answer your phone."

I frown, as taken aback by his question as I am by the disquiet in his eyes and the rigid line of his bare shoulders. If I could backpedal right now and retract my mention of her, I would. I wanted this to be nothing. I wanted him to shrug and say it's nothing, but it isn't *nothing*. It's clearly anything but *nothing*.

It's too late to about-face, but I can't watch this unravel, not now, even if I'm the one who pulled the string.

"I have to tell you something—" he says as I say, "I only wanted to let you know—"

We both stop.

He licks his lips, still unmoving, his face half-shaved. "Dori, tonight is your birthday celebration. Let me take you out—let's have our night out, and we can talk later, or tomorrow."

I'm a coward. A willing coward, complicit in my own fall. I've never told him that I love him, as if refusing to say it aloud would somehow shield us both, but it hasn't. Like an untamed, sentient thing, full of all I am and yet estranged from me, my heart discerns its own truth, and knows that this omission is a lie.

"Okay," I whisper.

"Okay," he says.

REID

I want to shake Brooke until her perfectly straight, Hollywood-white teeth rattle. God fucking *damn* her timing. I don't know what message she left, but I suspect it's a *Why haven't you signed that form yet* call—which can wait, because she's going to give me hell over my answer.

Dori and I finish dressing in silence, and when she's done, she looks more beautiful than she's ever looked—while clothed. The deep blue of her dress reveals the flawless tone of her warm skin, and matches my eyes besides. The clingy knit hugs the lush curves of her hips and nips at her waist, while the neckline plunges just low enough to give a hint of her perfect breasts. She was made to wear clothes that fit her like a second skin.

Still, nothing compares to how damned gorgeous she is when there's nothing between us. In my bed—or hers—with her modest demeanor suspended and her curious nature aroused, she's everything I could ever want.

"Your tie matches my dress," she says, running a finger over the silky pattern down the center of my chest. "And your eyes."

I packed a crisp white shirt and a dark gray jacket and slacks, plus an assortment of ties, intending to match whatever dress she chose today.

We're taking one last look at ourselves and each other before we exit the room, the mirror reflecting how very different but complementary we are—my build still angled and a bit boyish, but tall and broad-shouldered next to her smaller, softer frame of arcs and curves. Our coloring contrasts, too—my blue eyes and dirty blond hair next to her almost black eyes and smooth mahogany curls. I imagine pulling those pins from her hair, one by one, and pushing my fingers through the soft strands.

"How many hairpins did you *use*?" I ask, my words seeming like so much small talk while I'm picturing her beneath me in a few hours' time, hair spread across the pillow like a spill of ink.

She smiles, but permeating every tic of her mouth is an underlying sadness that I'm determined to wipe away, no matter what I have to do. I will make her forget that badly timed call—for tonight, at least.

"I'm not sure. A lot?"

Pulling her to me, I don't have to bend as far to kiss her. When I pull away, I smile down at her. "Mmm, you're wearing heels. Do me a favor—walk across the room and back. I won't get to appreciate this view nearly as much as everyone else will tonight."

She purses her lips, self-conscious, but she complies, turning to walk the length of the 2000 square foot suite.

Oh. God. Damn. Her hips sway, and my eyes are torn between following her curvaceous ass, her shapely, naked calves, or the arch of her neck—bare but for a few strategic tendrils allowed to escape the pins. She turns at the opposite end of the room, eyes widening in confusion at the look on my face, and I wonder how the hell that's possible—because she just looked in the mirror, didn't she?

As she returns, I find that it's no easier to decide what to focus on from this perspective. Same flawlessly-muscled legs and rounded hips, with the addition of those perfect breasts and her beautiful face.

"We need to leave now," I say gruffly when she reaches me. "*Right now*. Or else I'm going to toss you on that bed," I take her in my arms and whisper into her ear, "and fuck you senseless."

She leans into me and gasps softly, flushing scarlet, fingers crushing the sleeves of my jacket and digging into my arms.

"Let's just put that on the agenda for our return, shall we?" I kiss her one more time, gently, carefully, and then pluck her tiny clutch from the dresser and lead her from the room, never releasing her hand.

The paparazzi find us between the valet stand and the restaurant door, which is no big shock, considering I shaved and ditched the classic celebrity disguise—hat and sunglasses. They get off a few shots while bellowing my name. They don't know Dori's yet—too slow to match my designer-swathed date with her Habitat girl alter ego.

Once we enter the restaurant, all the diners and every employee from the maître d' to the chef are aware that a paparazzi-worthy guest has arrived. The whole place is either staring or trying not to. So much for a private, low-key meal.

"That wasn't too bad, was it?" I ask, holding Dori's hand across the tiny candlelit table, ignoring the audience and hoping she can as well.

"I'm still seeing spots, but no, I guess not." She blinks a couple more times. "How in the world do you see where you're going if you're alone?"

I nod. "Yeah, that can be tricky. If you're with bodyguards or other handlers, they just cannonball you through the crowd to where you need to be, almost like crowd-surfing. When I'm with other celebs, we stay in a herd as much as possible and head in the general direction of an entrance, exit, or car door."

She laughs lightly. "That's *terrible.*"

I arch a brow at her. "And she laughs! Where's the compassion?"

Attempting to suppress her smile, she fails entirely. "No, I'm serious! But I mean, a *herd* of you? How is that not a funny mental picture?"

"I'm glad my pain amuses you," I say, feigning a stern countenance.

She releases my hand and runs her finger across my palm. "Well, no herd tonight. And no bodyguard, either—unless I can stand in. I may not look very tough, but I pack a mean shin-kick."

Imagining her booting a hulking stalker photog in the shin is only amusing to the extent that I make sure it never happens—because I sort of believe she'd do it. "You're plenty tough, Dorcas Cantrell." When I reclaim her hand and brush my thumb over her knuckles, her lips part. "But your bodyguarding skills won't be necessary this evening. I'll get the maître d to help us sneak out when we leave. Don't worry over that now. Because right now, I'm just a guy, trying to have a romantic dinner with this beautiful girl…"

She lowers her eyes.

"You aren't worried, right?"

Her smile is wry. "No. But I'm *really* relieved to be wearing this dress, instead of an extra-large iced-tea-and-fruit-stained T-shirt."

Chapter 19

Brooke

Reid is seriously pissing me off, but what else is new? He's only been doing that for-fucking-ever. I get that he might be busy— *Reid-world busy*—which could mean anything from starting a new film project to banging a new girl, but he's had plenty of time to get the paternity test results and sign that freaking relinquishment form.

I texted him mid-week and he didn't answer. I called him last night and he didn't answer. I left him a voicemail he didn't return.

This is the sort of avoidance that makes me think something problematic is going on. I've worked too hard to get all my ducks swimming in a row, as Kathryn would say. I even called Daddy, which I'd been putting off doing. After that delightful meeting with my mother, I figured I didn't have anything to lose. So I gave him the shortest version possible of what I was doing, and he was silent for half a minute or so.

"Brooke, you're still so young—and there's more to being a parent than you know," he began, clearly about to launch into couldn't-be-less-welcome life advice.

"You think?" I snapped, and he shut up right quick. "Look. I'm not asking your opinion or guidance any more than I wanted *Sharla's*. This is an FYI call only. And if you want to tell the adoption caseworker what a horrible mother I'll be, then just *go ahead*."

He had the nerve to sound taken aback. "Brooke, I would never do that. I know I wasn't the best father—"

"Oh my God—really? Because you *keep having more*

children, which makes it seem like you think you're great at it." I wanted to rip the gearshift out and beat myself with it after saying that. I'd just tacked a bull's-eye right over my most emotionally susceptible spot. *Idiot.*

"The opposite, actually. I kept thinking I could start over and get it right."

Holy shit, I thought. *How deluded could he be?* "Well that's just stupid. You're screwing around with people's lives and breaking people's hearts. I can't imagine why you left Kathryn for *Sharla.*" I couldn't stop sneering my mother's given name like I was spitting out something poisonous. "Or why Kelley and Kylie weren't enough for you." *Or why I wasn't enough for you.*

"The problem, Brooke, is that with Sharla came you. With Vivian came Rory and Evan. The marriages may look like colossal mistakes from this distance, but I don't regret any of you kids. So I guess I can understand your motivation to get your boy back. And maybe you're doing it right. Getting the child without the dysfunctional relationship."

"You say you don't regret me, but you left me. You didn't just leave a bad marriage. You didn't just leave my mother, Daddy— *you left me.*" I bit back tears.

"I'm sorry."

"Yeah, well." I steeled my jaw. "Try calling Rory before he turns into a teenager who hates you. Try taking Evan to the zoo or something. Go to their soccer games, or school plays, or birthday parties, instead of just sending them *money.*"

I realized by the time I was fifteen that my father never slacked on his financial support of me. He paid his child support payments on time. He sent birthday cards and an escalating amount of cash every year. But I was jealous of the kids whose dads showed up for their *lives.*

"Do you hate me, Brooke?"

I sighed, too tired to hate more than one parent at a time with any real conviction. "I don't know."

He sighed in return. "You always were brutally honest."

I huffed an indignant laugh. "Mom just told me I was always a bitch."

"*What?* That's absurd. I think the whole state of Texas knows who the *bitch* is, sugar." He hadn't called me *sugar* since I was ten. The age I was when he left. My jaw clenched up again.

"I'm not kidding, Daddy. Call Rory and Evan. I'll keep you posted on River."

"His name is River? Brooke and River." He chuckled. "I like it. I'd like to meet him—"

"Not if you're going to disappear on him," I countered.

"I understand. Keep me posted. And don't worry about Sharla. She'll come around."

"No, she won't—but I don't care. You know as well as anyone—some things just don't work out."

Me: WHY aren't you calling me back? Have you signed the form???
Reid: Give me five minutes. I'll call you.

"Have you signed it?" I answer in place of *hello*, trying to keep the panic out of my voice, but there's something going on, and I know it. Something he's not telling me. I can feel it the way you feel certain storms out here in the hill country, right before they roll across the horizon. Like the air is charged. Electric. The invisible hairs on your body all standing up for it. Waiting.

"I haven't, and I'm not going to—"

"What? *What*? What the fuck, Reid—"

"Will you give me a minute, please? We need to talk about—"

"Reid, if you don't sign that form—"

"Don't threaten me, Brooke." His voice is solid, authoritative in a way it's never been, and I'm shot through with fear, because he has the upper hand, and he clearly knows it. "Please shut up and listen."

I say nothing.

"I can't sign the form because I don't want to relinquish my rights to him."

My whole body begins to shake uncontrollably, like it did the time I popped an amphetamine at a party—which scared me so badly I never tried it again. I yank on my boots, which look ridiculous at the end of my flannel pajama bottoms, but I don't care. Phone pressed to my ear, I tromp down the hallway and into the kitchen, where Kathryn and Glenn are making brunch together—a Sunday morning ritual. Jazz flows lightly from the sound system and the smell of waffles and bacon permeates the room.

"I'm walking down to the creek," I tell them, yanking a sweater from the coat rack and sliding the back door open.

Kathryn turns, spatula in hand, her smile fading as she takes in the phone and my freaked-out expression. "Everything okay, honey?" Her head angles and she takes a step toward me.

"Fine. Everything's fine." My smile feels like elastic play putty. There's nothing of me in it. "I'll be back up in a few minutes."

"I want to join your adoption application," Reid says as I pull the glass door shut behind me.

"Why are you doing this?" I'm trembling so hard that I'm afraid I'll drop the phone. Pulling the sweater's hood over my head as though the chill in the air is responsible for my body's reaction to Reid's words, I stomp in the direction of the creek. "Why?"

"I talked to my dad—"

"So this is a *legal* move? You're covering your ass or some shit while I'm trying to give him a home—"

"*No.* No, that's not it."

I realize then that he's speaking quietly. Almost whispering.

"Where are you?"

"I'm in San Fran with Dori. Her birthday is tomorrow, so we're here for the weekend. That's why I didn't call you back right away. That, and I knew how you'd react to this."

In the short amount of time I've been here, I've already begun to re-flatten a path from the house to the creek. "Let me guess. You still haven't told her."

"No."

"But you told your dad."

"Yes. And I plan to tell Dori. Today. I just wanted to wait…" He sighs. "I wish there was some way I didn't have to tell her. I don't know how she's going to react."

"You're at a hotel? It's like 8 a.m. there—are you in the room?"

"Our room has a private terrace. I'm outside." He laughs softly. "With a blanket. Jesus Christ it's colder here than LA."

"I don't want to talk about the weather, Reid."

I reach the creek, and my favorite rock, the flat surface of which is freezing cold. The slow trickle of the current is soothing, even so. I tuck the sweater under my butt and pull my knees to my chest, shivering and exhaling quick-fading clouds of warm breath.

"Okay. Yeah. I know." He sighs. "Dad thinks the best thing would be if we join the application you've already started."

"I don't understand why you're doing this, Reid. You've never expressed any interest in him—"

"I didn't think he was mine, Brooke. I got that conviction in my head years ago, and I just never let it go—not until we talked a couple of months ago. Not fully, to tell you the truth, until you sent me that photo. And now—the fact that you haven't once asked about the test results, well, obviously, you didn't need to ask. You knew what they'd be."

I close my eyes. Feel the speckled rays of sun touch my face through the trees. Listen to the creek babble. And forgive him, finally. "I did."

"Shit. I'm just so—sorry—"

"We were kids, Reid—I know that. We were too young to be *in love* or anything. We were just kids."

These are hollow words, of course. I loved Reid, once upon a time. For too long, I've held onto a silly little-girl belief that I didn't misread him completely. That some part of him loved me, too. It's time I get over that, and yet, I don't need or want to hear the blunt truth.

"Brooke—"

"Reid, don't." My words are barely audible.

"I just—I don't want you to get the wrong impression—"

"Okay, then let's just drop it?" I press my forehead to my knees, wrapping the sweater all the way around myself like a blanket. I can't deal with this right now.

"Brooke, I *worshipped* you. And what I thought you'd done, with those other guys—I could have handled it a million different, *better* ways. I know you hate me for deserting you, and I deserve that. I'd talked myself into the belief that he wasn't mine, and I let that color everything else. But I did love you."

Tears well up in my eyes and soak into the thin flannel covering my knees.

"Um. I need to go," he says. "I'll call you tomorrow, okay?"

"Sure. Okay. I'll talk to you tomorrow."

I hang up and realize two things. One, Reid has just told me that he once loved me. And two, I still don't really know why he wants to adopt our son.

Dori

When I woke up, the bedside clock read barely past 8:00 in the morning. Reid wasn't in bed next to me, and his impression wasn't warm against my palm. I got up and pulled on the robe, which never left its peg last night. Flushing from the memory of Reid's follow-through on his pre-dinner promise, I stepped through our shoes, my lingerie, his shirt and tie, dozens of hair pins, and his slacks.

I'd insisted on folding the dress over the desk chair.

He wasn't anywhere. I frowned, wondering if he'd left the suite to get something when I caught sight of him on the terrace, in his robe. Despite the sun's rays on the patio cushions, the air here is still quite cool this early, and our room is at the top of the hotel—even chillier.

And Reid was outside. On his phone.

I could have gone to take a shower. Or ordered coffee and breakfast. Or picked up the bits of clothing and undergarments strewn from the suite door to the king-sized bed, in anticipation of the fact that we need to pack up and check out in a few hours.

Instead, I went to the door and opened it, slowly. My body ached at the sound of his gruff morning voice—kept low, only a few words making their way to me: *Worshipped. Million. Better. Mine. Love you.*

I must have made a sound, because he turned and looked right at me, still talking. To her. I knew he was talking to *her*. He told her he had to go, that they'd talk tomorrow. He hung up as I backed into the room and followed me inside, closing the door behind him.

I didn't know it would come this soon.

Tossing the phone onto a low table, he reaches me in four long strides and grabs my shoulders, stopping me before I back into a wall. "Dori, we need to talk." He swallows, and I don't think I've ever seen him look this apprehensive. "I'll call for breakfast—unless you already have?"

I shake my head, *no*.

He leads me to the sofa and seats me in a corner before opening the room service menu and calling in a breakfast order. On this call, his voice is full of his usual self-confidence, but it vanishes as soon as he sits next to me, the dark blue of his eyes flicking away and searching the room as though he'll find the words he needs to say somewhere outside himself.

"Okay. Do you know who Brooke Cameron is?"

I nod. "Yes."

He exhales a long breath, one hand at the back of his neck. "Well, we used to go out." His eyes watch mine closely, reading and measuring. I don't know if I want to hide my thoughts or open them all to him. "A long time ago—five years."

Most people dismiss relationships that take place at fourteen or fifteen. Puppy love. Infatuation. A crush. But I know all too well how serious fifteen can be.

"It didn't end well." He runs a hand through his hair, unable to stop fidgeting. "It was pretty ugly, actually. I thought she'd cheated on me. So I broke up with her without even really ending it. A couple of months later, she called and told me she was pregnant."

Pregnant?

My brain calls up Colin, and what I would do or say if I ran into him now. He'd discarded me for no reason that I knew of, although Deb suggested the fact that he'd turned eighteen and I was fifteen was incentive enough. I never told him I was pregnant. I knew he wouldn't care.

"Dori?" Reid says, his hand on my face. I look back into his worried eyes. "Where'd you go? Talk to me."

I shake my head. "I don't understand. Why is she calling you now?" As soon as the words leave my mouth, I know the answer. *No. No. No.*

His jaw flexes and his throat works. "She gave him up for adoption."

I bite the inside of my cheek and my hands grip each other in my lap.

He cups his hands over mine. "God, your hands are freezing.

We can talk about this later—"

"*No.*" My voice is the only solid thing left of me, and he flinches. "Finish. Please finish."

He closes his eyes briefly before answering. "He was mine, but I didn't know it. I didn't talk to anyone about it, Dori. My parents didn't know. I've never even told John."

"How do you know he's yours?"

"We just did a paternity test."

Just. As in recently.

I'm missing something, and I don't know what it is. When children are adopted, their biological parentage is no longer an issue. "But—you said she gave him up. Why—?"

"A couple of months ago, she hired a private investigator to look for him. She was having nightmares about him and just wanted to make sure he was okay. The PI found out that he'd been removed from his adoptive home months ago due to drugs and gross neglect. He's in foster care now. So she's… she's applying to adopt him. And so am I."

The hands that he thought were cold moments ago flash like ice and then go numb. I can't feel anything. And then, suddenly, I feel everything. Waves of chills run from the back of my neck to my toes, millions of tiny pinpricks like sharp, agonizing barbs. As though some outside source grips my throat, my airway narrows and expands, over and over, and with it, my vision.

"I told you about everything that happened to me—with Colin," I gasp. "And you never said—you never told me—"

"Dori, I didn't—I didn't *know*. I thought Brooke had cheated on me. I swear, I didn't think he was mine. We were both so young and stupid and stubborn—we didn't talk like you and I talk—"

"Like you and I talk? Like when you told me you had a child with someone?"

He drops his head in his hands. "*I didn't think he was mine,* and I had nothing to do with her decision."

"So you left her to make that choice—alone? And now you get a second chance at doing the right thing because she made a different choice than I made?" I shift away from him, but he reaches out and grabs my wrists.

"Goddammit, Dori—no. It's not like that—"

"You said you're both adopting him. So you're… you're

getting back together?"

"No. *No.* Jesus. This isn't about me and Brooke—it's only about River."

His child has a name. Of course he does. "River?"

"He's four and a half. I have a picture—" He lets go of me, stands to grab his phone from the table and clicks through it. When he offers it, I reach to take it, thinking, *I don't know him.*

But I see him in his child's face. And if anyone needs saving, it's this little boy. His sadness is unmistakable, mirroring so many small faces from East LA to Quito—children shouldering the weight of the world. A world they didn't create, or ask to be abandoned to.

"Dad is telling Mom this weekend. He's talking with contacts in LA County Family Court tomorrow, and we're going to Austin on Tuesday to speak with Brooke's attorney, and possibly the case-worker and judge. Last, but not least—I'm not sure when this is going to break publicly, but once it does, it'll be a circus." He takes the phone from my hand and tips my chin, looks into my eyes. "Dori, say something."

The brusque rap on the door startles us both.

He sighs. "That's breakfast, I guess."

While he rises to let the attendant in, I stare out the window at the boats in the bay. From this distance, they look like models, or radio-powered toys. I imagine the holders of the remote controls are bored demi-gods occupying rooms like this on the top floors of tall buildings.

I feel his eyes sweep over me, neither of us speaking while our breakfast table is set up.

He is not the self-centered, arrogant boy who showed up at Habitat last summer, calling me a hypocrite for dismissing him and then proving to me that he was worth saving. Not the boy who urged me to be *reckless* with him last fall, because he was safe. Not the boy who showed up on the other side of my parents' screen door weeks ago, telling me he was *all in* before carrying me up the stairs and making love to me in my childhood bed.

This is Reid Alexander—the stuff of fantasy for ordinary girls. And in a few hours, this fantasy will be over. I'll return to my life, and he'll return to his.

Chapter 20

REID

Dori is as quiet on the drive back to the dorm as she was on the drive into the city two nights ago. I slide into a rare open parking spot and offer to walk her in, but she has that exam to study for, and if I get out of this car, there's the possibility I'll be recognized—and she clearly doesn't need to deal with that right now.

We angle over the center console to kiss goodbye until I murmur, "Screw this," slide my seat back as far as it will go and pull her into my lap. "Mmm. Better." Pushing my hand into her hair, I draw her mouth to mine and kiss her deeply, every slide of my tongue against hers, every shared caress a declaration of all she means to me.

Inhaling shakily, she rests her head against my shoulder. "You didn't exactly encourage a lot of study time this weekend, you know." Her hand lies over my heart.

"Well, *I* got plenty of study time. I'm pretty sure I could pick you out of a lineup of only belly buttons or kneecaps or pinkie toes now, let alone the parts I committed to memory ages ago. For instance—I could have identified you by those delicious lips two days after meeting you."

She blinks up at me and tilts her head back on my arm. "But you didn't kiss me until, you know, the pink closet."

I fix her with a suggestive look. "I remember—but those lips were one of the first things I noticed about you. I couldn't stop thinking about them, on or off site. I kissed you a hundred times in my imagination, and once I'd actually kissed you, all I could think about was doing it again." I run the pad of my thumb across her plump lower lip, recalling all the wretched time I spent trying to move on, trying to forget her. It had taken no more than two seconds of seeing her face again to realize that I hadn't forgotten a damned thing.

I wish I could read her mind. She's a pensive, deep-thinking girl, and it's not unusual for her to stare into space, lost in her thoughts. Normally, I'm fascinated when she does this—the shifting emotions crossing her face, marked by faint smiles, frowns or grimaces. That's not how I feel now, when I can't escape the uneasy awareness that her contemplations concern me.

"What are you thinking about?"

She blinks distractedly, and then stares up at me with eyes so dark and fathomless that I'm sure I'll never know all the mysteries behind them. Even if I can't follow her when she withdraws inside herself like this, I want her to know that I'll always be there to pull her back to solid ground before she goes under. That I won't let go.

"I don't want to say goodbye," she says, her eyes shining.

"Then don't say it," I say, ignoring the subtle premonition in her words. Ignoring the fact that she's not asked a single question about River, or Brooke, or the adoption. Ignoring my own hunger to hear her tell me, just once, that she loves me.

river

Wendy told me I might get a new mama. That I might go live with her.

The social lady came to talk to me about it—her name is Kris. She comes to talk to me sometimes. About Mama. Or about Wendy. Or about how I feel or what I think when I hide food. She said that I was just going to visit with the lady who might want to be my mama (except Kris said *mother*, not *mama*). Then she said, "Can you draw me a picture about that?"

That's what they always want me to do. Draw a picture.

I don't want a new mama. I want to stay here with Wendy, and I wish Sean would find a new mama instead. But I don't know how to draw that.

Chapter 21

Brooke

"So, what you're telling me is—we're making a *scrapbook*." Reid lifts an eyebrow and gives me a look of undisguised bafflement. Photos and scrapbooking supplies—borrowed from my stepmother—are spread across the huge, scarred farm table in Kathryn's kitchen where we sit side-by-side on a bench seat.

"My caseworker, Sheldon, calls it a *Life Book*. But yeah, basically, it's a scrapbook."

"And we have to do this because?"

I heave a sigh. I can't blame him—*crafts* are something neither of us does without a damned good reason, if ever. "River's caseworker will give it to him, to show him who we are and where we live. Where he will live. Hopefully, his foster mother will read what we write to him. Sheldon says some kids are thrilled shitless to leave their foster homes, and some aren't—so this helps."

Reid laughs. "Sheldon the social worker said *thrilled shitless*?"

I shrug and laugh, too. "Sheldon's pretty laid back."

He shakes his head. "I'm just trying to imagine Dori ever saying that to a client." One corner of his mouth turns up. "Nope. Nothing doing."

Not for the first time, I wonder about this girl who's so unexpectedly significant to Reid. He pulls his phone from his front pocket and checks it for the third time in the past half hour. Whatever he's looking for, it isn't there.

"While you've got that out, let's go hook it up to my computer so we can print out the photos you took." I get up and he follows me down the hallway to my bedroom.

As I'm booting my laptop, he examines my room. There's not a lot to it, frankly. I'm a minimalist everywhere I go. I stripped my apartment in LA of glass tables and white upholstery before I moved, but I don't do cozy—not naturally, which worries me where River is concerned. What if *cozy* is required for a child his age? I've never painted walls anything other than some neutral tone. There were no photos out, anywhere in the apartment. My living room furniture has never encouraged a spontaneous nap. I've never had a pet, not even fish. I kill plants.

"You're different here," Reid says.

I glance back at him as he's scooting onto my bed, one long leg off the side, foot on the floor, the other angling so the sole of his boot doesn't soil my white comforter. Reclining against the mound of pillows, he folds his hands behind his head, forearms flexed below the haphazardly rolled-up sleeves of his light blue button-down. His head tips to the side as he inspects the room, and me, and I turn back to the computer to keep from squirming.

I know what he means, I think—I'm just not sure whether I care for his spontaneous appraisal. I like being looked at when I know I've taken pains to look hot. Such is not the case at the moment. Ignoring both my blow-dryer and flat-iron, I haven't bothered to tame my naturally messy waves into the sleek, blonde waterfall mane I'm famous for. I'm wearing a long-sleeved thermal T-shirt in a plain heather gray over worn boot-cut jeans and my favorite leather-tooled Ariat boots. Nothing about me says *LA* right now—or Hollywood.

"What do you mean?" I ask, feigning unconcern as I pull up the photo folder labeled *Life Book*.

He considers before he speaks—which is either thoughtful or shrewd. "It's more than just how you're dressed, or the lack of makeup—though that's noteworthy. Your body language and expressions are—I don't know—more relaxed? And your accent is more prominent. You're less…"

I turn around and fix him with a sardonic look. "Less stylish? Less sophisticated?"

"I was going to say less *counterfeit*. I know what you think of your mother, and how much you don't want to be like her. But you *aren't* like her. You were never like her. Your stepmother? She's the one you sound like, by the way. I know that now that I've met her. Though your time in LA has probably weakened your accent permanently." He looks at me through dark, thick lashes some blonds would commit homicide for. "Which I've always believed to be a regrettable loss."

"What do you mean, counterfeit?"

His brows draw together. "You wear the LA-girl part well. But it's a role, isn't it? You were like this when I went by your apartment a few weeks ago, too. *This* is the real Brooke Cameron."

It takes everything I've got not to fall out of my chair. "Wow. When did you get to be so psychoanalytical? Is your girl responsible for this new, uncharacteristic awareness?"

He smiles. "Probably."

"Interesting. I think I need to meet her."

"You will, no doubt."

I angle my head, struck by the thing I've just figured out. He's in love with her.

"You're really serious about her."

He nods, but doesn't look happy. Hmm.

"You did tell her about all this—" I swirl a finger between us. "River, the adoption, etcetera. Right?"

He nods again, lips compressed. "She's had to deal with some rough shit lately. It's messed up her ability to trust."

"I'm sure *this* didn't help any—or you keeping it from her."

His mouth flattens and he shakes his head once. "Uh, no."

"So why'd you do it, Reid?"

"Why did I keep it from her?"

"No. That's yours to puzzle out. I want to know why you're doing this. Why you want to adopt River."

He flicks a blade of grass from his boot—slick, trendy and black—not cowboy boots, like mine, not work boots, like something Graham might wear. Perfect LA boy. But in Austin—straight-up hipster. Not that he'd care.

"I think it's a byproduct of who I've become since I've known Dori. Since I was sentenced to work on that house. It's like I see issues I didn't see before, and my connection to them. My obligation to do something, where I can." He looks me in the eye. "Where River is concerned, it's a pretty hardcore responsibility."

"I've *only* ever felt that sort of responsibility where River is concerned," I admit. "I doubt I'll ever have any weighty sense of social commitment, but I feel linked to River, even if I've never seen him."

Shrugging, he says, "He's part of you."

I bring the laptop to the bed and sit, handing it to him. "He's part of you, too."

He hooks up his phone and brings up the photos I asked for— of himself, his parents' house, and the room they've set aside for River.

"Wasn't this your bedroom?" I recognize the placement of the windows and the dark sliding closet doors. It's been five years, but I remember Reid's bedroom better than which house or condo Mom and I were living in at the time.

"I moved to my grandmother's suite a couple of months after—"

"After we broke up. You can say it. I won't shatter, you know." We sit shoulder to shoulder on my bed, which seems as unbelievable as the subject we're calmly discussing. "I know this might be difficult to hear, Reid, but I'm kind of over you."

He smirks. "Yeah, when you went all Operation Graham last spring and deployed me to seduce Emma—I kinda figured that you were well over *me*."

Graham again. I close my eyes and press my fingers to my chest. *Damn.*

"Still upsets you, huh? I guess you really did love him. God, there's no fucking way I'm ever taking Dori around that guy. Because seriously." His words are tongue-in-cheek, but the underlying tone is anything but.

"Last spring, I was so sure I could deal with all-or-nothing," I say. "When I lost him, I knew that wasn't true, but it was too late. In that moment, I'd have given anything to take it all back. Our friendship saved me—*he* saved me. No matter what I did or who I pretended to be, he was there for me. I don't know who I'd be if it hadn't been for him."

Copying the photos over to my computer so we can print them out, Reid says, "I'm sorry I did that to you, Brooke."

I shake my head. "It wasn't you. I've realized some things in the past few days. Like how I felt when my father left—when he stopped paying any attention to me. I was forever looking for something, or someone, to fill that void." I send Reid's photos to the printer in Glenn's home office, shut my laptop and slide it off my lap. "There are empty places in all of us, and some of them will never be filled. You couldn't fill the loss of my father, and I blamed that on you. Graham couldn't fill it, and I thought it was because I needed more from him than friendship. But that was never true."

He turns toward me. "Dori and I were friends first, I guess. But I don't think I could ever be *just friends* with Dori, even though that part of what we are is essential. I've wanted her almost from the beginning, and being with her only makes me want her more. It would kill me to be around her and never touch her. Maybe you'd reached that point with Graham."

I shake my head. "See, that's the stupid part. I *hadn't*. I convinced myself of that, but it was a lie. You and Dori—you've begun a relationship. Friendship only would be a step back that you don't want to make. But Graham never felt that way about me. Never. We were best friends for four years, Reid." Tears spill down my face. "I threw away the closest relationship of my entire life—aside from Kathryn—on a gamble to get something he'd made it very clear he never wanted."

Reid slides his arms around me and pulls me to his chest. I haven't cried about Graham in months. Instead, I've made myself endure that deep burn in my chest—the one that reminds me what I did—without giving myself the release of tears.

"I called Graham about the adoption," I say, quietly. Reid starts and looks down at me, surprised. "I knew River's case-worker was going to call him, and I was afraid of what he might say to her." I take a shuddering breath. "He told me I couldn't use River to fill my need for affection."

Pulling away, I grab a tissue and look back at Reid, whose shirt is wet with my tears. "Reid, River lost the only parents he's ever known. And he's understandably attached to Wendy, which will be another loss. If we do this, we can't back out." I take his hand and stare into his eyes. "Please don't do this if you can't be there for him. If you're going to start a new family someday and leave him behind. He doesn't need any more hollow places."

Staring down at our hands, he says, "I've thought for years that my father wasn't there for me, but he was. He was *present*—even if he didn't get me at all most of the time. Even if he didn't pay as much attention as he should have." Returning his gaze to mine, he says, "I'll be present, Brooke. I don't want to make promises I can't live up to, but I'll try my best to be more than present. Just promise me that if I fuck up, you'll call me on it. And you'll give me the chance to make it right."

I nod. "Okay."

Reid twitches his hair back and opens a palm. "So. Does *every* girl I know have to turn insightful all at once? I mean hell—I know I'm shallow, but Jesus. You'd think *somebody* would be content to remain superficial, just to keep me company."

The weight leaves the conversation, and I've unburdened myself—to *Reid*—without being demeaned for it. His wisecrack allows me to swim back to a place where my feet can touch bottom.

"Like John?"

"Oh, right," he laughs. "I forgot about John. Dude, I'm so covered."

REID

When Dori didn't answer texts or calls yesterday, I didn't freak out. She had classes all day, including that statistics exam she was worried about. It was her birthday, though, and I didn't get to talk to her. I told myself that her friends probably took her out to celebrate.

Even if it would have taken her thirty seconds to return a text.

Now it's Tuesday, she's still not replied, and every passing hour makes it harder to pass off her radio silence as the demanding life of a college student or a dead phone battery. I wonder if she's okay. I wonder if her parents would even try to call me if she wasn't. And then I wonder if I should call them. I try to remember her friends' names. (Kayla something. Aimee something. Shayma something.)

I'm not cool with the direction my thoughts are taking, because I *don't* do clingy or needy or dependent or possessive.

I've spent most of the day with Brooke, first at her attorney's office with Dad, and now at Kathryn's house making a scrapbook about us for River. After printing out photos of ourselves and parts of LA—hiking trails, parks, his bedroom-to-be at each of our respective places—we glue-stick them onto the pages, like kindergarteners.

"So, how do we plan to explain *our* relationship to him, since we're planning to move him from the one home he knows into two he doesn't know at all? Two parents who are already separated—that might be confusing."

Brooke chews one side of her lip, thinking. "Hmm. Well, we need to convince him that we're friends. That we aren't going to drag him into a tug-of-war. All our self-portraits are separate. Are there any photos in existence of the two of us together, happy? But not, you know, *happy*-happy. Maybe something taken during *School Pride*?" Glancing at my dubious expression, she waves a hand. "Yeah, never mind. We pretty much loathed each other for the duration of that whole thing."

After today's revelations, I feel even worse about how I treated Brooke then. Seriously, having a conscience is ass. "The only friendly one I know of is from five years ago—the one that got printed along with the pics of us at LAX a couple of weeks ago, along with all the theories about why we were flying together."

She rolls her eyes. "Right? Because nothing coincidental ever happens to celebrities." She thumps herself in the forehead and grabs her phone. "*Der.* Let's just take one *now*. Lean in."

We lean our heads together and smile, and she takes two or three shots. After we choose one and she sends it to her laptop, I say, "You know what the media is going to do with this story, right? River. Us."

Sighing, she nods. "I'm not sure what slant they'll take, but they'll probably either try to make us into a prepackaged little family, or we'll be the new young Hollywood poster children for teen irresponsibility. Like having a child is comparable to being jailed and rehabbed nonstop for a coke addiction. I wouldn't care what they say about me—"

"That's new."

She shrugs. "I just don't want River getting hurt because of it. Especially the whole illegitimate thing. So I'm thinking about giving Rowena an exclusive for the first photos of River—"

"What? *No.* Why would you even considering letting one of those vultures take photos of him?"

"Because c'mon, Reid, be realistic—they're *gonna take photos* of him. This is a huge story, and Hollywood babies are stalked hard. If we have Rowena do them, we diffuse some of the demand for him, *and* control how he's presented to the general public."

I grimace. "Alarmingly, that makes some sense."

"Of course it does. Look. He's four. If we can manage the way his story is told now, it will become the accepted account of his life. Once he's old enough to realize we're his real parents, it won't be a big deal."

"Except when he figures out that you and I were *happy*-happy at least once, which should absolutely be our secret code word for *sex*." I flutter my lashes and affect a feminine voice. "Reid, since you have River this weekend, I'm going to *happy-happy* my new personal trainer!"

"Shut *up*." She punches me in the arm just hard enough to bruise. "I don't do people who work for me. Gross. And trust me, you've been getting a lot more *happy-happy* than I have recently."

"Jealous?" She tries to punch me again and I block her and laugh. "Didn't you say you'd decided to do the season finale of *Life's a Beach*, along with that brainless beefcake you were involved with—what's his name—Xavier something-or-other? I'm sure he'd be game for a little happy-happy."

Hiding her face, she laughs. "Ugh! We were involved all of *once*—he was all pretty and no skill."

"Unlike yours truly." Grinning wickedly, I waggle my brows and she rolls her eyes.

"Christ, your ego always was ginormous. Unbelievably, it appears to have grown. How does your new girlfriend handle that thing? Or is that what you like about her being an ordinary girl—ass over elbows because hot superstar Reid Alexander is paying attention to her."

I feel like she's just poked my good mood with a pin. "Dori's not like that."

"Oh?"

"She's never been awestruck by me or impressed by the whole celebrity thing, whether I wanted her to or not. She doesn't think of me like that."

She arches a brow. "So you say. But you can't escape who you are, Reid, and neither can she."

And with those words, Brooke verbalizes exactly what I'm worried about. The odd solidarity building between us today served as somewhat of a distraction from my uneasiness concerning Dori, but that's all it was—a distraction.

"I'm going to step outside and call her," I say.

But of course, Dori doesn't answer. I disconnect when it rolls to voicemail, and then send her another text, in which I try to sound like I'm not about to lose it because she hasn't answered me since she got out of my car forty-eight hours ago.

Chapter 22

Dori

> Reid: You never told me how you did on the exam.
> Everything okay? Depressed to be the ripe old
> age of 19?

I stare at Reid's last text, again, and know I have to answer him. He's in Austin, with the mother of his child—a child I didn't know existed until two days ago. All Sunday evening, I thought about what he said. How he hadn't known the baby was his. That he didn't know how to tell me.

I inferred from these words that he didn't want to tell me at all, and I should be angry or tolerant or hurt over the lie. I am all those things—but over his child's existence, not over the fact that he didn't tell me. Once I got over the shock of it, I can see why he didn't want to tell me.

Because he feared I'd react like this. Maybe he even knew I would.

It's been hours since that last text, but when I answer it, he replies immediately.

> Me: I survived the exam. 19 is a weird age to be. I
> think I should feel older. Or younger. I can't
> decide.
> Reid: I'll give you a heads-up on 20 in 3.5 weeks. I
> suspect it may be more of the same.
> Me: At least it will be a different decade.
> Observable progress.

Reid:	True.
Reid:	We met with Brooke's attorney and caseworker. They're going to try to make this as simple as possible, so the process isn't extended thanks to me joining it.
Reid:	Can I call you now? Or tomorrow night when I'm home?
Me:	I've got a study group in a few minutes and a guest lecturer symposium tomorrow.
Reid:	Ok. I'm heading to Utah on Thursday morning to start shooting scenes there, but I'll text you.

A few photos of our night out in San Francisco made it onto the gossip sites. It took a couple of days for anyone to identify me, and even still, there are skeptics—because in that blue dress and heels, with Reid's shoulder partially blocking my face, I look nothing at all like that girl from Habitat. Nothing like an ordinary girl from LA.

The most vocal disbelievers think I'm someone minor from his last film, or the new one that begins shooting in a couple of days. According to rumors, taking a bed-to-bed sampling of the female cast members is customary for Reid Alexander. I've tried to get Kayla and Aimee to stop sending me links to the photos and stories—but they're far too excited to "know" a celebrity like Reid.

My mind drifts back a few months, to when we'd begun hanging out at his place. To the night I taunted him about having a popular novel with predominantly female fans on his bedside table. Brushing aside my snarky tone, he informed me he was up for the lead role in the film, as though this was no big deal. Deliberately, he gave me that lazy smile and asked if I thought he could *bring him to life* on the big screen.

He knew exactly what those words would do, once unleashed in my imagination.

Before I could hide my astonishment, he teased me by guessing that I was one of those "brainy" girls who only got in trouble for reading past lights-out. (I was.) Before I left that night, he'd kissed me—a lot—while a tiny sliver of my mind's eye was unable to stop picturing him as that brooding character I knew too well.

Thus began the weeks of what we termed being *reckless*—and I worry that from my viewpoint, at least, that word defines our entire relationship. Reid lives his life in a reckless way, and ever since his life collided with mine last summer, I've been unbalanced. The trajectory of my safe, small orbit cannot contain him, and no amount of wishing will change that.

He told me on Sunday that once news of River breaks, it will be a circus. I'm not sure what he means, not entirely, but I have a better idea than most. The *truth* will only be what the truth looks to be, not what it is. The media will toss out possibilities, and fans will gobble them down, making up their own storylines. They'll want to see Reid and his beautiful ex back together, saving their son from the horrors of drug addicts and foster care, and they won't want a plain-Jane nobody interloper in the mix.

Claudia drives Raul, Afton and me to Zachary's Pizza to brainstorm ideas for our group project. Afton and I don't own a car, and Raul's tiny, ill-maintained Fiat seats two and is forever running on fumes. He and Claudia argued about this all the way here and are still at it.

"You *never* drive, even that one time it was just the two of us."

Raul peruses the menu, his eyebrows arched defensively toward his black spiked hair. "So I'd rather bum rides or take BART everywhere and have a social life than buy gas for my little deathtrap—sue me."

"Bum is right," Claudia murmurs.

"You do know pizza can be delivered? We didn't have to show up in person." he says.

"Not from Zachary's. And other places are *so* not the same—"

"*Vraiment!*" Afton interjects in French, though by the looks they give each other, neither of them speak it. "This place is the best. Now stop fighting, you two. *God.*" She punctuates this edict with a pout, which ruins the stern mother effect.

Gesturing at her with his menu, Raul objects. "We're not fighting, we're sparring. It's what we do. If you don't like it, turn away." He makes a *move-along* motion with his free hand.

Afton rolls her eyes. "I vote thin crust spinach and mushroom."

Raul is horrified. "No way. I'm a man. I need *meat* and I want it *stuffed*."

"That's what he said," Claudia mumbles.

Before Raul can return fire, I notice one of the girls from my building who saw me with Reid the night he stayed in my dorm—one of the girls on the receiving end of that spontaneous wink of his. She's sitting at an adjacent table with several other girls, and they're all leaning their heads together and staring—at me.

"Uh-oh," Claudia tells me quietly. "I think your cover is blown."

"What cover? What's going on?" Afton is wide-eyed and speaking in a whisper that can be heard two tables away.

"Why. Are. We. Whispering?" Raul asks, whispering just as loudly.

"Can we go somewhere else?" I ask, and they all look at me like I'm insane. There's a mob of people waiting for tables, and we've got one.

A waiter appears, as though Raul's growling stomach conjured him. "What can I get for you guys tonight?"

As Raul and Afton order, Claudia scoots her chair a bit, blocking me from maybe two people at the table of six. "Just ignore them."

Ignore them. *Right.* I rearrange my silverware, all too aware that they've pulled out cell phones now and are taking pictures. Of *me.* When I was with Reid Saturday night, and he guided me into the restaurant with one arm around my waist, the paparazzi flashes were different. The photos were of him, and I was merely with him.

Here, I'm alone, ordering dinner with friends, living my average-girl life.

Except for the whole *strangers photographing me* part.

"Why is that gaggle of sororstitutes taking our picture?" Raul asks when the waiter leaves.

Claudia sputters, "Don't call them *that*, you sexist—"

"Have you seen the parade of them through my dorm room? No. You have not." One of Raul's roommates is a total man-whore, and is beyond skilled—according to Raul—at locating and successfully propositioning every willing girl on campus. "I can sleep through just about anything now. A condition which makes me sad for my lost innocence."

Claudia barks a laugh. "Oh, please. If *you're* innocent, I'm the Dali Lama."

"*Namaste*," he returns.

"Excuse me." Oh, no. Elevator girl—holding a magazine, folded open to a page splashed with photographs of various celebrities everywhere from fashion shows to deli counters to poolside. Right in the center: Reid in his gray suit and blue tie, and me, semi-obscured by Reid's body, in the blue dress. "This is *you*, isn't it? And when Geneva and I saw you in the elevator—that was *him*, wasn't it? I mean, I can understand why you'd want to keep it on the *down-low*, but come *on*."

I cross my fingers under the table. "We're friends." I don't even know why I'm lying. *I hate lying.*

She arches an eyebrow. "So what's he doing with *Brooke Cameron*? I mean—you said the guy you were with was your *boyfriend* before, when we asked."

Darn her memory. "He didn't want to be recognized."

"Because he didn't want it getting back to her that he was spending nights with you?"

My jaw falls open. Luckily, Claudia says, "Hey, look. We're trying to have a study group session here. She says they're friends, and she has no comment on what's-her-name. And please tell your friends that taking pictures of people they don't know is *rude*. Tah-tah and buh-bye."

The girl turns on her heel and shoots back to the table, where all six heads are conferring.

"Fudge," I say.

By Wednesday evening, there's an indistinct photo of Reid and Brooke Cameron outside a courthouse in downtown Austin on Tuesday morning. That's when the speculation starts in earnest. The photos of them in the airport and on the plane—each reading something, not touching and not speaking to each other—all of a sudden look like a lovers' spat.

That girl in San Francisco must be the cause of it, one site speculates. Brooke must have gone home to Texas, upset, and he followed her. But what are they doing at a courthouse?

Everyone has an opinion, and of course, neither of them can be reached for comment.

Reid: Why aren't you answering my texts or calls?

REID

Every time I get a text, I think maybe it's from Dori, but it's not.

This morning, Mom texted photos of the renovations in my old room. She and Dad set up home study appointments, and we've all filled out questionnaires that are every bit as intrusive as Brooke warned me they'd be. Mom is somehow *happy* about River, which floors me but doesn't seem to stun Dad, who says he knew it would go one of two ways.

He told her, she cried, and then she called to tell me she was proud of me.

She's only said that to me once before—the day I beat up a kid at school who'd lifted a girl's skirt in front of everyone on the playground and thought it was funny—until I busted his lip open. We both got suspended, though our exclusive private school had a zero tolerance for violence policy. Funny how zero-tolerance turns into we're-tolerating-it-just-this-once when affluent parents throw money at the problem.

That was ten years ago.

I just got a text from Emma, who I've only talked to twice since the Vancouver film festival last fall; getting a text from her is out of the blue.

Emma:	Dad called to tell me I'd gotten a call from a caseworker in Texas, and I assumed it was about Brooke, but it was about YOU?
Me:	Wow, that was fast.
Emma:	???
Me:	We're asking for joint custody

| Emma: | Hold on. I must be hallucinating. I read that you two have been seeing each other, which I thought could not be for real. But YOU and BROOKE - joint custody? Can you talk??? |
| Me: | Sure, I've got a few minutes. |

"I see you've been reading the gossip sites," I answer in place of *hello*, grabbing a bottle of water from the craft services trailer and moving away from the current scene being shot. I'm in full costume and makeup—including a couple of authentic-looking blades, one tucked into a holster on my belt and another in my boot, but I've got fifteen or twenty minutes until I'm up.

"Reid, you know I'm not allowed to read those. Emily reads them. I'm shown links or given summarized news on a need-to-know basis only."

"Still? I guess now she's protecting you from the legions of Graham-stalkers, eh?" She growls and I can't help but laugh. "Well, you can tell *Emily* that hearsay concerning Brooke's and my rekindled relationship is baseless. I'm with Dori. Not that she's talking to me."

"And the *joint custody* thing you just so casually mentioned?"

"Yeah, that's a thing. Not a thing that's out yet—but it will be. Soon."

She sighs. "Reid—you know that once that's out, it's going to underscore the perception that you and Brooke are together, and the media will push that angle full throttle. I don't know your girlfriend, but if it was me, I'd be *really* bothered. You need to talk to her."

"I *know* that—but she's not answering my calls or texts. Her parents hate me. I don't actually know any of her friends. I'm going to try to make a quick trip to Berkeley on Saturday, but right now I'm stuck on location in the middle of a fucking canyon in fucking *Utah*." I release a snarl of complete frustration and stop just short of running my hand through my perfectly-styled set hair. "And why am I talking to you about this?"

"Because I'm nosy?"

I laugh and heave a sigh.

"I know I'm not a *regular girl* compared to Dori—especially since I'll be banking on my previous film career to help me land Broadway auditions. But I do know how it feels to watch my movie star boyfriend be publicly salivated over by thousands of girls, to have him constantly rumored to be hooking up with other people. It's hard to take sometimes, even if I know it's total rubbish. And I trust Graham more than I've ever trusted anyone."

Her words are like a physical blow. "You think Dori doesn't trust me?"

"I didn't say that. Maybe she's feeling insecure? No one wants to admit to that. Insecurity makes you feel weak and powerless, and that's no way to have a healthy relationship. I would know. I was never more miserable."

"But she's not the insecure type. She's the opposite of insecure. It definitely feels like she doesn't trust me. But why should she? I fucked up, not telling her about River. Just like I didn't tell you."

She sighs. "You know, I've told you before—what happened between you and Brooke, before me, wasn't my business. I'd have gotten over the shock of that if it hadn't been for, you know, the parade of girls right after."

I shut my eyes. "Ugh, Emma—"

"Never mind that. I'm long past it. Here's the thing. Graham and I share past stuff—we talk about relevant personal history. But only stuff that impacts *our* relationship. Neither of us needs to know or confess every single thing that happened before we met. Once you decided to become involved with River—that's when it was time to tell her. And it sounds like you did. Eventually. Now she's just got to work it out in her own head. Maybe she needs time. Maybe she doesn't want to be in a stepmother position at her age. And if that's the case, you're going to have to make a choice between her and River."

I feel like she's just unloaded a ton of bricks on top of me, and I can barely breathe. Because what she just said—it's true. It's so fucking true. Emma would know what it takes to make that choice—to accept a child who doesn't belong to you, right in the middle of your relationship, like a ghost of some former love. Goddammit if my initial reflex isn't to back away from this child—who I don't know at all—if that's what it would take to keep Dori.

But what kind of man would that make me?

The PA calls out to let me know I'll be up in ten minutes. I hold up a hand and nod at him. *Fuck.* How can I shoot a battle scene now when I feel crushed into dust? I need every second of that ten minutes to get my game face back on.

"I've got to go. Thanks, Emma."

"I'm sorry, Reid—I know I didn't make you feel any better—"

"No," I laugh softly, once, "but you told me what I needed to hear. I'll look you guys up when I'm filming in New York."

Brooke: CALL ME WHEN YOU GET THIS
Me: Filming. Can't call. WHAT??
Brooke: We're getting a pre-placement visitation. We may get him early. His foster mother had some kind of health thing come up, possible surgery, and they don't want to bounce him into a new foster home and then to us not long after that.
Me: Shit. WHEN?
Brooke: Saturday. Can you be here? They need to see both of us interact with him. Are you doing the online parenting course?
Me: Yes and yes. I'll figure something out. Call you later.

***

Me: We're getting a visit with River Saturday morning, so I can't come to Berkeley this weekend – I have to fly in and out Friday-Saturday. So sorry.
Me: Dori, ANSWER me. Please.
Dori: That's ok. Shayma and I are helping with a free laundry thing for local homeless people on Saturday anyway. I was going to text you.
Me: Were you?
Me: If I call you tonight, will you answer?
Me: I miss you.
Dori: I miss you, too.

"Hello."

I didn't realize how much I expected to get dumped into her voicemail again until I don't. How much I missed the sound of her *hello* until I hear her say it.

"Hey. You answered." Right behind the relief is anger. I didn't expect that, either, and I start my silent therapeutic counting, hoping to head it off. But it doesn't work that way; the aggravation is filling me as fast as I'm emptying it, like a rainy day in a water-laden rowboat, with nothing to bail it out but a tin can.

"I'm sorry I've been so busy," she says, and I'm literally clamping my jaw shut on the words that want out.

I breathe through my nose and count. *One. Two. Three.* Until I can trust myself to speak. "Can we talk, please? Are you still upset?"

"I'm not upset, Reid. I just don't think we should rush into anything—"

"What do you mean by that—*rush into anything*? By *anything*—do you mean *us*? Dori, is this about River?"

"No. Maybe. It's not about *him*, specifically. You've got a lot going on with the movie, and River, and Brooke—"

"Dori, the stuff about Brooke and me in the tabloids is all speculation or make believe—you remember all the fabricated crap they printed when you *fell* on me last summer—that we were having a secret relationship—"

"We *did* have a secret relationship—"

"But we weren't having one *then*."

"That's your argument?"

"Well. *Yes.* I didn't say that they don't guess right sometimes. And do I *need* an argument?"

She doesn't answer. The silence is thick and solid. I want to reach through this phone and pull her to me.

"Dori?"

"You shouldn't have to explain yourself, Reid. You're right. I just want you to be free to do what you need to do—"

"And I'm not? I'm not free to do what I need to do?"

Silence, again. I'm arguing her into corners, because that's what I do. But if she goes mute on me, what good does it do me to be right? So I retreat to what I know. How I've been raised to handle conflict. It's simple, really. If the communication is making everything worse, then we'll just stop talking about it.

"Your spring break is in three weeks, right? We'll be done filming in Utah by then. I'll have some long workdays at Universal—but at least we'll both be in LA. We'll spend as much time together as possible. Everything will be fine. I promise." Without thinking, I ask, "Do you trust me?" As though this question isn't at the core of everything, and I haven't just circled back around to it, as unintentional as it was.

"You're doing the right thing, Reid, and I'm proud of you for it." That's the second time I've heard that sentiment in as many days, but this one feels like the prelude to something unwanted. "Spring recess is in three weeks, yes."

Everything is off. The cadence of her voice isn't quite right— it's flat, stilted, but I can't see how to fix this. Plus she didn't answer my question.

"I'll call you, after we meet him?"

For the beat of several seconds, I think she's not going to answer. Maybe she's already gone. And then she says, "Sure. That would be fine."

Chapter 23

Brooke

I've just gotten off the phone with Janelle, who is begging me, for the zillionth time and all that is holy, not to turn down *Paper Oceans*. She's had her first call from the producer and is freaking out that I'll say no to it. Attempting to explain my reasons does no good. "I'm done talking about this until you've got an offer on the table," I said, thoroughly irked. What I left unsaid, but she managed to hear anyway: *And then I'll turn it down.*

When the phone rings, I assume she's calling back with additional declarations of the Many Ways in Which I Am About to Ruin My Career, but the number on the display is unfamiliar and begins with 512. Local.

My hand shakes as I jab *talk* and say, "This is Brooke," in the most confident voice I can muster.

"Miss Cameron—hello, this is Wendy Long. I'm River's foster mother."

My fist clenched to calm the shaking, I strive to maintain my feigned composure. I know this woman has voiced concerns to River's caseworker, his ad litem, and the judge about me adopting him, though I'm not sure exactly what was said. Norman keeps reminding me that she's just looking out for his best interests, but I can't help feeling personally affronted.

I've got to do whatever it takes to mask *that* feeling.

"Yes, Wendy, good evening." *Shit.* I automatically used her first name—something I do to even the playing field in adversarial confrontations. *Awesome.* I thump myself in the forehead with that clenched fist. "Please call me Brooke."

"Oh, certainly. Brooke." Her drawl is heavy, words fading into soft endings, fusing and linking together, mirroring my mother's dialect. My brain screams *hick*, and I struggle not to assign that personal bias to it. "I thought we should have a chat about River before tomorrow's visit. Is Mr. Alexander going to be accompanying you? Is this a good time to talk?"

"Yes, it's fine. Reid will be in town this evening, and I'll pick him up on my way over in the morning."

"Ah. Um. All right. Well, about River. There are a few important things you should know about him before you meet."

"Okay."

"First off, and most importantly—he doesn't talk."

Everything I know about children, I've learned in the past few weeks. I may not know much, but I know that most four-year-olds are language-proficient and can supposedly talk your ear off. Kathryn says four is the age of *Why?*

"Kylie was more of a quietly observant child—oddly enough," she said, "but oh my Lord, Kelley asked *why* a million times a day. *Why do apples come in so many colors? Why did the dog eat that? Why do teeth fall out? Why can't I jump off the roof into the pool?* The house always seemed unnaturally silent the moment she fell asleep."

"What do you mean, exactly?" I ask Wendy.

"I mean he doesn't say words. He doesn't communicate by speaking."

"At all? Ever?"

"At all. Ever," she confirms.

"Is he developmentally challenged? From—what happened to him?" I bite my lip and taste blood, cursing his adoptive mother to hell. Again.

"I don't believe so. He understands what's said to him just fine. And he'll nod or shake his head, so you get your basic *yes* or *no* responses. And most notably, I've heard him verbalize words and short sentences in his sleep a few times—usually during nightmares. So he *can* talk. He just *won't*. It's possible that he doesn't even know he can."

I frown. "What's been done to address that?"

"He sees a therapist every week, and his social worker every month."

"What the—what good does a *therapist* do if he can't—or won't—speak?"

"He has River draw pictures about his feelings. He's real good at that. He's smart, and he's a good little artist." I hear the affection lacing her words and almost lose it. "He's just had a rough time of it."

"Yes. He has. I intend to end that, Ms. Long. I promise you."

"Please, call me Wendy. And I want to believe you, Ms—er, Brooke. But the stories in the tabloids, about you and Mr. Alexander both… Well, I'm worried. I'm sure the gossip is played up and all to sell papers. I mean I seen one last week that said a lady gave birth to a thirty pound baby, and I'm here to tell you, that's just not possible."

"Well—"

"Don't get me wrong—you two are both young and nice-looking, and I don't mean to pass judgment on you for your lifestyles, whatever they are. It's not my place to say, you understand, except where River is concerned. He's not…" She swallows audibly. "He's not a knickknack, or a pet. He's been hurt, and all the pretty clothes and new toys in the world aren't gonna fix him. He's like a little flower bud that just won't open up, and to be perfectly frank—with what he's seen, I don't know if he ever will."

Tears stream down my face and clog my throat. "Thank you for your honesty, Wendy. Now let me give you mine." My voice is earnest, pleading—such a foreign effort for me, but I need her to believe me. "I don't know anything about raising a child, except how *not* to do it. I know he needs a home. He needs love. And I mean to give him those things." I take a shuddering breath. "If he never wants to speak, then I'll just have to get really good at artistic interpretation. He can draw on the damn walls if he needs to."

Reid slides into the passenger seat of Glenn's king cab pickup wearing his sunglasses and a Cal baseball cap, an open plaid shirt over a white T-shirt, jeans, and boat shoes. He looks like a cute college boy, not a Hollywood sex symbol.

"Brooke Cameron—sporting western boots one day and

driving an F-250 the next. Will wonders never cease. What's next, a ten-gallon hat?"

I flip him off, but he just arches a brow and smirks.

"Aww, c'mon, I was just funnin'." His drawl is all kinds of exaggerated. "No need to get hostile."

I roll my eyes behind my own mirrored sunglasses and pull into traffic as soon as he's buckled up. "There's more hostility where that came from, Reid Alexander." Like slipping into a broken-in pair of boots, I affect the accent he professes to love. "You just keep that smart mouth shut or you'll be meetin' your son sportin' a fat lip."

Luckily, he grins that full-wattage smile and shakes his head without any more flippant commentary. Cocky son-of-a-bitch.

As we leave downtown and head south on I-35, he turns the alt rock station down and asks, "You nervous?"

I sigh. "Hell, yes. You?"

"I've never felt so panicked about meeting anyone in my entire life."

Nodding in agreement, I say, "That pretty much sums it up."

"How long will this visit last?"

"Wendy said about an hour, unless River makes it clear he's done, and then it would be best to leave. We don't want to make him uncomfortable."

When I tell Reid what I learned from Wendy yesterday concerning River's muteness, his periodic nightmares, and some of the details about his adoptive parents, he mutters, "Shit," and stares out the passenger window for several minutes.

Two years ago, River's adoptive father died in a tragic car accident. I vaguely recall him, out of all the prospective adoptive parents Kathryn and I sifted through that summer. Blond, handsome, mid-thirties. Financially sound. What I remember best is something he wrote at the end of his prospective adoptive parent statement: *I hope to be the same loving, wonderful father to my child that my dad was to me.* That sentence was the tipping point for my choice of them over another couple.

His father is deceased, his mother is in her seventies and living in a retirement home. No chance for a home with them.

River's adoptive mother had been estranged from her parents for years, and they were unwilling to consider caring for River, whom they didn't regard as a grandchild. Soon after her husband's death, she'd sunk into an addiction she was unwilling or unable to abandon, even though it meant losing her child—a little boy who had no one else to depend on in the world.

Except for me.

"What are we supposed to say to a kid who doesn't talk?" Reid asks, finally, all hints of his earlier levity gone.

"He can understand what *we* say. And I brought the *Life Book*—it's on the seat behind you."

He turns to snatch the scrapbook we started when he was here earlier in the week, leafing through the pages as I spot the exit up ahead. "This is great, Brooke," he murmurs.

"When I was six or so, Kathryn made me a scrapbook of my own. I was jealous of Kylie and Kelley having books of their baby photos and stories about their first few years of life."

"Your mom didn't make you one?" he asks, and I glance at him like *Really?* "Guess that's not much of a surprise."

Sharla making a scrapbook? Definitely not.

"Kathryn told me to bring a few photos the next time I came over. Over the next few weeks, I pocketed snapshots of myself that I found in drawers or boxes at home. There weren't many, even though I was basically an only child. Kathryn bought a handmade journal at some craft fair, stuck glittery pink adhesive letters on the front that spelled out *Brooke's Book*, and composed the story of me."

I haven't thought of that thing in years. I'd forgotten about it until just now.

"Do you still have it? My mom's definitely not crafty, but she kept photo albums of my childhood. Up until I was ten, anyway."

I bite my lip until it goes numb. "No. I don't have it. I made the mistake of taking it home. Sharla found it. She was furious. Ripped the pages out and tore up all the pictures."

"Holy shit, Brooke." He stares at me. "That's fucked *up*."

"Yeah. What a great role model for a mom, huh?"

His hand clenches into a fist on the console between us. "Your role model is Kathryn, not Sharla. You know that, right?"

I did know that, somewhere in my head. I'd just never acknowledged it consciously.

"Yeah. You're right."

I turn down a street of analogous one-story homes, all of them small, each with a big front yard, a driveway on the right-hand side, and a cyclone fence. A few pecan trees and crepe myrtles dot the landscape here and there, but this flat stretch of acreage was probably reclaimed farmland when the subdivision was built, so there were no old oaks, like those surrounding Kathryn and Glenn's place.

"This is it," I whisper, spotting the mailbox house number, which is surrounded by a hand-painted swirling heart motif. My heart thumps so hard that I feel each beat like someone is pounding on my chest from the inside, trying to escape. My hands grow cold, though it's a beautiful late-winter day, the temperature in Austin within a degree or two of LA.

As we walk up the long, cracked sidewalk, I alternate between examining the chalked pictures and inscriptions decorating the concrete and staring at the quiet little house I recognize from the photo Bethany Shank brought to me not even two months ago. Reid, silent and following me, takes my hand as we reach the front door. He removes his sunglasses and I remove mine, and for a moment we stare at each other. I've never seen him look so resolute.

"Here we go," he says, pushing the doorbell. At the echo of chimes inside the house, my heart rate surges. Reid squeezes my hand and says, "It's all good, Brooke. We can do this."

I can't let go of him.

And then the door opens, and the middle-aged woman I recognize from the background of my only photo of River stands there, a faint smile wreathing her face. Her hazel eyes are clear and kind.

"Brooke and Reid, I presume?" she says, and we both nod. She pulls her arm gently from behind her, her hand attached to a little boy who appears slowly on the right side of her hip. All I see are dark blue eyes, impossibly huge in his small face. "This is River."

186

Dori

Shayma has nudged me at least ten times this morning—whenever I'm not paying attention and someone asks me a question about operating the washers and dryers, how many tokens are allowed per person, or where the nearest public bathroom is located. After my last space out, she says, "Girl. Where is your head this morning?"

While my roommate is one of the few people with confirmed knowledge about Reid and me, I've never been a big fan of sharing too much information with anyone, even trusted friends. I love Aimee and Kayla, but I'm pretty darn sure they've told every living soul at UCLA that they're friends with Reid Alexander's girlfriend. Shayma knows we're going out, and that we met when I supervised him (or rather, *tried* to supervise him) at Habitat. She also knows I don't publicize our relationship, so neither does she— which places her in a select class of friends.

Occasionally, she surprises me with facetious questions like, "So is Reid Alexander a good kisser?" or "I'll bet Reid Alexander is *RAWR* in bed, isn't he?" I'm glad she hasn't yet discovered my glowing, telltale ears. The wide-eyed look on my face is indicative enough of my discomfiture, I'm sure.

"How do you deal with all the making out your boyfriend does in those movies?" she asks now in her naturally discreet voice (thank goodness), after handing a stack of washer/dryer tokens to a guy who in all probability hasn't washed any of his clothes in months. The smell makes my eyes water involuntarily until he shuffles over to a machine with an armful of grubby laundry and the small box of donated detergent I just handed him. I suspect he'll need more than the one box.

"And the rumors with ex-girlfriends or not-girlfriends. That alone would drive me batshit crazy. My mawmaw—the self-proclaimed seer?—is a practicing Cajun Voodoo Queen. She'd be happy to whip up a little gris-gris for you."

At the word *voodoo*, I arch a brow. "I'm afraid to ask what a *gris-gris* is."

"It's a protection amulet. Sometimes for luck, but usually to ward off evil. I imagine ex-girlfriends qualify. Also, I figured you might not want to follow the still-practiced but ethically-murky voodoo superstition to make a man stay faithful."

"Now I'm really afraid to ask."

She leans closer and whispers, "You put a drop of your blood in his coffee."

"Ugh!" I looked down at the latte in my hand, appalled.

"Right?" she chuckles. "I overheard Mawmaw telling my momma to do that to Daddy when I was little. And my ordinarily sane legal secretary mother was *listening*. I never asked her if she did it. If she did—it didn't work. If she didn't—well, who'd want to keep a guy that way anyhow?"

"But using an *amulet* is a-okay," I laugh.

She shrugs and smiles. "That's the first time I've heard you laugh in a few days." When I pin my lips together and sigh, she says, "Amulets are about warding off bad stuff, not binding people to do things they might not otherwise do. But I'm with you. If and when I get a guy I'm interested in keeping around, I want him to stay because he wants to stay. Not because I poked a voodoo doll of him in the junk with a pin."

During a show we were watching on Hulu last night, an ad for the MTV Movie Awards popped up, which is on next month. Reid and his *School Pride* costar, Emma Pierce, have been nominated for Best Kiss. As the clip played, Shayma gave me a sidelong glance, but didn't say a word. An unwelcome mental image of the two of them reenacting the lip lock that made every girl I know swoon (Claudia excepted) at the upcoming awards show made me feel temporarily homicidal.

"Maybe I should tell Mawmaw to make a gris-gris for Emma Pierce," Shayma suggests now, and I suppress an actual growl. "Though supposedly, she and Graham Douglas have been a legit couple for months. They went to the Vancouver Film Festival together last fall, and she popped up for a romantic weekend in Dublin a couple of months ago, when he was filming there. They're spotted together all the time—alone or with friends, sometimes with his daughter. In particular near NYU, where they're rumored to be *condo-shopping*."

I narrow my eyes. "You looked all of that up last night, didn't you?"

"No! I looked it up this morning." Shrugging, she counts out tokens to a tired woman with two small children in tow, all three of them holding a basket of clothes, and I plop a trial-sized box of detergent in each of their baskets. "You looked like you might go postal when that ad came on, is all. A little abnormal for such a peaceful girl, if you ask me."

Rats. My nonexistent poker face betrays me again.

Chapter 24

REID

River doesn't speak a word during the visit, of course, but he seems curious enough that he doesn't signal an end to our stay. The first hour is spent under Wendy's supervision, and he never ranges far from her. Brooke and I sit side-by-side on the worn sofa, our legs wedged behind a coffee table that—while smelling of wood polish—has been crayoned and scratched and generally battered to hell. Propped next to his foster mother's chair, River leans his thin frame against her as though her bodily support is necessary to his ability to remain upright.

"We made a book for River to keep—well, Brooke made most of it." I remove the book from Brooke's lap and lean over the table to put it into Wendy's hands. River inclines closer, eyes a little wider and head angled to study the cover, which depicts a beach view of the western horizon over the Pacific at sunrise. "It has some pictures of Los Angeles, where we live—parks and other cool places. And a few pics of us."

I reach over and squeeze Brooke's cold hand as Wendy turns the pages, reading the descriptions to River, who doesn't take his eyes from the book until she's done. And then he reaches over, turns back to page one, and looks at her expectantly until she begins to read it again. Brooke clutches my hand as if she is hanging over a deep gorge, her eyes never moving from him.

Handing him the book after the second read, Wendy says, "River, why don't you show Reid and Brooke your room? And put this with your other books."

He eyes us for a moment before hugging the scrapbook to his

chest and leading the way down a short, dim hallway, and into a cramped bedroom that contains a set of bunk beds, one separate twin bed, a dresser, and a bookcase. There is no room for anything else. While we stand in the doorway, he walks to the single bed and slides the book beneath his pillow. The pillowcase is covered with cartoon depictions of cars and trucks in primary colors, and it occurs to me that here is a boy who would have loved my yellow Lotus.

Going to his knees on the tiny wedge of open carpet, he pulls a box from beneath his bed. I tug Brooke into the room by her elbow and urge her to sit down on the floor beside me. "What have you got there? Ah, Legos—they were my favorite thing in the world when I was your age. I wanted every set that came out." What I don't say: I *got* every set that came out. All stored somewhere in my parents' house, no doubt.

The three of us are sitting on his bedroom floor building things when Wendy appears in the doorway and announces that it's time to wash up for lunch. I check my thick-banded watch and am dazed to find we've spent nearly two hours here. My eyes meet Brooke's and she nods, subtly. Time to go.

I clear my throat. "We should go get lunch, too." River finishes snapping a plastic brick onto what appears to be a freelance spider the size of my hand that he's fashioned out of the black and gray rectangles. He's used two red squares for eyes—at least I think they're eyes—on a creature that only exists in nightmares for most little kids.

With an intense blue gaze, full of his hesitation and all the reasons for it, he examines me and then Brooke, alternating between us. Brooke seems as guarded as River, and almost equally quiet. I have no idea what she's thinking; I can't read her. It's not like we're all that familiar with each other now, as weird as that is, considering the fact that we're attempting to adopt a child together.

"Thanks for letting us come play, bud." Still sitting cross-legged, I hold a fist toward him—something I might do with John or any other guy under twenty-five. He considers my knuckles, his pale brows drawing together, and for a moment I'm sure I've made a careless miscalculation, but after a quick glance at my face, he raises a very small fist and bumps mine lightly with it.

And then he smiles. It's fleeting and subdued, but it's

definitely a smile.

"It was so nice to meet you, River," Brooke says then, her voice soft. After a glance at me, he offers his knuckles to her, and she bites her lip and bumps them gently, her eyes glassy. At which point I figure I'd better get her out of here.

Brooke and I walk to the truck in reflective silence. At the curb, I turn and look back at the house. River is standing with Wendy in the doorway, his expression disturbingly stoic. I wave, and Wendy waves. River stands like a toy soldier, straight and unblinking, but the fingers of his right hand wiggle.

Neither of us speaks a word during the twenty-minute drive to my hotel. The enormity of what we're doing is too staggering. We need time to select the words and formulate their order. When we arrive, Brooke parks the truck and automatically follows me inside, and I'm vaguely aware of fellow guests identifying us between the door and the elevator.

Brooke and I both released box office hits almost three weeks ago, and I'm the lead in the in-production film version of one of the decade's most popular novels. Our STARmeter ranks are glowing green, and our days of occasionally roaming around in public sans bodyguards are all but over—especially when we're together. It's clear we're about to be together a lot.

Following me from the elevator to my room, she collapses on the small sofa next to my open suitcase and stares out the lake view window at the cloudless sky.

I got a late checkout approved, but it's already noon.

"Lunch?" I suggest, and she nods.

Grabbing the room service menu, I ask what she wants, and she waves a hand, mumbling, "I don't care."

After calling in sandwiches and fries, I grab a couple of bottled waters from the mini fridge and slump into the armchair next to her. While she sips silently, I swallow half my bottle.

"So what now?"

Her eyes shift to mine and I blink, hard. She looks wrecked.

"I want him, Reid. I've never wanted anything so much. Is it wrong? That I want him?"

For the space of a breath, I wonder why she'd think that

wanting River could be wrong. And then it hits me. "You don't trust your own intentions."

She shakes her head, her eyes welling up.

I lean up and take her hand for the third or fourth time today. It's still so cold that it feels bloodless. "Brooke, I've never seen you be less sure of yourself, and yet more on a mission. I knew when you said you were going to give up *Paper Oceans* to get him that you'd rocketed past my preconceived notions about Brooke Cameron." The image of River thumping his small knuckles against mine knocks the breath out of me. And that brief, barely-there smile. "But I guess I'm drinking the Kool-Aid, because I want him, too. I can see that he's good there with Wendy, but she's a short-term solution and always was. My dad was right. If we don't do this, we'll live to regret it—sooner rather than later, I imagine."

She frowns in confusion. "Your dad said that?"

"Yeah," I chuckle. "Shocked the shit out of me."

"So he's really okay with you doing this?"

I shrug, thinking about the fact that my parents' house is in an uproar of make-ready for a four-year-old they didn't even know existed a couple of weeks ago. Dad wore his courtroom face this morning at her attorney's office, though Brooke's counsel was genial, and by the time we'd left, the two of them were strategizing together as if they'd always done so. Evidently, there's a potential issue with the fact that I'll only be twenty, and the minimum age to adopt is twenty-one. They plan to carefully approach the judge with the contention that I was fifteen and had no legal counsel when I effectively gave up my parental rights.

"He's more than okay, and so is Mom. It's bizarre. In their defense, I think I set their expectations of me pretty damned low in the past few years."

She laughs softly, one tear escaping and trailing down her cheek. I reach to wipe it away, but that simple touch erases her smile. She swallows and sits back abruptly. "Thanks for upending your schedule on such short notice to come with me today."

My elbows on my knees and my hands clasped, I sigh. "You don't need to thank me anymore. We're in this together. I'm not doing you a favor. I'm doing what I should have done in the first place—taking some fucking responsibility."

I finish packing while we eat, and she agrees to drop me at the airport so I don't have to bother with calling a car. When we exit the hotel, there's a single photographer waiting outside. Snapping up from leaning against his van, he hollers our names, but neither of us takes the bait. *Nice try, dickwad.* Luckily, the truck is parked in the opposite direction, and since there's only one of him, he doesn't get too close—though I'm sure his zoom lens does.

Dori

My cell recorded a missed call from Reid, though I never heard it ring or felt it buzz. It figures that when I fully intended to answer it, my phone goes on hiatus. When I try him back, his phone is off—the call goes straight to voicemail—and I presume he's somewhere between Texas and Utah. I leave him a message telling him I'll be studying in my room tonight.

"Call me when you're back to your—trailer, I guess? Talk to you later. Bye."

I try to imagine Reid in a production trailer, but having never been inside one, all I can picture is the interior of a motorhome purchased years ago by a pair of retired neighbors, after they sold the home they'd owned for forty years. They were very proud of the cramped, nomadic house and the miniature everything—from the fridge to the shower to the "bedroom" that was little more than a wall-to-wall bed at the back of the vehicle.

During the "tour," Deb leaned to me and murmured, "What happens when Oscar slams on the breaks to take a sharp corner and Ethel is in bed or in the shower? Naked, wet, pissed-off old lady tumbleweeding up to the cockpit, that's what."

I nearly choked to death trying to contain my giggles. When Mom turned and bestowed a narrowed look on the two of us, Deb blinked and appeared angelic, angling her head toward me. "She swallowed her gum." She slammed a hand on my back several times. "Cough it up, Dori, cough it up."

In between devising a citations page for my Intro to Psychology paper and studying for a quiz in Intro to Sociology, I text with Aimee, who is incensed that she and Kayla won't get a normal spring break because UCLA does quarters instead of semesters.

Aimee:	We only get TWO DAYS of your spring break before we start another quarter! What about the college experience??? This is false advertising.
Me:	Didn't you look at the academic calendar before applying? Or registering?
Aimee:	Obviously, no. ☹
Me:	I'm sorry. ☹ I'll be home all week, though, and you go to school in LA.
Aimee:	But you'll be making time for REID, I'm sure (not that I blame you). And Nick?
Me:	Nick's spring recess is a week before mine, so we'll only overlap the first weekend. And Reid, if he's in town, yes. He's filming, though. So I'm not sure of his schedule yet.
Aimee:	DUH. He'll be filming at Universal, so he'll be in town. I have it on Perez authority.
Me:	I'm rolling my eyes at you so hard right now.

Ten minutes later, I get a text from Kayla.

Kayla:	Hey, check out the link I just messaged you. I don't want to be the bearer of bad news, but there are some things you have to KNOW!
Me:	Ok.

The link goes to one of those websites I wish didn't exist, where the lives of people like Reid are dissected and displayed. It's there that I find a somewhat indistinct photo with the caption: *Reid Alexander and Brooke Cameron! Together again?* They're entering a hotel elevator. And if that isn't conclusive enough— there's an incontestable photo of the two of them a couple of hours later, exiting the same hotel and climbing into a pickup truck.

Brooke Cameron is beautiful. This isn't an envious or unrealistic statement—it's just the incontestable truth. She's one of the prettiest girls I've ever seen. Who had Reid's baby. And was with him in Austin on Saturday. Entering and leaving a hotel.

Suddenly, I'm so tired.

I'm tired of feeling jealous—an emotion I've never truly experienced before Reid, which has somehow become all-consuming. And relentless. And just so *exhausting*.

Closing out of the website, I barely register the tears streaming down my face, but I can't let them blind me to reality. If I talk to Reid, my tongue will burn with the need to ask him what's going on between them, if anything is. And even if nothing is—yet—I can't believe that it won't. Or even that it shouldn't.

I didn't see this coming—not this soon. Not this way. But that doesn't matter, because I always knew he would return to his Hollywood lifestyle, and his peers. I can't blame him, and I don't. Because in pursuing the adoption of his son, he's choosing the difficult thing. He's choosing the right thing. And I admire him for it.

He believes that I helped him become a better man, that I'm a good influence, and it's true. Because that's what I was meant to be, for him. I see that now. I was never meant to be the girl he wanted forever. It doesn't matter if I fell so, so hard—if I'm crazy in love with him. When you love someone, you want what's best for that person, not what's best for you.

I didn't change Reid Alexander. I just helped him uncover who he always was, at his core. Now, it's time for me to let him go be that man.

Reid:	Missed Calls (3) Messages (2)
Reid:	Okay, you said you'd be in tonight. I've called, and I've left messages. I wanted to talk to you about today.
Reid:	Are you angry with me? Did I do something I'm not aware of doing? I don't understand.
Reid:	Missed calls (2)
Reid:	If I wasn't stuck in the middle of the damned desert, under contract, I would be banging on your dorm room door and to hell with who heard or saw me. I'm worried.

Reid: I'm going to have to call your parents. (And I can't BELIEVE I just wrote that.)

Reid: Dori, not again. Please, goddammit, not again.

Chapter 25

REID

"Hello?"

"Mrs. Cantrell—this is Reid. Alexander."

"Yes, Mr. Alexander?" Her tone is somehow accusatory—and what's with the *Mister Alexander* crap?

Ten seconds in and I'm already pacing the length of this fucking trailer, wondering what sway her parents have with her, still. Wondering if I can fault *them* for her withdrawal. Knowing, after that meeting two months ago, how elated they would be to see this relationship collapse, which makes me furious.

One. Two. Three. Deep breath. *Four. Five. Six.*

"I haven't heard from Dori in several days. I just want to make sure she's all right."

She pauses before answering. "Dori is fine. I appreciate your concern—but she's fine." *Without you*—that's what I hear. *She's fine without you.*

"You're aware, then, that she's not returning my texts or calls. And clearly, you also know why." One hand at the back of my neck, I'm fighting every innate compulsion I have to keep from demanding that she tell me what the fuck she knows that I don't. "Would you mind, very much, sharing that information with me? Because I don't have a clue what's going on."

"Don't you?"

"What does that mean?"

"Do you read the celebrity gossip sites, Mr. Alexander?"

I huff a breath. "Not if I can help it. I ignore them as much as possible, in fact, because they're mostly lies and misconstrued half-truths, or unabashed invasions of privacy. Dori knows what's true or what isn't. At least, I thought she did. I thought she trusted me."

"And what is the truth? That you've been photographed numerous times with another young lady—one you used to—date?"

"Dori knows why—"

"Yes. She told me about the child you fathered, and what you and your ex-girlfriend are doing now—which, for the record—is admirable of you both. But it's also not something my daughter needs to find herself caught up in or distracted by—"

"Maybe you're right. Maybe it's not something Dori should have to deal with. Maybe it's even more than she can handle." Christ. Speaking that sentence makes me feel as though I just stabbed myself in the chest. I can't accept that it's true. "But why isn't she talking to me about it? Why does she think that dropping off the face of the earth is the way to resolve this?"

Her answer is quietly devastating. "I imagine she's protecting herself from being further hurt by you."

When I recover my breath, I blurt, "Further? What do you mean *further* hurt by me? *I love her.* I don't intend to hurt her. I don't want to hurt her. I almost relinquished rights to my son because I don't want to lose her—because I was afraid of this reaction." I can't tell her what may actually be behind Dori's reaction—the needless guilt she feels over a choice she made years ago—a choice that, at the time, was right for her. "Even so, I never imagined her doing *this*. She's not a coward, and this is the most cowardly thing I've ever known her to do."

"So you believe that shielding herself from certain emotional damage is cowardly?"

"*Certain emotional damage*? You make it sound as if this outcome was inevitable. Like there wasn't any other possible result of a relationship between us, and we were doomed from the start. But that deduction isn't something you based on the knowledge of my son or anything to do with Brooke Cameron—it comes from your prejudice against *me*. Against my *lifestyle*, or my career, or my previous reputation—"

"Isn't that how we all assess people and predict outcomes, Mr. Alexander? By their previous reputations? Let's say you're correct.

What about your lifestyle or reputation would benefit my daughter? What about your career would ever make her feel safe? Standing aside and watching while you're physically involved on-screen and constantly rumored to be offscreen—whether it's true or not—with other women? Why would I want that for her?

"And then, let's add the existence of a son with one of those rumored other women. What will happen to her once that secret comes to light? What will people say? Of course I don't want that for her. Why in the world would I?"

I'm shredded by the recognition of how right she is. Even if her daughter is the only person I've ever met who *didn't* ultimately judge me by my reputation, but by what she saw in me—and God knows how she managed that. I have only one truth to stand on.

"I. Love. Her."

"If that's true," she answers evenly, "you'll want what's best for *her*. Not for yourself."

Brooke's words about Graham slam into me and I fall to my knees in the middle of the trailer. I feel like my heart is imploding. Every scrap of anger or righteous indignation evaporates. Every argument turns to ash. Because of course, she's right. If I love Dori, I'll want what's best for her. And only Dori can know what that is.

> Brooke: I saw the judge this morning. The case is being accelerated. We're getting an overnight. First, here, tomorrow night. (If you come to Austin, Kathryn says you can stay here. A hotel would blow our cover.) If that goes well, each of us will get him in LA for a few days. His caseworker will travel with him.
>
> Me: DAMMIT. I can't get away right now. I am LITERALLY in the middle of the desert. They had to set up a special tower just so we could all get cell service. If I could leave this set, I'd be in CA. Call me in a couple of hours? I've got a scene to shoot.
>
> Brooke: K

Two hours later on the dot, my phone rings. Brooke.

"Hey. So he's going to stay at Kathryn's with you overnight? Will the fact that I'm not there be a problem?"

"No," she answers. "I explained that I'm not working right now, but you are, and that if we get him, we intend to trade off projects. That one of us will always be with him." Brooke always did think fast on her feet. "Reid?" A new hesitation creeps into her voice. "Are you sure about this?"

"About River? Yeah. I'm sure." I don't have to ask if she is.

She releases an audible breath at my answer—as though she's still expecting me to back out any minute. It's so difficult for her to count on anyone. To trust when someone says they'll be there for her. With our history, it's a damned miracle for her to have confidence in anything I promise. I can't blame her for asking.

"Wendy is having surgery two weeks from Monday, so that's when the overnights in LA will take place. One of the little boys she's been keeping will be moving to a new foster home, and the other is moving toward a family reunification that might be too early. She couldn't say much about either one, but it sounded like she was freaking out over both of them. I think we've suddenly become the best case scenario."

That seems like a wrong sort of thing to feel fortunate about, but I'm a dick, so I'll take it. "Yay for other people fucking up?"

She laughs shortly. "I guess. Will you be back in LA by then?"

"Yeah. We're wrapping up here in the middle of bumfuck nowhere. Probably fourteen, fifteen days left, and we'll be doing the studio sections next, at Universal. I should be back in town right before he arrives."

"And you'll have the home study and parenting course stuff by then?" she presses.

I roll my eyes, but tell myself she's just making sure of essential details. No need to snap back. I set my jaw. "Yes."

"Okay." She takes a deep breath and launches into part two of this call. "I think it's time to call Rowena." I curse and start to object—*again*—but she barrels on. "I know you have a preconceived perception of her after last spring—but Reid, she's our best shot at maintaining *any* control over how this news breaks. The public will want photos of our child. You know they will."

She's right—River is going to be top photo stalker material. The only way to neutralize that is to provide the pics ourselves. With a jolt of comprehension, I realize I've got to trust her. And this Rowena person. *Ugh.* My opposition dissolves unsaid.

"What did you mean before, when you said you'd be in California now if you could?" she asks, undoubtedly to change the subject before I can build a case against her sycophantic paparazza.

"Dori. She stopped talking to me about a week ago."

"A *week*? What happened?"

"I have no idea. That's a major component of the 'stopped talking to me' bit."

"Don't be an asshat. Did you two have a fight? Did you do something stupid like screw some girl who took photos of your naked backside and leaked it online?"

I would take exception if that exact thing hadn't transpired a couple of years ago.

"No fight. No girls. The photos of you and me in Austin are all over, of course, though she hasn't said a thing about them. But she knows about River. I guess she just decided she couldn't deal."

"That sucks. She should know not to pay attention to the crap online, although it's occasionally true. If she can't handle it, though, maybe you're better off without her."

I couldn't have asked for a better time to film a withdrawn, brooding character. My Darcy role was a bit brooding, but he was mostly sarcastic and arrogant.

With the amount of time I spend alone—either in my trailer or walking at a barely visible distance from the huddle of trailers and sets, I think my costars have decided I'm one of those method actors who insists on remaining in character on and off screen. I've caught insinuations that indicate as much, but I've no need to artificially immerse myself in the moody temperament of my current character.

I get him. Jesus Christ, do I get him.

And though I'm certainly drawing on my personal thoughts and emotions during filming to portray him (*actual* method acting) I'm not drawing on painful experiences from my past. All I have to do is conjure Dori, and the agony blazes through me, on cue.

Brooke

It's been six days since I've seen him.

Kathryn has been the voice of reason at every turn. "Don't overwhelm him with *things*, Brooke," she says, when I want to buy him every Lego set I can find online. We choose a half-dozen, and put four of them away for later. It takes me almost an hour to narrow to a couple of plush animals—a teddy, of course, and a floppy-eared puppy (to compensate for the fact that Kathryn urges me not to buy him the real thing).

One wall of his room at Kathryn's has been painted green—his favorite color, according to Wendy. His room at my condo will include lots of green—I've hired a *tromp l'oeil* artist to paint a roadway with colorful cars and background scenery all the way around at eye level. The ceiling will be baby blue, with fluffy clouds scattered from one corner to the other. His closets will be painted with chalkboard paint, so he can draw all over them.

It appears that I can't help but overdo.

I worry over this, too, but Kathryn laughs and shakes her head. "This is you, Brooke. Just try to pull back a little. Remember, what he needs is your love. That's why poverty-stricken parents can still do a wonderful job of raising a child."

What she doesn't say: *That's why wealthy parents often fail at it. They substitute* things *for* affection.

"I'll remember."

One thing we agree on is half-filling his built-in bookcase with books—dozens of picture books—favorites from my childhood, and anything new that catches my eye. Their spines are multihued and inviting when we line them up on the shelves—a miniature library. Wendy says River likes to be read to before bed, and I wonder to myself if he'd like to be read to on the flat rock by the creek, in the middle of the day, for no reason.

I buy Matchbox cars and a track with a double loop in the middle that Reid assures me every boy ever born would like, and authentic-looking construction trucks that will look even more realistic with their working parts encrusted with dirt.

I choose a green toothbrush and three kinds of toothpaste. A nightlight shaped like a racecar that switches on and off. A pair of galoshes in John Deere green, even though the forecast calls for a cool, sunny day.

River's caseworker is picking him up from Wendy's after his afternoon nap, and bringing him here. Kris has been here several times during the home study, so she's already familiar with the place. She and Kathryn hit it off immediately—lucky for me. It took Kris longer to warm to me, but that's the upshot of being a woman and having a blunt personality.

Sometimes people just don't like me. Go figure.

Glenn is planning a cookout for dinner. He's one of those guys with the manly black canvas apron boasting, *Licensed to GRILL!* and all the long-handled accessories you can shake a stick at. On the way home from work last night, he stocked up on supplies: sirloin patties and beef hot dogs, buns, pickles, sweet relish and shoestring potatoes.

Kathryn's charged me with assembling a fruit salad to keep me occupied (read: I'm driving her up the wall with my anxious patrolling around the house). One minute I'm happy and ridiculously domestic, and the next I'm positive someone will call to tell me they've made a mistake. I never should have been considered to be River's mother. It was a court error—haha, so sorry.

When the phone rings, my hands jerk reflexively from the task of chopping the heads off strawberries, and I feel the sharp sting of the blade cutting through layers of skin.

"Ouchgoddammit! I mean—darn it!" In a matter of seconds, my index finger develops a streaming red gash.

"Maybe handing you a paring knife wasn't the best decision," Kathryn observes, turning to grab first aid supplies from the pantry while I cleanse the cut and press a paper towel to it to stop the bleeding.

Glenn snags the phone on the third ring. "Y'ello?" His expression appears concerned, which makes my heart flip over— until he says, "And it's only making that noise when you're coming to a stop, but not when you're idling? Uh-huh. Do the noise one more time for me."

I'm an idiot. This call is on the landline, not my cell. And it's obviously Kelley or Kylie with some sort of car trouble, rather than the State of Texas calling to stamp out my delusions of motherhood.

"Let's see that grisly wound." Kathryn takes my hand and examines the cut. Light green eyes sparkling, she says, "I think we'll be able to save the finger. Let's bandage that up and then give you something less disaster-prone to do while we wait."

As though I'm six again, my stepmother seats me on the corner barstool, applies ointment to the gash and covers it with a neon pink bandage.

"Reid told me that you're my role model, instead of Sharla," I say, and her worried gaze flashes to mine. "I must have known that, deep down, for years. But I never really acknowledged it. I always thought who I was—who I'd become—came down to blood, but that's just not true. I don't know who I'd be without you. Which seems pretty damned unfair, given the fact that my existence ruined your life."

Pressing a kiss to my forehead, she sighs. "Oh, honey—take a look around. Does my life look ruined to you? I have *three* very beautiful, talented daughters, a loving—" We hear Glenn outside, preparing the patio cooking area and belting out his own version of an eighties pop song, in which *grills* are crazy about sharp-dressed men. "—slightly insane husband, and I'm preparing to become a grandmother *twice* in the next few months! I have a wonderful life, Brooke, and I'm happy you're part of it."

When the doorbell chimes, I freeze in place. I can't breathe.

"Go answer the door, honey," Kathryn urges, slipping outside with Glenn so River won't be overwhelmed with new faces, everyone hovering, before he even gets in the door.

I walk to the door shaking, and pull it open, hoping my smile looks friendly instead of panic-stricken. There he stands, gripping Kris's hand as securely as I'd held Reid's on Wendy's front porch just a week ago. Next to him is a miniature rolling case shaped like a rather squared-off frog. Green, of course. He makes no move to enter, and his unsmiling expression doesn't waver.

According to Wendy, River is forty inches tall and weighs thirty-four pounds, putting him in the sixteenth percentile for both height and weight. The medical consensus: nutritional deprivation for some portion of his first few years; with proper nourishment, he may be able to make up for some of it. In our pre-visit call last night, she notified me about his food hoarding, and the psychological causes of it. "Also, he sometimes experiences nightmares—and occasionally, night terrors. Most nights, now, he sleeps just fine. But these are a possibility since he'll be in an unfamiliar environment."

I calmly accepted everything Wendy said, asking pertinent questions and taking meticulous notes, and when I got off the phone, I walked to the creek, sat on my rock and cried until my throat was raw.

I squat down to his level and fix a careful smile on my face. I'm an actor. *I can do this.*

Years ago, I found a skittish litter of kittens living under Glenn's tool shed. They were lightning-fast balls of fluff, and I wanted to hold one of them more than life itself. So I sat in the grass all afternoon, as close to motionless as I could manage, cooing and sweet-talking as though I was the safest girl who ever lived.

Moderating my voice in that same way, I speak to my son, to whom I am still a stranger.

"Hello, River. I'm glad you've come to visit. Would you like to come inside?"

Like those kittens, his dark blue eyes regard me warily, assessing whether I can be trusted. An eternity passes before he nods, once.

Standing, I welcome Kris as well and offer to take River's case. His soft little fingers brush mine as he passes the handle to me, and I turn and lead the way through the living room and down the wide hallways, biting my lip.

"Your room is right next to mine. Here we are."

Pausing in the doorway, he angles his head and scans the room—eyes moving deliberately over each individual object. I place his case on the bed and wait. When his gaze reaches me, he doesn't skip past. I'm given the same careful regard as everything else. The thing that finally lures him into the room is the golden-coated stuffed puppy. Drifting closer, he comes to the opposite side of the twin bed, chewing his bottom lip. Kris remains in the doorway.

"I think that puppy needs to be held." My voice is still whisper-soft. "Know why?"

His eyes flick to mine.

"Because we're having *hot dogs* for dinner, so he's a little worried."

One eyebrow quirks up, and I suppress a gasp—for the beat of two seconds, he is Reid, and I know in that moment that he's going to be fine. I've never known anyone as stubborn and indomitable as this child's father, unless it's his mother. He's survived the hand he was dealt because he's tough as nails, as small and breakable as he appears.

I quirk a brow back at him. "We're going to eat outside. You can bring him along if you want. He doesn't have a name yet. I was thinking about calling him Hot Dog, but maybe that's why he's worried about what's for dinner."

His mouth twists on one side this time, his eyes shifting back to the puppy.

"Kris, would you like to stay for dinner?" I offer.

She shakes her head, smiling. "I think you've got this. Let me know if you need me—you have my numbers?"

I nod. "Programmed into every phone we've got, and your card is on the fridge."

"Awesome." She turns her smile to him. "Goodnight, River. I'll see you tomorrow after lunch, okay?"

When I turn back, he has the puppy clutched to his chest. He looks at me one more time before nodding to her, giving her permission to leave him here with me. Alone.

Chapter 26

river

Brooke is pretty. Her hair looks soft, and I like her smile. Kathryn is nice, and even Glenn is nice. He's way, way bigger than Harry, but he doesn't scare me. He shows me how he makes broccoli taste better by sticking the tree part into a bowl of cheese.

I didn't know cheese could come in a bowl. I like it.

Brooke and Kathryn don't eat the cheese, but Glenn does and I do. I try my potato sticks and my hot dog in it, too. (The food hot dog, not the puppy Hot Dog.) I try dipping a berry in it, but that isn't very good.

After we eat, I pick up my empty plate. One of my chores at Wendy's house is to help clear the table. Kathryn smiles and says, "Thank you, River." She shows me where to put it in the kitchen.

Brooke asks if I want to walk to the creek and we go back outside. There is no fence around their house. I can only see one other house and it is far away.

Brooke makes me step around a big ant pile out in the grass, but the ants are all running around carrying things and I want to look. She says it's okay to watch the ants if I don't get too close. There are so many ants that I can't count that high.

"If you get too close, they think you're a big monster, and they all bite you to make you run away," she says. "See, one bit me last week." She shows me a red spot on her ankle.

I don't want to make those ants scared.

She has a real creek in her back yard. There are trees on both sides of it. We climb onto a big rock and sit near the edge. I can see down into the water. There's sand and rocks at the bottom. I don't see any fish, but there are bugs buzzing around on top of the water and we hear a frog.

"This is my favorite place in the world," Brooke says.

My favorite place used to be Mama's closet. It was dark all the time, and Harry never found me there. This rock is better, I think.

Brooke makes her sweater like a pillow and lies on her back. She says, "I like watching the clouds go by through the trees."

I make my jacket a pillow and lie down, too. She points to a cloud and says it looks like a squirrel. I think it looks like Hot Dog. I hold him up above me so I can see him next to the cloud.

"You're right. That cloud *does* look more like Hot Dog," she says.

I have a bad dream after bedtime. When I wake up, Brooke is sitting next to me instead of Wendy. *I want Wendy. I want Wendy. I want Wendy.*

"I'm sorry you're scared and in a new place," Brooke says. "I know how that feels."

She rubs my head a little, like Wendy does when I have a bad dream. Wendy had to cut my hair really short because Sean got lice and he gave them to me. I like bugs, but I didn't like *those* bugs. They itched.

Brooke says it's a little dark in here, and she goes to open the curtain wide. "Is this better?" she asks, and I nod. There are lots and lots of stars in the sky, and we can see the moon.

"Would you like me to sing you a song? I don't know very many, but I know a couple that my daddy used to sing to me when I was a little girl and I had bad dreams."

I nod again, and she picks me up. She sits in the big chair next to the window and sings *Twinkle, Twinkle Little Star.* That's a song Wendy sings to me sometimes. I hear her heart go *thump, thump* under my ear. The stars twinkle in the sky, like they're listening to her, too.

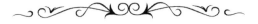

Brooke

Usually, prospective adoptive parents meet the kids at a fast food place or a park, before they do overnights. But that's not an option for us. I can't be seen in public with River yet, or we risk alerting the gossip rags to his existence, and the rumors will go nuts.

He's been to Kathryn's for two more overnights, during which I got him used to the idea of talking online with Reid. Not that he talks—but he listens.

Reid signed on once in full costume—sword and all. River's eyes widened while Reid told us about rappelling down a sheer cliff that day—how the winds were so gusty that his hair kept sweeping straight up, and the director kept yelling *Cut!* so someone could spray his hair back down while he hung in place in a rope.

"It looked like this," he said, making his hair stand straight up and managing to tease a smile from our son.

Our son. Every time I think or say it, it becomes less odd and more real.

River's next overnight will take place in LA. He'll stay with me three days and nights, and Reid four. Kris will send daily reports to the judge. When I asked her point-blank if the judge was considering an early placement due to Wendy's health issues, she told me she couldn't reveal that sort of thing. And then she arched a brow and smiled.

I'm filming the season finale for *Life's a Beach* this week. It's odd working with my old cast mates, most of whom would give anything to land either of the film parts I've done since I left. There are also a couple of new girls who were hired as replacement-blondes, which puts me on the receiving end of some spiteful glares and mumbled asides. If I decide to return to the show, their dreams and jockeying for the position of top bitch are *over*.

So sad, so sorry.

Should Xavier and I both choose to stick around, the writers will devise an angsty continuation of the boiling-point romance between the now of-age Kirsten and her sexy long-time obsession,

Kristopher. A passionate consummation will finally occur (during ratings week, no doubt), and then some justification for them to part will be devised, of course. Fans will be glued to the screen every week—whining and panting for our characters to screw each other again until Stan and the writers finally decide to land them in bed. Or more likely, on a picturesque, isolated beach—as if those are *all over the place* up and down the coast of California.

Yawn.

Xavier is as dense as ever, but we still have unrestrained chemistry on film, so Stan is downright smug over his own genius in getting both of us to agree to do the finale. We do a scene that takes two hours of body contortions and crude (on Xavier's part) lip-locks, and at the end of it, Stan tosses his arms in the air and says, "Am I not goddamned brilliant?"

He's so pompous I want to choke him. But we're almost done with the episode, and it's been a long day, so I smile tightly and devise a half dozen ways of killing him in my pretty little head.

Not an hour later, in front of the entire cast and crew, Stan bestows a smarmy, veneer-toothed grin on Xavier and me. "I guess you two tried the wonderful world of movie-making and decided that a nice, steady, big-network paycheck is something to be missed after all, huh?"

As if we failed on the big screen, like so many optimistic television actors before us.

Xavier grunts in response, but he's focused on a three-meat sandwich one of the giggly production assistants ran out (literally) to get him—so his grunt could be a sound of carnivorous appreciation.

I hold my tongue, just barely, until I slide into my car and call Janelle, who's left me five or six messages. I don't bother to listen to them before calling her back.

"Brooke!" she shrieks, and I dial down the volume on my phone. "You got the offer!"

Crap. I was about to beg her to find me another rom-com, or a soap, or hell—a set of commercials—anything but more Stan, as long as it's filmed locally. I don't want to talk about *Paper Oceans* today. Last week, I hinted at the fact that I'd most likely ask her to turn it down, and she *cried*. I have never heard Janelle cry, and Christ on a cracker, I hope I never do again.

Not to mention the fact that I do desperately want that part.

And after today, I'd like to tell Stan to take his Kirsten Wells beach-bunny role and stuff it back up his ass.

"I'm driving," I say.

"Ohmygod! You know how I feel about talking and driving!"

Yes. Yes, I do.

"Then don't leave me a hundred messages while I'm *filming*—I thought someone died. I'll call you later."

"That doesn't sound like a promising reaction. *Brooke.* Please. Do. Not. Turn. This. Down."

"Getting on the freeway!" Total lie.

"Okay, okay—call me tonight."

Shit.

I'm meeting my personal paparazza at my new place in about an hour. Despite Reid's reluctance to use Rowena to introduce River to the world, I have faith in her—to a point, of course, restricted to her job. She's always shown me in the light in which I wanted to be seen. She's never sold a pic I hated. She's even been handy a couple of times dispelling rumors I didn't want to spread.

Even so, we've never met at my place before. My home has always been totally off-limits to the media—including Rowena. My new condo is situated inside a walled, guarded community. Ins and outs are filmed, and all non-residents are stopped by a security guard at the big iron gate at the front. Unauthorized visitors are sent packing.

The doorbell signals her arrival.

"Hello, Rowena." I'm trying my best to be nonthreatening.

She's wary, like a wild animal being lured into a trap, but too hungry not to follow the smell of food. I shake her hand, which I guess I've never done before, because her hand is *tiny*. I knew she was skinny almost to the point of malnourishment, but up close, she looks like she's got all the might of a parakeet. I can't imagine how she heaves that camera equipment around.

"Ms. Cameron," she nods, entering haltingly. It's like she expects to encounter a tripwire and be impaled on my wall any second. I've asked her to call me Brooke a dozen times before, but I realized a while back she was never going to, and I gave up.

She's brought her gear, but it's all zipped inside a tattered black bag. Glancing around surreptitiously, her desire to fish out her camera is unmistakable. We sit on my new sectional sofa, skirting easily around the rounded corners of the reclaimed wood coffee table. There's a pink-tipped ivy plant of some sort in the center of it, an indoor potted tree by the window and several hanging and potted plants on my top-floor patio.

I hired a plant person. Seriously.

"I've got a proposition for you. It involves top secret information, and of course, a story I want told—photographically —in a certain light."

"I'm listening," she nods. Her ambitious eyes give me pause.

"What I'm about to tell you cannot leave this room. Ever."

Her eyes widen slightly. I've trusted Rowena with a lot over the past few years, but I've never prefaced anything like this.

"You've always been more than fair, Ms. Cameron. I'll of course agree not to share any information you entrust me with."

I take a deep breath and keep my eyes directly on hers. "I'm adopting a son."

She blinks twice, stunned. "Congratulations." Whatever she expected, this isn't it.

"Thank you—but it's more complicated than that sounds, which is why I need you. There's no ringing biological clock, no philanthropic statement. This isn't a foreign adoption. I'm adopting my own child, a baby I gave up when he was born four and a half years ago." Her eyes bulge. I've never seen this much emotion on Rowena's face. "I assume you've made the leap everyone else will make—the question of *who's the daddy*. Well, you're in luck. If you agree to take photos of the three of us that he and I will approve prior to release, we'll give you an exclusive."

I don't have to tell her that once this comes out, it will be huge. If she times this right, and gets ahead of everyone else, she'll make a freaking fortune.

"Oh my God," she says. And then she does something I never, ever expected to see Rowena do. She bursts into tears.

Brooke: Rowena is all set.
Reid: K. What's the plan?
Brooke: I was thinking we could go somewhere semi-public and have her photograph us "candidly" - like we arranged to happen with you and Emma last May, outside the airport.

Reid: Shit. How did she ever forgive me?

Brooke: You told her the truth when it counted, even if it
          made you look bad. For what it's worth, I
          admired you for that. Hated the shit out of you
          at the time, but admired you. You were a better
          man than me.

Reid: Haha.

Brooke: So, one of the hiking spots in the Hills, really
          early on a weekday? OH – I know – let's do it
          the day he transfers from me to you. The kid
          swap. Like divorced couples.

Reid: Yeah - perfect. That will answer the "are they a
          couple?" question, too.

Brooke: Ok, cool. Rowena is on this. She was stunned
          that you stepped up, btw. I think you've gained
          a new fan. She's a single mom, apparently.
          She said her guy used to knock her around.
          She left the day he hit her kid.

Reid: Jesus.

Brooke: She says she's always liked me because I
          don't take shit off anyone, lol.

Reid: Haha. Truth.

Reid: So have you heard anything more about Paper
          Oceans?

Brooke: Yeah. Janelle got the call earlier today—
          they've officially offered it to me. But I'd have to
          be in Australia all of June. I can't do it.

Reid: Brooke. This is your CAREER. Say yes. I'll
          take him in June. I'll probably be done filming
          by then. If not, it'll be a small overlap. He and
          the au pair we're hiring can come to New York
          with me. It'll be fine.

Reid: Unless you want to do Life's a Beach instead…

Reid: I've heard that Xavier guy is an exceptional
          kisser…

Reid: And Stan is a gem of a producer and not at all
          egocentric…

Brooke: I'm crying. Holy shit. Are you sure? Are you
          SURE?

Reid: YES. We'll be fine here without you. This is going to be his life. He'll adjust. I can do this. And yes, I even promise to call on the all-knowing and ever-powerful Graham if I need advice.

Brooke: Is it okay if I kind of love you right now?

Reid: Yeah. Is it okay if I thank you for letting me knock you up?

Brooke: God, we're weird.

Reid: Hell yeah we are.

Chapter 27

Dori

"Hey, Deb." I lean to kiss her temple and she blinks, but her fixed expression otherwise remains like the face of an impassive wax figure. "I thought you might be getting tired of tulips, and also, one of Dad's rosebushes bloomed. They're pink—which I know you think is such a cliché flower color. But they smell *so* good that I didn't think you'd mind."

Depositing last week's purple tulips in the trash can, I rinse and fill the vase in her bathroom sink. It's been five weeks since I've seen my sister.

Five weeks since we buried Esther. Four weeks since Reid and I were in San Francisco. Three weeks since I've spoken to him. Two weeks since he stopped texting and leaving voicemails.

"I like Cal. My roommate, Shayma, is from Louisiana. You'd love her. She's a business major, but she does community outreach projects with me."

Shayma hadn't asked about Reid—or the fact that I hadn't mentioned him in a while—until a couple of days ago. When I told her I hadn't had a chance to talk to him in a few days, she pursed her lips and said *um-hmm*, but nothing more.

"I'm taking all intro classes this semester, but most of my professors are pretty cool. And you were right—the campus is one funky place. There's a full-scale T-rex model in the Life Science building. The grounds are beautiful, but the architecture is all over the place. And there's tons of activist history intact—like the building that's missing an outside handle because during protests *fifty years ago*, students chained the doors shut, and the administration took one handle off so they couldn't do it again. In the upper plaza, student groups hand out flyers and sell things to raise money for charity. Sometimes, opposing groups have tables feet apart, but everybody stays remarkably civil."

Running a brush through Deb's short hair, I recall what it looked like before her accident. She had beautiful shoulder-length hair, chestnut with auburn highlights she did herself. Now it's short, dull, and frizzy; I make a mental note to bring conditioner with me next time. The bare spots from her surgeries have finally grown back in, though the surgical scar will remain a sort of odd, random part at the back of her head.

"Berkeley feels like a small town, even though it's not. It's definitely not like LA or San Francisco—which you can see from certain spots on campus, if the fog hasn't rolled in."

Deb's chair is positioned so she can "see" the view from her window, which is no more or less ridiculous than me taking her for a stroll on the grounds. My parents insist there is no proof that she's totally oblivious to what goes on around her, because her brain registers some activity. In some ways, this is more horrifying than if she'd remained medically unresponsive, because no one can assure us that she isn't aware to some degree and simply unable to respond, though her doctors continue to reiterate that her brain activity is too inconsequential to represent comprehension.

My parents continue to hear what they want to hear.

I continue to speak to my sister because I have to talk to *someone*.

"I haven't spoken to Reid in a while. I miss him. Sometimes it feels like my heart is going to burst, and I almost want it to."

When I was very young, I had chronic ear infections and a grandma with unconventional ideas about what constituted a helpful story. "Back in my day, there were no antibiotics for such things," she told me during one particularly excruciating episode. "Your eardrum just swelled up 'til it popped."

"Oh, Mother! Don't tell her your horror stories!" Mom said, aghast.

"Well after it popped, it stopped hurting!" Grandma huffed. "Problem solved."

I keep waiting for my heart to pop.

"He has a son. River. He thinks that's why I stopped talking to him—he thinks I'm angry he kept it from me. He doesn't understand how easily I could forgive and understand that choice. It's true that when he told me, and I looked at his picture on Reid's phone, that was when I felt myself detaching. But anger wasn't the reason for that."

I place a blanket over Deb's lap and take a light sweater from her closet. Clothing her is very much like dressing an infant on the cusp of being a toddler—she doesn't help, but she doesn't fight against me as I bend her elbow gently and pull her arm through the sweater.

Once outside, I resume our one-way conversation.

"I'm such a coward—I'm terrified that if I meet River, he'll become important to me. And when everything ends with Reid, I'll lose him, too."

I find our spot—a secluded bench surrounded by waist-high camellia shrubs covered in white blossoms. Taking a seat, I face Deb's chair to me and stare at her beautiful hazel eyes. She blinks slowly, seemingly focused on something in the distance over my shoulder. Positioned as I placed them before we left her room, her hands rest in her lap, fingers twitching as they sometimes do—just another involuntary movement, doctors insist.

"I know you'd tell me I'm being spineless," I say to Deb now. "Only you'd say it more gently, like: *Dori, you're braver than this*. It's true, though—I'm gutless where Reid is concerned. If I talk to him, I'll want to believe in everything he says."

My eyes fill, my heart compressing as I wait for the *pop* that never comes. "I know I'm hurting him, and I hate that." After his last text: *Please, goddammit it, not again*—I almost caved. It took every ounce of willpower not to answer him. "But it wouldn't be fair to try to keep him when I have nothing to offer him in return."

I swipe the tears away before they have a chance to track down my face.

"There's something I never told you about that decision I made four years ago." I take a shuddering breath. "I've never felt a middle ground between acceptance and remorse. Every day for the last four years, it's been one or the other. Black or white. There was no gray, but I could bear it, because I had you. When I lost you, I began slipping into perpetual guilt. Carrying that secret, alone, for the first time, while trying to balance the idea of a benevolent God with a God who could let this happen to you—it was like falling into quicksand."

Reid saved me from going under. He'd needed me to help him see who he could be, and in return, he allowed me to be myself in a way I never have. I was content to accept that happiness as long as it lasted. To try to make him happy while he was mine.

"Deb," I whisper, leaning closer. "I feel hollow. I feel separate from everything and everyone. Nothing is touching me except the things that hurt. You always told me that if I helped other people, even if I was just going through the motions, it would keep me grounded. It would eventually help me define and know myself again. But it's not working this time. I don't know who I am, in relation to anyone else. I've lost *me*."

When I get home, Dad is brewing his Saturday afternoon "sermon-busting coffee."

"Hey, sweetheart. How was Deb?"

I almost say *the same*, but that's not what he means. "The roses looked beautiful in her room, and when we got back in from a circuit in the garden, the whole room smelled rosy."

He smiles. "You don't think she minds that they're pink?"

I don't think she notices that they're pink.

"No, Dad." I smile, handing him the keys to the Civic.

"If you might need the car later, just keep those," he says.

I shake my head. "Nick is coming over. We're going to get an early dinner and catch up before he goes back to Wisconsin tomorrow. Our breaks are on consecutive weeks instead of the same one."

"Oh? That's a pity." He looks hopeful, and I bite back the desire to tell him that ship has long since sailed.

"It's okay." I shrug. "At least I get to see him once."

He clears his throat, and I know before he speaks what he's about to say. He and Mom are so transparent. "Seeing Reid this week?" he asks as I'm walking toward the stairs, my face turned away so he won't notice the way I close my eyes and breathe through my nose, schooling my voice not to betray me.

"No. I don't think so."

"Oh. Have you two—"

"Dad, I'm not ready to talk about it," I say, and thankfully, he drops it.

I'll never be ready to talk about it.

Nick arrives an hour later. The doorbell echoes through the house, and then I hear his voice in the foyer, comparing notes with Dad on the Badger basketball season. My father never took that relaxed tone with Reid... but I have to quash my irritation over that. There's no purpose to it, after all.

"Hi, Nick," I say, arriving downstairs. He beams and hugs me, and as he releases my shoulders, I ask, "Have you *grown*?"

His brows elevate hopefully. "I dunno. Have I?"

I laugh. "I think you have! Boys add the freshman fifteen in a whole different way than girls! Seriously unfair."

He smiles down at me. "You *do* seem shorter."

"Shut up." I punch him halfheartedly and we turn to go. "I'll be back in a bit, Dad. Don't get into any trouble while Mom's at work."

"Aw, pumpkin—you're no fun!" He says in pretend objection, chuckling and shutting the front door behind us.

We turn to cross the porch and stop on the top step.

Reid is halfway up the walk. When he sees me with Nick, he stops abruptly, too. In the span of those two seconds, a smile blooms and dies on my face. Whipping his sunglasses off, Reid glares at Nick and then at me. His jaw locks, fists clenched at his sides, as we all stand immobile and dumbstruck. He's clearly angry, but so beautiful I can hardly stand to look at him.

"Dori?" Nick finally says, breaking the tense silence.

"Would you mind waiting in the car, Nick?"

He glances toward Reid, "Are you sure—"

"Yes. I'll be fine."

Reid's eyes flick to him as he passes. Nick is taller than average, but shorter and leaner than Reid, whose in-production body looks big and defined in comparison. Nick keeps a wide berth and avoids eye contact as he walks to the sedan he borrowed from his mom for the night. Reid's spotless Ferrari is parked right behind it.

I start down the steps. "Reid. What are you—" I swallow the uncomfortable lump in my throat and start over. "What are you doing here?"

He watches me approach, but makes no move toward me.

"You stopped talking to me, Dori. I came to find out why." He glances over his shoulder at Nick, who waits by the driver's side door, resting his arms on the roof of the car and watching us. "Or should I take this as an answer?" When he looks back at me, the pain is evident in his eyes.

I shake my head, coming to stand in front of him. "No. Nick has nothing to do with us."

"Is there an *us*, Dori?" I flinch at the raw torment in his voice, and his hand moves as if to touch me, but he drops it back to his side. "I made promises to you, and I intended to keep them. I know I was wrong to hide River from you, and I'm willing to do whatever I need to do to make up for that. But you have to talk to me. If you're going to end it, you have to tell me why. You can't just disappear like you did before."

Mom told me he'd called, though her memory was suspiciously vague as to the content of their conversation. From his perspective, my withdrawal is exactly like last time. But last fall was about submitting to pressure from my parents. This time is all me and my personal demons.

"This isn't like last time."

"Isn't it?" he says softly.

My heart clenches rhythmically instead of beating. "We can't talk about this now—"

"Because going out with *some other guy* is more important to you?"

I wince at the indignation in his voice, and the way he pivots from hurt to anger.

"Nick is leaving town tomorrow. We made plans."

He stares at me, hard, silent.

Laying my hand on his forearm, I note the immediate tautness of the muscle under my fingers. Like he can steel himself against my touch. Like he wants to.

"Can we talk tomorrow, Reid? Please?"

The tension melts from his shoulders with a sigh. Carefully— as if he's afraid to startle me, he lifts his hand to curl one finger under my chin and gazes down into my eyes. "*Will* you talk to me, Dori?"

His thumb grazes over the indention in my chin as though it's meant to rest there before it slides up to outline my lower lip. When he leans to kiss me, my body responds without regard to how this connection tears at my heart. My mouth opens to him, yielding against all the rapidly disregarded rationales for why I can't surrender to what he thinks he wants right now. My hand slides up his arm and under the sleeve of his T-shirt, tightening on his bicep as he slips that arm around my waist and pulls me closer, urgently.

I want this. I need this. And when he kisses me, he knows it.

Stroking my tongue with his, he's both fiercely possessive and gentle, and I want nothing more than to wrap myself around him and be carried away to a place where I don't have to think. A place where there's no guilt or fear, no right or wrong, no divine punishments or senseless accidents or indeterminate states.

When he draws back, his chest rises and falls with mine. "I'll be back tomorrow afternoon," he says, turning to go without looking back, pulling his keys from his pocket. He ignores Nick completely as he gets into his car and drives away.

I walk unsteadily to Nick's car, belatedly aware that at least three neighbors came outside in the last few minutes to sweep clean sidewalks or check empty mailboxes and watch Reid Alexander kiss me.

REID

As soon as Immaculada leaves the kitchen, Mom walks in with her coffee cup and heads for the impressive-looking coffee maker, which supposedly makes all sorts of coffee drinks. If it's in operation, though, there's a good chance it's just making coffee.

"Reid?" She pulls out the adjacent seat and glances back at the digital clock over the stove. "Goodness, you're up early," she observes, sitting next to me.

I shrug. "I'm still on production schedule, I guess. Just as well—we start up at Universal on Monday."

"So soon?"

I arch a brow at her. "Time is money, Lucy."

She laughs at my overdone impersonation of my father and every producer in Hollywood.

Truth: I couldn't sleep most of the night, thinking about how Dori responded to that kiss. She wants me still. I don't care what she *says*—or refuses to say, since she hasn't been speaking to me. Come to think of it, her avoidance feels even more suspect, because I've seen Dori angry, and nothing about her reactions yesterday denoted anger, even in the face of my obvious jealousy toward her friend.

Dr. Shaw will be happy to know I didn't lay a verbal insult (or a fist) on *Nick*—the guy I mistook for her boyfriend last summer at Habitat, because he clearly *wanted* to be her boyfriend. Considering the fact that for about two minutes yesterday afternoon, I thought that guy was the reason she wasn't calling me back—I think I showed extraordinary restraint.

"River's room is completely ready," Mom says, breaking into my mental recap.

"Mom, are you sure you're good with River living here? I know you and Dad thought you were almost rid of me. And it's not like I can't afford my own place."

She smiles and lays her hand on top of mine. "Reid—this house is ten thousand square feet, give or take a few closets. We have staff who've been with us for years and are utterly trustworthy. It's private. It's safe. This is the perfect place for him. And for you, for now. Not forever—for now."

I nod. I'm still stunned at how my parents have reacted to this.

Mom sips her coffee and I sip mine, both of us lost in our thoughts.

And then: "You haven't said very much about Dori the last few times we've spoken," she says. "How are things with her sister? And her first semester at Berkeley?"

I shake my head. "I'm not completely sure on either count."

"Hmm." Her *hmm* doesn't sound surprised.

"When I met her, I saw her altruistic side and thought *do-gooder*. I saw the girl with no makeup, wearing the least flattering outfits a girl could wear—especially knowing *I* was going to be around—" Mom rolls her eyes and shakes her head at me "—and I expected *boring*. She wore these T-shirts every day, supporting all kinds of causes, and I decided she was judgmental and sanctimonious."

During our very first dinner out, Dori admitted that she was a bit sanctimonious. Her admission was coupled with that mischievous smile of hers that I'd begun making deliberate efforts to trigger. That may have been the moment I fell in love with her.

"But I was so wrong about her. Even when she questioned her own goodness, she managed to see something good about me. And then her sister had that accident. It destroyed her. It obliterated her faith in everything." I bite the inside of my lip. "Everything except me. I somehow got her to trust *me*. And then I *lied to her*. And I can tell myself it was a lie of omission like that's something *other*. Like that's something *lesser*. But it was still a *lie*, and I knew it every goddamned day that I didn't tell her."

"Reid, if she's lost her faith in God, that isn't yours to resolve—"

"Yes it *is*. She was trying, Mom—she was trying so hard to rebuild it. And then her dog died, and I didn't tell her about River. And now I have a son, who I can't turn my back on—"

"Of course you can't. Dori wouldn't expect that. She wouldn't *want* that. I know she wouldn't."

"That's what's tearing me apart. I don't know how to fix this. How do I *fix* this?" I stare into her eyes—my eyes, mirrored back at me. "I can't lose her. I love her."

"I see that, Reid. But if I've learned anything in the past few months—and I think you have, as well, it's that people must fix themselves. That's the only way change has any hope of becoming permanent." She squeezes my hand.

Winking at me from her ring finger is the huge, flawless, round-cut diamond my father presented on bended knee when they were young.

Not as young as I am.

My dad was twenty-nine or thirty when he proposed to my mother. He was thirty-five when I was born, very legitimately. Thirty-five. Not fifteen, and too much of a dickwad to even consider the fact that a girl he'd had sex with—a girl he'd *made love to*—could possibly be pregnant with his child, no matter what else he thought she'd done, or with whom.

Mom follows my eyes to her hand and back to my face. She angles her head. "Reid?"

"Mom. I need to ask you something."

I hear the melodic chirrup of the Cantrells' doorbell when I press the button, because all the windows and the front door are wide open. It's a beautiful spring day in LA.

"I've got it!" Dori calls as she descends the staircase, alerting me that one or both of her parents are home. Just like the first time I ever heard her speak, I'm struck by the musical sound of her voice.

I watch her appear a bit at a time—bare feet on the steps and then her perfect legs in a pair of khaki shorts, followed by one of her more hideous T-shirts—a tie-dye done with too many colors, rendering it a sort of repulsive brown, for the most part. It sports the name of a chorale outreach program for teens, sponsored by her high school choir. Finally, her beautiful face dips into view.

How could I have ever thought her plain? I must have been blind.

As she reaches the screen door, I say, "You can't scare me off with that butt-ugly T-shirt, you know."

She clicks the lock on the door and admits me, glancing down at herself. "It works on most people. I could stand on the porch like a scarecrow and no one would come near."

"Except me." I pull her close and wrap my arms around her. "You know, if I keep you close enough, I can't actually *see* it. Plus, it's actually very soft, even if it is the most revolting T-shirt ever made."

Her mouth quirks. "It does sort of look like it was tie-dyed in poop."

I laugh. "Yeah, it does."

I'd like to sweep her up, take her to her bedroom and strip it off. That's not an option at the moment. One, her parents are home. And two, we need to talk.

As if she's reading my mind, she shifts her eyes away from mine. Lucky for me, her hair is pulled back into a ponytail, and those exposed, pink-tipped ears tell me she *can* read my mind. Sucking her bottom lip into her mouth, she reveals her anxious mental state.

Time to be serious, as much as I'd like to help her avoid it.

I take her hand and lead her to the sofa. The ceiling fan whirrs overhead, and Esther's dog bed is still in the corner, though her collection of toys has been packed away. Rose bushes provide bursts of color across the tiny back yard, and the aroma wafts through the open windows, as potent as a hothouse. As luxurious as my parents' house is, I love it here. I love her watery-colored bedroom and those fish swimming across her ceiling. I think River would love it, too.

Her hand lays palm up in mine. Skimming the contours of her fingers, I concentrate on calming her. Her eyes are still downcast, watching my finger trace slowly over her skin. I know from that kiss yesterday that she wants me, but she's always been capable of pushing those desires aside. If we don't go deeper than that—if she won't let me all the way in, apart from her physical response, I won't be able to keep her.

"I want to apologize for not trusting you," I say, and she frowns as her eyes snap to mine. This is not what she expected me to confess. *Good.* "I was afraid of what you'd think of me if, or when, you found out about River. But you've been the one person to continually see anything worthwhile in me, to help me see it— and I should have trusted in that."

I recall the words she said when she found out about him: *You're doing the right thing, and I'm proud of you for it.* Her eyes go glassy, and I cup her face in my hands as the realization hits. Fucking hell, how did I not see this? "You have faith in me—but not *me with you.*"

And that does it. She shuts her eyes, and I know I'm right.

"You love your parents, but you think they don't know you. You may still believe in God, but not that he cares about you. You're disconnecting, trying to protect yourself. But baby, it's not going to work. I'm here to tell you—it's not going to work."

All of a sudden, she's crying, and I'm praying this conversation isn't going to push her further from me.

I stand and pull a small, square box from my pocket. Go to my knees in front of her, so we're eye-to-eye. "Dori, I have faith in us. I don't know how else to prove to you that I want you forever." I open the box and set it in her open palm, and she gasps. "My grandmother willed this ring to me, to give to the woman I want to spend the rest of my life with. When she died almost six years ago, I had no idea what my future held—or that someone like you would be part of it. That River would be part of it. I don't know where I'll be in another six years, but I know I want you there with me. With us."

She stares down at the enormous sapphire stone, surrounded by slivers of diamonds and set into a platinum band. I don't tell her that this ring also belonged to my great-grandmother. My maternal great-grandfather was one of those dudes who pulled his money from the stock market months before the crash, keeping his family beyond solvent at a time when many of his peers lost everything. Their son presented this ring to my grandmother, and it skipped a generation and came to me.

I close the box and shut her fingers around it. "Take this. When you're ready, I want to put it on your finger. I want you to meet my son. I want you to let me bring you into my world—because I need you there. The media crap is just PR. Piece of cake for you, trust me. There are a hundred people ready to help us nail it. Let me help you rebuild your faith, because that's who you are, and I love who you are.

"Remember last fall, when you needed to be reckless, and I told you to use me? Well, now, it's time to be *fearless*. I can't promise that you won't be hurt again, because life can suck. And sometimes, it hurts like hell. I'm asking you to have faith in one thing, for now: the fact that when we're alone, I'm just Reid, and you're just Dori, and we're going to love each other for the rest of our lives."

She's staring at me, the velvet-covered box clutched in her hand. I lean forward and kiss her, tasting her tears or my own, I don't know which. "Come to me when you're ready to be fearless. Unless you can look me in the eye right now and tell me you don't love me."

Lower lip trembling, she says nothing, and I kiss her again before I leave.

Chapter 28

Brooke

"*Brooke*," Janelle answers. "Please tell me you're calling to say yes to *Paper Oceans*."

"I'm calling to say yes to *Paper Oceans*."

"*Oh, thank GOD!*" My agent begins to squeal with joy and I jerk my cell away from my ear. Jee-*zus*.

"Janelle—I have one condition," I yell toward the phone.

The squealing ceases. "Okay. Let's have it." She sighs. "I'm your agent—I was born to bitch up and negotiate. Hit me."

Ugh. Dramatic much?

"No negotiating necessary. This one is for Stan: tell him to go ahead and kill off Kirsten Wells, because she is *never coming back* to that damned beach."

She shrieks with laughter. "Okay, seriously? After what he said to you on set last week, he can suck my—"

"All right, then!" I stop her before she finishes that thought and I'm stuck with a mental image I'd prefer to bypass. "We're good. So, other than the occasional PR-necessary interviews and whatever pre-planning meetings the producers might need me to do beforehand, I'm officially out of commission until June. I'll be back and forth between LA and Austin until then."

"Oh. So you're going through with the adoption?" She sounds confused.

I grit my teeth. Janelle is a determined *I will never, ever have children* sort of woman. I was, too, not long ago. An aversion to parenthood was something we had in common. I can't expect her to suddenly relate to my new priorities—though I do expect her to work around them.

"Yes. Reid has agreed to keep him while I'm filming in Australia. He'll be between films in June."

"Huh. Impressive. You two are behaving better than most of my divorced-with-kids cohorts—and they're in their thirties and forties. Those poor kids are like the rope in their parents' I-hate-you-now tug-of-wars. Thank God I don't have to ever speak to either of my douchebag exes again."

I know instinctively I'll never have that sort of issue with Reid. Whatever his past or present faults, he's stepped up in a way I never could have foreseen him doing. If he wasn't in love with Dori, I could fall for him all over again.

But he is in love with her. And I need his friendship too much, for River's sake, and for my own. I learned my lesson with Graham, whose friendship I'm determined to earn back. Someday. If Emma allows it.

"Heads up, Janelle—Rowena is getting an exclusive photo op of Reid and River and me. She's going to 'catch' us doing our first custody swap. Expect the story to break by the end of the week—I'll need you to consider who to give the print story to. It'll be jointly done."

"Wow. You're using Rowena for this?" she says. "So, it will be a breaking story—photos only, instead of an official announcement. That's *ballsy*. But why am I surprised? Of course you'd approach this the way you do everything else: head on."

Can't argue with that. "I've gotta go. River will be here any minute."

"Thanks for the *great* news!" she squeals. "I'll be in touch!"

I have *got* to get some earplugs.

I've never made so much queso in my life, and I'm from central *Texas*. River seems to like to dip everything he eats in a bowl of cheese, and given the fact that we're trying to get his weight up, his pediatrician has given the green light to unlimited amounts of it. To my son, everything is better dipped in cheese—except fruit. But hand the kid a chicken nugget or a green bean or a stick of celery, and into the queso it goes.

I also did something that Kris was none too sure about: I

bought a dorm-room sized fridge for his bedroom. "Maybe not the best precedent." Kris said, but I know she was thinking what I thought when I bought it: at least the food he hoards won't spoil. And it may get him to do it more openly, which could result in his no longer feeling the need to do it at all, at some point.

He also likes to sit in his closet, occasionally, with the door almost all the way closed. So we constructed a little tented-off area in the back with blankets and pillows, and a safety light, though he sometimes sits in the dark. If I can't find him, I know that's where he is. I sit on his bed and call to him nonchalantly, telling him it's time for lunch, or bath, or pajamas and a book. Eventually, he emerges, always holding Hot Dog, who will need a bath of his own soon. His fur is sporting all sorts of random stickiness and, unsurprisingly, cheese smears.

"Hi, River," I'll say, as though it's perfectly normal for a kid to want to sit in a dark closet. He'll climb up beside me, and I'll smile as though it doesn't break my heart that he needs to hide. That he still gets that scared. That he still doesn't speak.

I've had him for three days, and he's going home with Reid now. "He's had one bad dream this week," I tell Reid quietly, as River stands at the hiking barricade, checking out the big Hollywood sign in the distance. He holds a finger out, tracing the letters in mid-air. "He yelled, 'No' and 'Don't hit Mama.' But he stayed solidly asleep."

"Jesus," Reid says, watching him. We're both smiling, because Rowena is a small distance away, taking photos. My smile has never felt so unnatural.

"I'll call you if I have any problems." He looks down at me, and the worry in his eyes is plain. "You might want to keep your phone on 24/7."

I smile up at him. "You'll do just fine. But yeah, I'll have my phone on and *on me* for the next four days straight."

River's second favorite place is the huge sandbox on my enclosed patio. Daddy sent it, along with a note: *Brooke, I got Evan one of these, and he loves it. I thought River might, too. Evan is the starting forward on his soccer team, which I'm now assistant coaching. Rory's interested in cars, so we're taking a long weekend to go to the auto show in NYC. Thank you for your advice. It was spot on. Love, Daddy.*

Reid plans to take River to the private beach owned by John's parents. "John thinks he's become an uncle," Reid says. "I had to talk him out of buying River a kid-sized sports car." I shake my head. *John.*

"Did you pack that bulldozer you said he likes?"

I nod. "And the crane. So you can *both* play."

We laugh and River turns to look at us. His sweet little face is so serious, but at least he isn't frowning.

"Ready to go, bud?" Reid says, squatting down. River walks over and straight into his arms, and I bite my lip and keep my face turned from where I know Rowena is until my fake smile is back in place. I watch as Reid straps River into a booster seat in the back of his dad's SUV, and hands him Hot Dog. "I'm guessing Immaculada is gonna get hold of that dog sometime in the next few days," he murmurs, "and send it through the wash."

"Good," I murmur back. "I think we could stick him to a wall and he'd stay there right now." I run a hand through River's soft hair, wavy and the perfect beach blond, like Reid's. "Goodbye, River. Have fun with Reid, and I'll see you soon." When I lean to kiss his forehead, he turns his face into mine. Not quite kissing me back, but accepting my kiss.

I've always said I would never need a man, and no boy would ever save me.

I was wrong.

Dori

Me:	I'm ready to talk, if you're free.
Reid:	River is here for his second overnight. His bedtime is 8. Mom is reading to him now, and he's looking pretty sleepy.
Me:	Oh! I don't want to interrupt your time with him.
Reid:	Come at 9. He'll be in bed – you won't be interrupting. Please come.
Me:	You're sure it isn't too late?
Reid:	No such thing, Dori. I'll open the gate – just park in your usual spot.

I have a usual spot, even if it's been over two months since I've been here.

I take a deep breath and stare at the house where Reid grew up. It looks like a castle to me—a beautiful architectural monstrosity. But to him, it's just home. He doesn't see the world as I do—not because he willfully refuses to, but because *this* is his reality. His celebrity is his reality. His career. His reputation. His son.

And he wants me to be part of this life of his.

Unbeknownst to me, Mom was eavesdropping on our conversation on Sunday afternoon. I didn't know until the next day. When she appeared at my bedroom door and asked if I had a moment to talk, I was separating the last of my clean laundry—hanging what I need for the coming week at home, packing what I'll take back to Cal next weekend.

"Sure, Mom. Kayla and Aimee aren't coming to get me for a couple more hours."

My friends planned a night out that included a movie: *Hearts Over Manhattan*, having no idea, of course, that it starred the mother of Reid's child—whose existence was still a secret.

Mom perched at the end of my bed and glanced around my tidy room. "I've missed you, Dori. When Deb first left for college, it was difficult to watch her go, but her leaving didn't silence the house—though it certainly quieted it."

Deb, as tone-deaf as she could be, was the one who sang at the top of her lungs in the shower. She howled with laughter when talking on the phone or watching television. She banged pots and pans while cooking. It was impossible for her to enter or leave a room quietly. But she was so sweet and constantly happy that Mom and I, naturally more restrained, couldn't criticize her innate exuberance.

Those memories are bittersweet now—rare moments that bring both laughter and tears, and leave my emotions a tangled mess.

"You were only ten when she left for college," Mom said, smiling. "You still wanted to tell your dad and me all about your day, or help make cookies, or play with Esther. The house still felt full with you in it, and now, it's so quiet."

I slid a hanger through another shirt and hung it in the closet, unsure how to respond.

"I was listening to some of your conversation yesterday. With

Reid."

I turned to face her, stunned. My mother had never been the purposefully overhearing, snooping around sort of parent. Neither of my parents was. Of course, that was before I spent the night with Reid last fall.

"What he said—that you don't think we know you, that you don't think God cares about you—it's true, isn't it?"

I shrugged—because it was unerringly true. How can you tell a parent who's always loved you that she doesn't really know you at all? But I couldn't lie to her, either.

"You've been very patient with me while I figure some things out. Like the fact that you're a smart, loving young woman, and it's time I trust your decisions about who you choose to love. If my interference in your relationship with Reid is what's caused you to think I don't know you, Dori, I'm even sorrier. You're my daughter, and I want what's best for you. But that's for you to decide, as hard as it is for me to admit."

I crossed the room as she stood to hug me. "I'm sorry, Mom."

Shaking her head, she said, "You have nothing to apologize for." She pulled back and took my face in her hands. "If you see something good in that boy, then there's something good in him. I trust your judgment, Dori. I always have."

"There's a lot of good in him, Mom. And I want to tell you about all of it. Well—most of it." I blushed, knowing Reid would laugh at that accidental disclosure.

A tap on my window breaks me from my reverie. I blink, because Reid is standing right there, waiting for me to exit my car.

As I release the seat belt, he's opening my car door, and the hinges protest as they always do, though I'd swear they squeal louder when I'm parked in his driveway.

"Hey," he says. "I'm glad you came." I fall in beside him and we walk inside. "He's asleep. Would you... do you want to see him?"

I nod, chewing my lip.

Tiny lights line the baseboard along the hallway between River's partially open door and the steps up to Reid's room, like the aisles in nice theaters. Reid pushes his son's door open and enters, barefoot. I slip my flip-flops off in the hallway and follow him.

The room is dark, but there are two nightlights, and after a minute, our eyes have adjusted well enough to cross the room. Along with shelves of toys, I spy a television and game console, a huge overstuffed chair, and a perfectly-proportioned desk.

The bed is raised, with a ladder at the end, but isn't quite high enough to be a bunk. His small body curled around a stuffed dog, River is wearing pajamas covered in cartoon ants, of all things. Unmistakably blond, his hair is longer than it was in the picture on Reid's phone. His lips are parted, the lightest snore emanating from him.

I've always loved kids, but knowing this little boy is Reid's takes that appeal a step further. I have to clench my hands into fists to keep from reaching out to touch him. "He's beautiful," I say.

Reid stares down at me with dark eyes, his hair almost as light as River's—no color, as though he's a black and white version of himself in his white T-shirt and dark jeans. He takes my hand and leads me from the room.

Instead of taking me to his bedroom, he steers me to a small parlor off the main living area, and we sit on a sofa, side by side. He turns to me and seems to brace himself for what I have to say.

I pull my Mary Poppins bag from my shoulder and reach into it, pulling out a gift bag. "It's a belated birthday gift. I had to get creative, since you have everything. Or, you will now—after you unwrap that."

Surprised, he opens the bag and flings the tissue paper to the floor. When he pulls out the T-shirt, he laughs. Aimee, Kayla and I scoured the local thrift stores for the last two days to find a MADD T-shirt similar to mine. They were horrified that I'd give Reid something "used," but once I had the idea, I couldn't let it go. They forced me to swear I wouldn't tell him they had any part in finding it.

"Should I try it on now?" he asks, one eyebrow quirking up.

Good golly, he's hot, and I'd love for him to strip off his shirt and not put *anything* back on. But we're not done.

"I have one other thing to give you."

He pushes the shirt and wrapping materials to the side while I reach into my bag and pull out the small velvet box. His eyes flick from the box to my face, and he doesn't move.

"What you said the other day—you were right. I've been disconnecting myself. I haven't believed my parents know me. I haven't believed that God cares about me, or my sister. I haven't been sure he exists at all. And I haven't had faith in a future with you."

I take a deep breath and hold the box out to him. He swallows, jaw clenched, and opens his hand. When I place the box in his palm, he closes his fingers over it.

I lick my lips and take a deep breath of my own. "You said you have faith in us. You told me to come to you when I was ready to be fearless. The truth is, I don't know if I can be fearless. I've lost myself, Reid, and I'm still so scared. But I'm ready to try. If you still want to, I'm ready."

He blinks, stunned, and opens the box. Taking my left hand from my lap, he pulls the ring from its silk-sheathed slot, and slides it onto my finger. The dark blue stone and surrounding baguettes fill the space below my knuckle, and somehow, it fits perfectly. He leans closer, his lips a whisper over mine at first, and then he kisses me deeper, gathering me closer, our breaths mingled and shared until we're both winded, chests heaving like we've each run a mile uphill.

He stares at my hand in his for a long minute, his thumb caressing the edges of the band on my finger, before his eyes lift to mine. "When do you have to be home?" His voice is low and tinged with an ache that echoes back from my heart.

"I told them I might be a little late," I say.

Before I can say another word, he grabs my right hand, jumps up and strides through the house to his bedroom. He programs an intercom system inside his door—the display reads: *River's room: ON.* "I can hear him; he can't hear us," he says.

Elbowing the door shut, he tugs me into the circle of his arms.

The second his mouth crashes into mine, I'm on fire. Engulfed. I open my mouth and he kisses me harder as I press against him, locking my arms around his neck. His hands are hard on my back, fingers digging in, sliding down to my hips, gripping me tight as his tongue thrusts deep into my mouth, stoking the fire at my core until it's raging through me.

One knee slips up the outside of his thigh and he immediately grasps my leg, wrenches it higher and around his waist. As the other follows, he lifts me effortlessly, and I hook my ankles at his low back. Cushioning my head with his hand, he slams me into the wall. His lips leave mine with a loud *pop*, sliding along my jaw, raining kisses down my neck as I'm gulping in air. Seizing handfuls of his hair, I pull him back to my mouth, kissing him urgently, our tongues tangling.

Shoving my tank up, his hands cup my breasts, thumbs teasing beneath the smooth satin, and I can't get close enough to him. Without his hands bracing my weight, I've slipped just low enough to feel him hard against me, too many layers between us. Panting, he unhooks my front-closure bra and shoves the cups to the sides, and despite my determined muteness so far, I cry out when he sucks a nipple into his mouth, hard. Arching into him, I bite my lip until it stings, and I'm rewarded with his growl as he swings me around, strides toward the bed and drops me onto it.

I'm transfixed by the sight of him jerking his shirt over his head without bothering to unfasten the buttons. He slings it to the ground, inside out, as I shrug out of my tank and bra. Stepping up and unzipping my shorts, his dark gaze is on my face. My heart thuds as I return his stare and begin unbuttoning his jeans slowly, brazenly.

Seconds later, he's tossing my shorts to the floor and pressing me to the mattress. As soon as our mouths meet again, my heart cracks open, and the memories are a tidal wave, beginning with that first spellbinding kiss in the pink closet. He seems heavier, bigger, harder all over than he was even those few months ago, but his beautiful face is still all angled symmetry, except for his full mouth and the thick, curving lashes ringing his dusk-blue eyes.

His kiss is the same—hot and demanding, but never stingy. Perfect. *I'm good for you even if you don't know it yet*, he told me, and then he waited months for me to know it. To believe it. To stop doubting him.

Tears seep from the corners of my eyes to snake into my hair, and I hold on and kiss him back, measure for measure. "I love you," I say, finally, and he freezes and pulls back, watching me. "I love you," I repeat, "and I'm so scared, Reid. But I have faith in us."

Fingertips stroking the edges of my face, he shifts his weight from me, pulling me into his embrace. "That's what faith is, right?" he says. "Believing in what can't be known? Fall into my arms, Dori. I'll catch you, every time, and I won't let go." His lips brush over mine, feather-light. "Say it again, please. I've waited so long to hear you say it."

"I love you." I push him gently to his back and lean over him. Stare into his eyes. "I love you. Please don't let go."

"I've got you. And I'm not letting go. Again. Please."

"I love you."

He closes his eyes and whispers, "Again."

"I love you."

"I love you, too," he breathes.

"I know," I say and he laughs, flipping me onto my back, lacing our fingers and pinning my hands.

"Again."

I stare into his eyes, a slight smile pulling at my mouth, and I see myself as he sees me. I feel loved, and scared, and hopeful. I feel found. And I think, *Here is the beginning of my faith. Here is my forever. Right here. Right here.*

"I love you, Reid."

Epilogue

REID

New York City – June

Sitting across from me, Emma's eyes widen slightly, focused over my shoulder, and Graham coughs into his fist in a transparent attempt to conceal laughter.

I glance over my shoulder to see Cara and River emerging from the mouth of the hallway that leads to two bedrooms— Graham and Emma's on one side, Cara's on the other. Emma is still attending NYU, but she's planning to postpone her fall semester for a role she just landed on Broadway, and she may or may not return next spring. When Graham is filming on location, Cara divides her time between the apartment and Graham's parents, ten minutes away.

They were both more than excited to meet Dori and River, who flew into JFK last night. I have three more days of filming. Brooke left for Brisbane yesterday, but not before multiple confirmations of contact numbers and appointed Skype times.

"No, walk like this." Hands on her hips, Cara strides forward—her feet echoing *thump thump thump* on the worn wood floor. A pink sheet, tied around her neck, billows out behind her, and rhinestones glint regally from the top of her head. Her expression grave, she turns to look back at River. "Now you try."

Stepping into the room, adorned in a purple sheet, my son's stride is not so forceful. Unlike Cara's exaggerated stamping, the pads of his bare feet make no sound, and his gait is careful. I wonder again at genetics, and how Brooke and I could mesh genes and produce such an unobtrusive kid.

And then I notice his head. More specifically, what's *on* his head—which explains Graham's amusement.

"Son of a *bitch*."

My voice is muted, but Graham coughs once more to cover it, stifling another half-laugh. I'd really like to punch him, because somehow, some way, this is his fault. Dori places her soft hand on my forearm. My eyes jerk to hers. Dark and dancing with laughter, they almost convince me to laugh, too. Almost.

"Is my *son*"—I inhale through my nose and keep my voice very low— "wearing a *tiara?*"

Hands raised in placation, Graham clears his throat, "Eh-eh," when I shoot him a direct glare.

"Cara loves to play princess." Emma's voice of reason pulls me from contemplations of violence. "She must have convinced River to be her prince."

"He's not the prince, he's the *king*," Cara chirps, drawing all eyes to her. Her hands clasped daintily in front of her, she rolls big brown eyes and tilts her tiara-clad head at the four of us, like we're all a little stupid. "He's *carrying* the prince."

Sure enough, in a hold that would be better suited for a football than a baby—which I'm kind of thrilled shitless about at the moment—my kid cradles a blanket-swathed baby doll in his arms. "Jesus Ch—"

Dori's fingers slide across my arm, a gentle reminder to swallow my words, and I breathe an involuntary sigh. I'll never understand how she does that with a single touch.

"What's the little prince's name?" Dori asks, and Cara turns to carefully take the doll from River, as though it's made of glass, and wouldn't just bounce across the floor if one of them dropped it.

"Well *I* wanted to name him Tristan or Edward."

Cara frowns at her father when he chuckles again and Emma swats him, but Graham just pulls her closer and kisses her temple, and she settles into his embrace. "Those are very *princely* names," he assures his daughter.

"Yeah." She rocks the bald-headed baby doll, the eyelids of which are closed because, I assume, it's horizontal. "But we named him Reid, because River said princes get named after their grandfathers."

Dori's hand stills on my arm.

"He said what?" My words are thin, but they seem to echo across the loft.

She continues to stare at the doll. "Okay really, he just said, 'Reid,' when we were choosing a name, which is you, so obviously that's what he meant."

"He said, 'Reid'?" My voice is a whisper.

Cara nods, unaware of what it does to me that the boy who never speaks when he's awake chose to utter *my name*, even if I didn't hear it. Dori knows, though. Her eyes are glassy when I slide a look at her, and her beautiful face swims through tears I'd rather not shed in front of Graham and Emma.

River tugs the purple sheet behind him as he rounds the end of the sofa, his eyes on mine, puzzled and anxious. That's the last thing I want him to feel.

I open my arms and he climbs into my lap, still staring. His eyes are such a stormy, serious blue. Wisps of wavy blond hair poke up and out from around the tiara. Every feature is small and vulnerable. He scares the absolute hell out of me. My feelings for him scare the absolute fucking hell out of me. And that's how I know they're right.

Drawing the purple sheet up to my shoulder, he leans closer and I fight the urge to crush him close, watching Dori over his head. Her tears are incompatible with her blissed-out grin, like rays of sun hitting the ground during a rainstorm. Silly, beautiful girl— wearing my ring, sharing my bed, accepting my child, my past and my future.

My son's small finger touches the outer corner of my eye, releasing a tear. *Damn.* I know Graham and Emma are watching, but no matter how exposed I feel, I can't move. I don't breathe.

"No cry, Daddy," he whispers, warm breath under my chin, his cheek against my heart.

And then everyone is wiping tears away, and Graham and I look at each other in silent agreement that this moment is between the four of us and is going nowhere. Ever.

Cara takes River's hand and tugs. "C'mon, River." Sliding off my lap, he allows himself to be led away, and none of us can contain our laughter when Cara murmurs, "That's another thing you need to remember about families—sometimes everyone is just *weird*."

ACKNOWLEDGMENTS

My first thank you goes to my readers. Coming to the end of a series as a reader or a writer is simultaneously exhilarating and heartbreaking. I've enjoyed this journey so much, and I appreciate every reader who was in the trenches with me as I told Reid's story. I'm grateful every single day for each one of you.

Thank you to my beta readers: Ami Keller and Robin Deeslie, who've given me indispensable feedback for five books running. You two are the most wonderful friends, and I miss seeing your faces every day. Thanks to my wonderful author friends who provided criticism and cheerleading as needed: Elizabeth Reyes, Tracey Garvis Graves, Colleen Hoover and Abbi Glines. Your advice is always constructive and gently given—and that is never taken for granted.

Thank you to the amazing team at Penguin/Razorbill UK, especially my editor, Alex Antscherl, and editorial manager, Samantha Mackintosh. I've never been so nervous handing a manuscript to anyone, and you both made it painless. Thank you for your guidance, patience, and faith in me, this book and this series. A special thanks to my agents, Lauren Abramo and Kate McLennan, for keeping me calm while writing to someone else's deadline for the first time. That was no mean feat, ladies.

This book required more research than any novel I've written before. (Except for that Viking romance I wrote when I was nineteen, which thank goodness no longer exists. But let's not talk about that.) Much appreciation to the fantastic people who helped me get my CPS and adoption facts straight, gave personal tours of UC Berkeley, and answered texts at 2 a.m. about filming schedules: Carol Gardner, Holly Durham, Michele Bland, Marie Peterson (along with Ashley, Giana and Bryce), Liz Reinhardt and Zachary Webber.

Thanks to my parents for your unceasing encouragement and love. Thanks to Keith, Hannah and Zach for the inspiration you provide and for your understanding of my constant distraction when on a writing deadline. And as always, thanks above all to Paul, who cares for me in more ways than I can count, who has faith in me when mine is nonexistent, and who loves me no matter what.

ABOUT THE AUTHOR

Reading was one of my first and earliest loves, and writing soon followed. My first book was about a lost bear, but my lack of ability as an illustrator convinced me to abandon that effort and concentrate on passing 3rd grade. I wrote sad romantic poetry in high school and penned my first half-novel when I was 19, for which I did lots of research on Vikings (the marauders, not the football team), and which was accidentally destroyed when I stuffed it into the shredder at work. I'm a hopeful romantic who adores novels with happy endings, because there are enough sad endings in real life.

TammaraWebber.com
Facebook.com/TammaraWebberAuthor
Twitter.com/TammaraWebber